Nova's Blade

Will SciFi

www.willscifi.com

www.facebook.com/willscifiauthor

willscifiauthor@gmail.com

This book is a work of fiction. Names, characters, and incidents are the product of the author's imagination or are used in a fictional manner. Any resemblance to actual events, locales, or persons, living or dead, is coincidental.

Copyright © 2021 by Will SciFi

All rights reserved. No part of this publication may be reproduced, distributed, or transmitted in any form or by any means, including photocopying, recording, or other electronic or mechanical methods, without the prior written permission of the publisher, except in the case of brief quotations embodied in critical reviews and certain other noncommercial uses permitted by copyright law. If you would like permission to use material from the book (other than review purposes), please contact the author at willscifiauthor@gmail.com. Thank you for your support of the author's rights.

Prologue

The crowd's roar fills Astra's ears with pain. Blood leaks out her busted eardrums. Disorientated, Astra staggers back as blood pours down her head. A woman stands on the other side of the ring, holding a bloody dagger. She charges at Astra, yelling.

She slices Astra's forearm. Astra lunges back, holding her bloody arm. Looking down, Astra sees the spikes at the bottom of the ring. The woman stalks towards Astra, relishing her impending victory.

"You have nowhere to go!" the woman snarls with bloodlust in her eyes.

Dropping her arms, Astra stops in her tracks. The woman smirks and lunges forward. Stepping to the side, Astra grabs the woman's arm and snaps it. The woman screams, dropping her dagger as her bones rip through her flesh. Astra catches the dagger. She rams the hilt into the woman's nose, smashing it completely.

As the woman reels back, Astra drives the dagger into her throat. The woman gags, coughing up blood as she stares at Astra. The woman drops to the ground. Exhausted and beaten, Astra falls down, catching her fall with her hands. The arena erupts in cheers.

A robot floats down from the sky, scanning the woman's body. It throws its arms up, signaling the victory, to no surprise to the cheering crowd. As Astra rests in a puddle of blood, confetti falls down. On the big screen above, her photo appears with the word 'WINNER.'

Covering her mouth, Astra cries with gasps. Reporters and people in suits storm the ring, flashing cameras at Astra.

Blaze Neroburn comes into the ring, wearing his aqua blue suit with his baked tan face. His straight white teeth shine.

"Ladies and gentlemen, after outlasting 31 competitors in an unique fashion with the utmost determination, your Last Valkyrie, Astra!"

The cheers pour as Astra embraces the crowd with tears and waves. As reporters flash their cameras and shout questions, a young man comes through the crowd with a bouquet in his hands. He's tall and built like an athlete with a sharp jawline. They lock eyes, ignoring everyone around them. The man hands Astra the flowers.

"You were always my favorite," the man says.

Clutching her chest, Astra smiles. She tosses the flowers out the ring. Members of the audience punch and wrestle each other over the flowers. Astra jumps into the man's arms and gives him a hard kiss, smearing her blood all over his face. As they make out ferociously like animals, Blaze steps to the camera.

"You see this ladies? This could be you, if you stop playing. So get up because this is a love to kill for!" Blaze cheers.

CHAPTER 1

I open my heavy eyelids with tiredness. I don't even want to move as I rest with my cheek in the pillow, staring at the wall. I came home late at 2am, and it's already 7am. It's a few hours before work again. Another over time shift moving moon rocks because some idiot didn't do their job right, so I had to pick up the slack.

It's funny how I stand still as if a jolt of energy will replace my fatigue. Not moving, I relish over the dream I had, hoping it will ease my headache from the lack of sleep. I dreamed of the beach my parents took Luna and me when we were kids. I wish I was back there, feeling the ocean brush against my feet as they dug into the sand. After not moving for several minutes, I force myself out of bed. My joints crack as I stretch with a loud yawn.

I pull the lever, opening up the shed door from my room. The rust on its chain causes a loud screech. I try my best not to let the door fall and wake everyone up. The sound of the television comes from the living room. Oh well. I let the door crash into the ground.

"Good morning," I yawn.

"How did you sleep?"

"Fantastic."

In the living room, my mom sits in her floating chair, tucked in her covers as she watches the television. Her unused oxygen tank sits in the corner.

"Mom, you have to use that," I say.

"I was just taking a break," she sighs.

"There are no breaks. This is your health. Please."

I grab her bony and skinny hands. She has black circles around her eyes. She frowns then smiles.

"Okay," she agrees.

"Thank you."

The news anchor on tv interviews 'The Hottest Couple of the Year'. It's the title the media runs wild with.

"Astra, it's been a year since you outlasted 31 women to win Last Valkyrie. How has life been as a Belenus?" the anchor asks.

"Beyond amazing," Astra rejoices. "I come from poverty, so this new world is a blessing. But I won't let the money and fame get to me. I'll use it to help those who aren't as fortunate as me."

She goes on to talk about her new foundation which aims to help kids in poverty. The anchor eats it up. A recast of last season plays. Highlights show the Valkyries on dates with the Chosen One, Davion Belenus. The clips show the Valkyries training, battling in the arena, and killing each other in front of thousands of screaming fans. It ends with Astra and Davion's wedding. Astra continues, but this is enough for me. I head to the kitchen. My mom's eyes stick to the screen.

"Don't tell me you like that garbage," I sigh.

"It's not a crime to be happy for others," she defends.

"If you say so."

As a kid, I watched Last Valkyrie religiously with my family. Modern day gladiators fighting to the death was a spectacle for me. But it wasn't the violence that attracted me, it was the charismatic Valkyries. Their larger than life image, radiating a godly presence reeled me in for years. I dressed up as my favorite Valkyrie each Halloween - Nokomis.

She rode a mechanical griffin to the ring with her shining gold armor. She moved fast in the ring, bouncing around and flying in the air for attacks. How she fought, told a story. That story said, 'I'm going to give you the greatest show on Earth. Why? Because I'm the greatest.'

After she won, she became more popular than the other winners. When she went back for another season, a move that had never been done before, I was delighted. Surprisingly, she was decapitated in the first round. This was a shock to everyone, seeing our hero defeated like that.

Speculations for her sudden defeat came: she was past her prime they said, marital problems, even suggestions that she had a death wish. Regardless of the reasons, her death left a stain inside me. I lost my love for the sport. The fantasy was over. Now I can't stand the show. As I eat my protein block, I open the blinds, letting in light.

"I don't see how you can stay in this house with the lights off. You're living like a vampire," I say.

"It's called saving money."

I shake my head. Cherry perfume fills the atmosphere. I already know who it is. The dolled up face smiles at me with brown lipstick.

"How do I look?" Luna asks.

"The same as usual."

Her face tenses up.

"Okay, you look nice. Happy?" I say with a smile.

She giggles and dances away, fixing her hair. I have to give it to my sister. She's great at perfecting her looks. New week, new hair color; this time, it's velvet curls. The hours she spends on her makeup makes her round face more stunning. But she doesn't even need makeup to look beautiful.

"Nova, can you pick up the chicken from Ms. Blackford before you leave?" my mom calls out.

I look to my sister for answers. I trip over my tongue, but she smiles back.

"Why didn't you ask her? She's been up longer than I have," I complain.

"Because I asked you, that's why."

Luna shrugs like it's out of her hands.

"I'll do it when I leave for work," I groan.

Luna skips over to my mom and kisses her.

"And today marks the 11th anniversary of the Siege on Hyperion Industries," the news anchor reports. "Please have a moment of silence as we honor the 27 brave souls who died that day."

Different photos of people display on the screen. We are silent. The face above the name Orion appears. I bow my head, shutting my eyes to close out the tears.

"CEO Augustus Hyperion will give a speech today to commemorate their memory."

I roll my eyes as we scowl at Augustus' face on the screen. I snatch the remote off the table and change the channel.

"See you later," Luna says.

We wave at each other. She lifts the shed door, encasing the house with sunlight. My mom covers her eyes as the sunlight hits her face. The door shrieks really loud as Luna closes it, putting us back into the darkness.

"It's so bright," my mom groans.

"That's because you've been in here too long."

I replace her iv packet with a new one.

"When are you going to go outside more?" I ask.

"I do, sometimes," she sighs.

I stick the needle into her veins.

"Sometimes isn't enough."

"Don't worry about me, I'll be fine," she promises. She swallows some pills. "I'm running low."

"I'll pick up your medication when I get off work."

"Thank you."

"I told you, you don't have to thank me. It's my job."

"I could pay you, if you want," she jokes.

Our smiles are cut short when a loud bang hits the top of our shed.

"Those annoying kids," I scorn.

"Make sure to pick up some flowers too."

I march outside where two giggling kids jump from one shed to another. Pollux and Castor - those irritating twins.

"Hey!" I scream, startling them. "Get off of there now! If I catch you again, I'm telling your dad!"

Their faces turn white as they jump off. They look down, trembling as I approach them. Now I feel bad.

"Hey," I say calmly. "I know you want to have fun, but it's really dangerous up there. You can get hurt, and I doubt your dad wants to pay the hospital bills. Do you?"

They shake their heads.

"We're sorry. Our football got stuck up there. When we got it, we thought we would have some more fun," Castor explains.

"It's okay," I say.

They take off, tossing the ball back and forth. I arrive to a shed. A big meaty lady with curls in her hair comes to the door.

"Good morning Ms. Blackford. My mom brought you her plants," I greet.

Her fat cheeks lift, and her face lights up, seeing the bag of plants.

"Thank you so much. This will be great for my soup!" she cheers in her soft voice.

Despite her six foot frame and intimidating look, her voice can put babies to sleep. She hands me a bag of frozen chicken.

"Tell your mom I said thank you. I hope she is doing well."

"She is," I lie.

Ms. Blackford is the neighborhood's chef, operating a restaurant from her own shed. With the high prices of actual food, many of us have to eat protein blocks made from insects. They come in all kinds of flavors. Thankfully, Ms. Blackford hunts animals and grows food for her restaurant. She believes the people of the sheds suffer from bad health due to the protein blocks, and it's why most of us never live past fifty.

Although she doesn't have enough supplies to feed everyone all the time, it's good to eat fresh and natural. Unlike the expensive foods in the stores, hers is low cost. She has to make money, but she puts people first.

"Tell Luna to stop being a stranger, I'll feed her right. She'll get a student discount on Fridays," Ms. Blackford offers.

She hands me a bouquet of flowers.

"Fresh from the store," she says.

"Thank you."

The twins' father is smoking a cigarette by his shed. Too bad he wasn't out earlier.

"Good morning, Mr. Archer."

"Alright Nova. Going to work?" he asks, waving through the blue smoke.

"I have one stop before I go," I say, holding up the flowers.

"Tell your dad I said hello."

"Will do."

"You be safe now. God bless you."

Every morning before I go to work, he blesses me. Years ago, he lost his wife in a mining accident on the moon hence his good faith.

At the cemetery I place the flowers on a headstone with the name Orion on it.

"I love you dad," I utter.

**

My head slants against the window on the bus as protestors march in the street with signs. I don't care what the signs say. One catches my attention. A little girl holds it proudly. 'Over 300,000 girls go missing each year. Will I be next?'

"God, if I could afford new knees, I'd be out there protesting with them," an old man behind me says. "Young lady, you ought to join them on your free time."

"Like my presence is going to make a difference," I chuckle.

"If everyone had your attitude, what would have happened to all the great movements? One person can make a difference."

I get a good look at his rough face. He's blind in one eye and has a scar on his cheek.

"All these marches and protests just so we can fight and kill each other. What's the point? There will be another injustice tomorrow, and people will forget about the one today," I argue.

Chuckling, he sits back in his chair, conceding the argument as if he knows it's pointless. As the bus drives, a line of protestors block the street. The bus honks.

"Run them over!" a passenger screams.

A masked individual boards the bus. I am sure they're with the protestors. God, the theatrics are getting annoying. I will be late for work, if this bus doesn't move.

"Please pay the fee to enter," the robot driver says.

"Shut up!" the protestor barks.

The protestor smacks the robot with a billy club, knocking its head off. A passenger wrestles the protestor to the ground. As I watch, my necklace tugs against my neck. I do not notice until it's completely snatched off. Another masked person runs out the back with my necklace.

"Hey!" I scream.

I run after them. This has nothing to do with the protest. These bums are just thugs looking for a score. I chase the masked individual down the busy street, running through pedestrians.

"Someone stop them!" I yell.

Nobody does anything, looking at me like I'm crazy. I follow the goon into the busy street. A car slams on its brakes, honking at me.

"Get out the way!" the driver yells.

This distraction increases the distance between me and the perp, but it only fuels me. I keep pursuing. I don't care how long this chase goes on, or how tired I get. Adrenaline pumps through my veins. Take my money, my bag, even my life. But nobody steals my necklace. I crash into someone coming out a store. Looking up, I am relieved to see a cop.

"Officer, help! That person stole my necklace!" I beg desperately.

The cop reaches for his belt. A gun is over the top, but at this moment, it's whatever it takes. My relief ends when the officer grabs his scanner. He points it at my head.

"What?" I gasp.

"Hold still," he instructs.

"What are you doing? They're getting away!"

He scans me. The scanner beeps.

"Sorry ma'am, but you don't have a subscription to our services," he says with monotone.

"Huh?"

The bold yellow letters on his vest reads *MOA Corporation Police*.

"Oh come on. I don't have time for this! It's an ongoing crime!" I plead.

"If you would like to purchase a subscription, I can help you through the steps," he continues like a robot.

The perp is out of sight. I throw my hands up in the air, admitting defeat as the cop leaves. It's no use.

"This can't be happening," I whimper, almost breaking out in tears.

This is what happens when someone robs you in an area you don't pay services in – more robbing. I don't understand why we have to pay for our own police department, but this is how things are. Someone's breaking into your house, pay a monthly fee to a police department before they rob you. You get shot in the street, whoever is calling the police better make sure they're a subscriber. They don't even stop a murder unless they know the victim is a paying customer. It's worse when bystanders do nothing because it will add to their bill, covering someone outside their family plan.

I have to wait another hour for the next bus, making me late for work. I stand in the pickup line at work, trudging with my head down.

"You got quadrant 5," the clerk at the booth states to the person in front of the line.

He scans their badge, bored out of his mind as he slouches in his chair.

"Next!"

I move to the front. He raises his eyebrow with surprise, bringing some life to his uninterested face.

"Your quadrant was called an hour ago, Nova."

"I had trouble getting to work," I grumble.

He scans my badge.

"Well, you got quadrant 5."

He nods over to a group of people, males and females chilling in the corner smoking. Their tattoos show through their sleeveless shirts, obviously for show.

"Come on Faz, just give me a ride to my quadrant. I'll make up the work."

"Rules are rules, unless you want to speak to corporate."

He chuckles as I storm away. As I put on my gear in the locker room, the group from outside strolls in, consisting of three women.

"Hey you're the new girl they added to our quadrant?" one asks aggressively.

She has pointy blue hair. They gawk at me. I give her an uninterested glance and continue to dress.

"Yeah," I utter.

"Well, we don't need a newbie messing up what we have, so you better stay out of our way. Don't try to be a workhorse, and you'll be alright. Got it?"

"Yes sir," I say, saluting her.

Her two compadres giggle. I sense that makes her mad. She marches up to me. Her height forces me to look up as she's a few inches taller than me. I remain calm. Her tough act doesn't scare me.

"You got something you want to get off your chest? Because we can work on it," she threatens.

"No, I don't need any work on mine. It's fine," I glance at hers. "But judging from the looks of it, you wouldn't know what I mean."

Her friends laugh, awing to stir trouble.

"She got you, Jax," one teases.

Without waiting for her to respond, I put my helmet on.

"Now if you excuse me. I got work to do," I say through my helmet.

I slam the locker door and strut away.

CHAPTER 2

I step out the moon rover and halt at the massive crater below us. Its ginormous size births doubt inside me.

"What's wrong, you scared?" Jax teases, slapping me on the back.

They laugh, leaving me behind. Closing my eyes, I take a deep breath. The jetpack takes me down into the hole. As I descend, the area grows brighter from the light poles at the bottom. Several bulldozers are down here. I go for the nearest one.

"Oh no. We already have ones we use regularly. There's an extra one up ahead," Jax mentions.

She points to a bulldozer off to the distance, away from the others. I sigh, heading over there. Despite humans building cities on the moon for almost a century, so much of it is still uninhabited. Our job requires us to make way for more cities. Experts say it will take a few more centuries until there are cities across the moon. I won't have to worry about a job anytime soon.

I am happy to be away, ready to work in my own zone. It's a simple job: pick up the moon rocks, dump it in a pile, repeat. In my old quadrant, the mining quadrant, I worked the drill which required less maneuvering with the vehicle. We specialized in mining minerals and resources. All I did was press a button. Now I have to manage the stick in the bulldozer. It's not something I am use to, but I have enough experience.

Despite how simple our job is, they do not automate it. Ever since the first moon skyscrapers fell due to a robot's error, society doesn't trust robots to build cities. Corporations tried to move on from it, promising it was rare, that their robots improved. But people never forgot the deaths of thousands, refusing to live in cities built by robots.

I turn on 21st century classical music in my suit, going in a deep focus. Like always, the hours become minutes to me, passing quickly as I work intensively. I move so many rocks, making many holes.

"Wow, look at her go," a woman says.

The day will soon be over. I can't wait to go home and put this terrible day behind me. I try my hardest to forget my necklace. What will I tell mom? Probably nothing. It's too small to notice until one day she will say, 'I notice you don't wear your necklace anymore.' Then I will be in deep trouble. Moms always have a way of figuring things out. Just focus on this task. The bulldozer's claws get stuck in a wall. I try to pull back, but the dozer doesn't move.

"Man!" I blurt.

"What's wrong?" Jax asks over the com.

"Nothing."

"It doesn't sound like nothing."

"The claws are stuck."

"I'm coming over."

I keep moving the stick back.

"I got it," I say.

"Yeah right you do. Don't move it, you may cause a mess."

I groan. Now she wants to help? After all the trouble she stirred, I am not falling for it. She can back off. I put my hands on the handles, gaining the strength to pull it.

"I said, I got it!" I bark.

I yank the handles back. The bulldozer breaks free of the rocks. I don't need her. My confidence turns to surprise when a long crack goes up the wall. Small rocks fall down then bigger rocks.

"Oh no," I gasp.

"What did you do?!" Jax yells.

A chunk about the size of a car drops. I pull the bulldozer out, but a rock blocks my escape. The bulldozer is useless now. I get out and hit the jetpack button, propelling me diagonally in the air. I hit the ground. The rocks do not stop, now raining down rapidly all around us.

"That's it. We're leaving. Everyone get out of your bulldozers and get to the top now!" Jax screams.

Another voice shoots through the intercom.

"I'm stuck!" a woman cries.

A small rock pins her leg to the ground. Jax and the others fly away, leaving her behind.

"Don't leave me please!"

The top of the crater intimidates me as I watch the others fly away. You don't owe her anything. Just press the button and save your own self. Yes, but if she dies, it will be my fault. I fly towards the woman as rocks continue to crash down. She is about 50 yards from me. The closer I get, the more rocks I have to dodge. She doesn't register my presence as she freaks out,

20

trying to move the rock. I assist in moving the rock, but it's too heavy.

"Turn to your side, and on 3 press your jetpack button!" I order.

She gets to her side. Turning around, I put my heel in a small space between the ground and the rock.

"1.2.3!"

We press at the same time, igniting our jetpacks. The rock slightly moves, just enough for me to pull her out. She hobbles up, groaning in pain. We shoot into the air as the crater turns into an avalanche, pouring down massive rocks. One falls towards us. We jump out the way, barely missing the rock.

The destroyed rim of the crater becomes visible as we get closer. Fully out, we plant hard on the ground. The avalanche stops. We surprise the others. Jax is more disappointed as she scowls at me.

"I guess you had some beginners luck," Jax scorns.

I rush at her, but the others get in my way.

"What in the world was that? You left her to die!" I yell.

"You caused all of this," Jax argues.

Dropping my hands, I step back. The crater is in darkness from the destruction. She's right. This is my fault.

**

"You cost this company a lot of money Nova!" Glen, the manager, screams at me in the office on Earth.

I say nothing, keeping my head down in shame. Even if I try to save myself and justify what I did, it's pointless.

"You're fired," he declares.

The words hit me like a bowling ball in the gut as my mouth drops. This isn't shock from the firing. I knew the punishment was going to be more than a suspension without pay. I just can't believe I'm jobless now.

I plod in the parking lot, facing the ground. Being jobless is a new concept to me. I've been working since I was thirteen. When you no longer can do something so crucial to your living, you feel like something's missing. You feel naked and weak. Who will pay the bills, buy groceries, and get mom her medicine? The fact I have to ask these questions makes me feel pathetic.

I hear footsteps approaching fast. As I turn, a hard punch blindsides me in the mouth. Blood flies out my mouth. On instinct, I strike back without looking at my attacker. My fist connects with someone's jaw. The woman lands on the ground. It's one of Jax's pals. As I step forward, another blindside hits me in the temple.

I stagger back, punching my second attacker twice in the face quickly. She stumbles. I go for a knockout blow when someone trips me. The two women grab my arms, holding me to my knees. Jax marches up to me, fuming with anger.

"You cost us weeks of work. I got a kid to feed!" she howls.

I head-butt her in the nose. She screams as her blood flies in the air. My arms slip free. I elbow the other two women. Jax hits me with a flurry of punches to my face and stomach, dropping me back to my knees. She kicks me in the ribs. I shriek, hitting the ground. The kicks continue as I lose my breath. They stop. I wheeze, coughing up blood. Jax gets on top of me, pointing a knife at my throat. The tip of the knife pokes my jugular. I try my hardest not to show fear as I look directly in her eyes, but my heart pounds. Her blood drips on my face.

"Do it Jax!"

"Kill her! She can't afford good cops."

The tip of the knife presses further against my skin. At any moment, the cold metal will pierce my throat, pouring my blood everywhere. I can't blame Jax. It's what I deserve. Hopefully my life insurance plan from the job is still valid. Jax pulls back the knife, getting off of me.

"No need to. She'll be homeless in a week!" Jax declares.

I remain on the ground, staring at the night sky with a racing heart. It feels like the sky is falling down. My bruises reflect back at me in the window on the bus. I have a busted lip, and a scrape on my head. I lock eyes with a little girl in front of me. She inspects my face with curiosity. Her gentle eyes are the only source of happiness I have today. She hands me a lollipop. They say don't take candy from strangers, but I need something to take my mind off of things. I take the lollipop.

"Thank you," I say.

She smiles and turns back around, sitting next to her mother.

CHAPTER 3

Entering into Shed Court, I hear a cry.

"Phoebe, what's wrong?" I ask.

Sitting on the porch, she holds up a circular disk. A foot size hologram pops up, projecting a young man in a military uniform. He takes a deep breath.

"Phoebe, I know I said I will come home in a few weeks, but the terrorists did another bombing. My patrol has been extended. I don't know when it will be up, but I'll keep you updated. Please stay strong, and tell Saylor I love you both," the hologram says.

She breaks out in more tears.

"I just keep waiting and praying for him to finally come home, but he never does. I don't know if I'll ever see him again!" she cries.

Sitting next to her, I place my arm around her.

"Warrick will come home. He promised it, and he never breaks his promises. That's why you two are still together."

Wiping her tears, she smiles.

"How's Saylor doing?" I ask.

"She's doing okay. She wakes up crying at night sometimes. She really misses her dad."

"It's going to be okay, Phoebe. He survived this long. You really think those terrorists can stop a man like that?"

"I guess not," she giggles, giving me a hug.

Warrick is her boyfriend. They've been together since the 9th grade. I met Phoebe in my later childhood when I first moved to Shed Court. While others hated me for being an outsider, she welcomed me, not letting any of them pick on me. We stayed close friends for years, but after graduation, things changed. I started working full time, and she had Saylor. When Warrick got deployed to Mars, things really changed, and we went our separate ways. We never forgot each other.

Luna's voice steals my attention. It comes from a group of guys standing in a circle. The guys wear the same blue jackets, smoking and drinking. I march over there, hearing her voice clearer. She's in the middle of the circle vaping. I push past the guys.

"What are you doing?" I blurt.

She drops the pen and backs up, gasping in surprise.

"Nothing, just talking," she quivers, trying to play it off cool.

"Go inside now," I say, clenching my teeth.

"Why? I'm just hanging out."

"Now!"

The guys laugh as Luna stomps away.

"She's 16, you know that?" I assert.

"Oh my god, would you just relax Nova? Vaping isn't going to kill anyone," Dirk, the tallest one of the bunch, groans.

"Stay away from my sister," I order.

I walk away.

"But you can bring yourself back here girl."

He pulls my arm. I punch Dirk right in the nose. He lands hard on the ground.

"Man!" one of them shrieks.

They laugh at him. Holding his nose, his hands fill with blood.

"You can't hit a cop!" Dirk snarls.

"Whoever said you are a cop?" I bark.

He jumps to his feet enraged. I square up, ready to throw down. He's bigger and stronger than me, but I don't care. I've been waiting to give him a beating ever since he called my mom a zombie.

"Hey!" a voice calls out.

Another blue jacket runs on the scene. He steps in between the two of us. It's Atlas.

"What are you doing?" Atlas questions Dirk.

"She started it!" he argues.

"What are you 5 years old? Get out of here!" Atlas orders, shoving Dirk. "All of you, go! We have cases to solve! You don't get to chill!"

They dip out, murmuring insults at me.

"What was that about?" Atlas asks me.

"Your 'brothers in arms' are losers. They need to leave my sister alone."

He frowns with embarrassment.

"I'll take care of it. You know I can arrest you for assaulting a cop?"

I smirk, wanting to see him try.

"Please, when you guys can actually solve a crime, then worry about me. Until then, do your job and catch the actual criminals."

"What happened to your face? Did they do that?" he asks.

"No, it was from work," I say hesitantly. "I got fired."

Wait, I don't owe him anything.

"Deuces," I mock, putting up the peace sign.

That reminds me. I cover my bruises with makeup before going home. It's hard to believe we pay those chumps to protect and serve us. Shed Court's finest as they like to call themselves. Our police are rent-a-cops. They're fresh out of high school and fools in their early twenties, who throw on badges just to do drugs and chase after girls.

I step inside my house when my mom confronts me. Luna paces back and forth.

"Nova, what's going on with you and your sister?" my mom asks.

"She's controlling like she always is!" Luna yells.

"Luna, please," she begs. "Nova, what's the problem?"

"She was smoking with the cops and thinks she knows everything. If she keeps messing around, she's going to be in a world of trouble."

"Didn't I tell you not to hang out with them?" my mom asks Luna.

Luna cowers back with silence, surprised my mom doesn't take her side.

"You're hard-headed you know that?" I rant. "You never listen, and that's your problem. You keep doing the same thing over and over again, and we're tired of putting up with it."

"I don't have any friends at school! I do the best I can there, and what am I left with? Nothing, so excuse me if I just want to have some freedom in my life! Can I at least do that?!" Luna protests.

She storms off.

"Luna, we're just-." my mom begins.

Luna marches past her. The door to her room slams. Through the dark circles on my mom's eyes, she has regret and pain.

"Nova, you didn't have to antagonize her."

"It's the truth. She has to listen," I defend.

"But you know how she is. I thought maybe we could talk together. You know like a family like we once were?"

She sighs, drowning her head in her hands. She throws her wig off, revealing her bald head with just a few strands of thin hair.

"Where are you when I need you Orion?" she prays.

It hurts me whenever my mom's in pain. It hurts more whenever I cause it. I traipse into Luna's room with shame as she draws. Crumpled up pieces of paper are on the floor. I pick one up, seeing a drawing of a coffee shop.

The drawing is detailed. The occupants of the coffee shop have their own unique characteristics, giving life to their faces. Ever since Luna was a little girl, she could draw. It wasn't taught, she was just born gifted. 'You got yourselves a little Picasso,' friends told our parents.

"These are beautiful. They should be framed not thrown away," I speak.

"What do you want?" she asserts, focusing on her drawings.

"Can I talk to you please?"

She spins around towards me, crossing her arms.

"What?"

"Sometimes I can be hard on you, but I do it because I care. I'm sorry for attacking you like that."

Lowering her arms, her face relaxes.

"What you're saying is you're my sister, so it's your job to be so uptight," she chuckles.

"Oh don't be a brat," I tease.

I stick my arms out. She ponders, then runs up. We hug. She looks at the canvas in the corner where empty vials are at.

"The school won't let me borrow anymore paint from them," Luna sighs.

"I can buy you some more," I offer.

"It's okay. I need to get a job anyways and help around too."

At least one person will have a job in this house. I still do not know how to tell them.

"Can I come in?" my mom asks.

"Of course," Luna welcomes.

Her chair floats her over to us, and we hug.

**

I am reading *Last Days of Olympus*, a memoir by the final American president, when someone bangs on the shed's door. Who in the world is that, this late at night? It better not be those stupid twins again. I slam by book and rush to the door. It's Atlas.

"Finally have enough evidence to arrest me?" I taunt.

"I was thinking about what you said about your job situation. I can help you. We'll both get what we want."

"I'm not going to let you pimp me out, if that's what you think."

His eyes widen as he gasps. It's hilarious how seriously he takes everything.

"Oh my god, no," he stammers. "You really think-."

"Just tell me."

"There's a lady down the block whose granddaughter is missing, and I'm investigating it."

"I fail to see how this concerns me."

"You need a job. Be a cop and work with me on this case."

I laugh in pity.

"Why would you want me to be a cop? I'm not police material, not that the others are. What about your pals?"

"When you broke Dirk's nose, it put us at odds, so they're not helping out right now."

These clowns are so ragtag, that if I join, it'll be a huge addition to their department.

30

"So what do you say?" he asks.

There's no way I want to be a cop especially for these chumps. But there are bills to pay. Pick up a few paychecks and dip out when I find something better because everyone knows Shed Court PD pays not a lot of money. I grab my keys.

"Just don't call me partner," I say.

CHAPTER 4

"That I will bear true, faith, and allegiance to the same, and defend them against enemies, foreign and domestic," Atlas reads from a paper.

He waits for me to recite it as I hold my hand up. I sigh and recite it nonchalantly. I recite a few more pointless lines.

"So help me God," I repeat with fake enthusiasm.

"Congratulations," he says, sticking his hand out.

I leave him hanging. He goes over to a safe that has a retinal scanner. It scans his eye. He retrieves a gun and puts it in his holster.

"When do I get my gun?" I wonder.

"Until you're trained, I'm the only one who carries, but I have something for you."

He hands me a blue jacket and a baton, the same kind he has.

"You have to wear it, it's the uniform," he instructs.

Snatching them out of his hands, I grin quickly.

"Let's just get this on the road," I say.

We go to a shed down the block. An elderly woman comes out sniffling. She holds tissue as her eyes are red.

"Hi, Ms. Kader," Atlas greets, showing his badge. "I'm Officer Atlas, and this is my partner Officer Nova. We spoke over the phone."

"Yes, please come in," she offers sullenly. "Can I get you anything?"

"It's fine. You said you know the boy who kidnapped your granddaughter Cammy?" Atlas asks.

"Yes it was her boyfriend Enzo! Him and his pals are always hanging out with her, and one night she didn't come home. I know it's them."

"What makes you think that?"

"Sometimes she came home with bruises. I tried to get involved. She never claimed it was him, but I'm not stupid. She talked about leaving him, but feared he wouldn't like that. On the day she went to break it off, she never came back."

Atlas writes down notes as I walk around the living room, surveying the area. There are pictures of the grandmother when she was younger with a little girl who I assume is Cammy. There's a picture on the ground. I set it back on the desk. It's a picture of Ms. Kader by herself.

"Do you know where this Enzo lives?" Atlas asks.

"No. Him and his friends move around from shed to shed. That's how I knew he was trouble. A guy who can't hold anything down is no good."

"You mind if we check the room?" I ask.

"Of course not."

The room is a pigsty. Clothes, vaping pens, and food wrappers are on the floor.

"I'm glad I don't have a sister," Atlas says.

He goes over to the laptop on the bed.

"I hope those passwords she gave us work," he adds.

Four passwords later and nothing. We have one last chance before the computer locks. Atlas groans as he stops typing.

"Now what?" he complains.

I survey the room. There has to be some kind of clue here. In this mess, who knows? My eyes stop at a book on the floor.

"In all lowercase try Hartman," I tell.

"What?"

"Just do it."

Shaking his head, he types. The laptop chimes as the home page appears.

"How did you know?" he asks with surprise.

I point to the ground at an old ripped copy of *Last Days of Olympus* by Cole Hartman.

"What are the odds," he laughs.

We search her history to see the social media accounts she has. There are over fifteen, so we go to the one with the most recent activity.

"There, that's the last post," Atlas points out.

It's a video posted three days ago at night. The video plays. Cammy marches with ruined makeup and teary eyes, holding the camera to her face.

"This is the last time I'm putting up with this loser! I'm done! Enough is enough!" she fumes.

She approaches a shed that has a car.

"Wow there's no privacy," I remark.

"Check it out," Atlas says, pointing to the geotag in the post. "That's where she was at. She was trying to tell us."

This will be interesting. The destination in the post leads us to a lone shed on the outskirts of Shed Court. Nothing's around, but bare land.

"You remember Mrs. Foxwell from 9th grade English," Atlas asks as we pull up.

"The one who made us do all our work on paper, and we couldn't use ebooks?"

"Yeah that's her!"

"That lady was so far back in the 20th century, I was surprised she had autopilot in her car. What about that dinosaur?"

"I saw her last week at Blok Factory."

I gasp.

"What in the world was she doing buying protein blocks?" I stammer.

"She said she was giving them away to the shelter."

"I bet she makes the kids give up their electronics before she feeds them."

We laugh. As we step out, we stop laughing. The atmosphere changes. Atlas' hand wavers around his baton.

"Be alert at all times," Atlas says.

He bangs on the door repeatedly. My phone rings with a text message from my mom.

'Please don't forget my medicine again. Keep the change. Love you!'

I forgot to get her medicine after work because I was too busy getting beat up. My mind was focused on my job. I make a note in my phone to go to the pharmacy after this. This time there will be no distractions. Atlas keeps banging.

"Hold up!" a voice calls from inside the shed.

A bony fellow with purple spiky hair lifts the door. He's vaping.

"Who are yall?" he questions, eyeing us up and down.

Atlas shoves his badge in his face.

"Shed Court 86 Police. Are you Enzo?"

"Yeah, what'chu want?"

"It's about your girlfriend Cammy. Her grandmother reported her missing."

"Ex-girlfriend," he mutters, grinding his teeth. "Besides I haven't seen her since."

"Since when?" Atlas questions.

"Since…." His eyes turn to the sky as he pauses. "Last week."

"Sure," I say, hovering my hand around my baton. "We're coming in."

I barge right past him. Atlas rushes in behind me.

"Wow, what yall doing?" Enzo asks.

"We can't just barge right in," Atlas whispers to me.

"The video was three days ago. He's lying," I whisper back.

That, or he can't remember. He has blisters on his face. Whatever drugs he's on fried his brain so bad, he probably can't remember his own birthday. Two of his pals are sitting on the couch smoking. Their eyes are red as they reek of some terrible weed.

"Yo, who are these clowns?" the one with dirty blond hair coughs.

"It's 5-0," Enzo informs.

Goldilocks puts his hands up.

"Officer, I didn't steal anything, it was him!" he laughs, pointing to his buddy playing a banjo.

They crack up.

"Nah, it's about Cammy, they want to know what happened to her," Enzo says.

"That girl is bad," Banjo laughs.

Enzo lightly kicks Banjo in the leg.

"That's my girlfriend you talking about," Enzo grunts.

"Ex-girlfriend," I remind.

"Huh?" he utters with confusion, squinting his eyes trying to figure it out. His eyes open as he catches my meaning. "Oh yeah. Like I said I haven't seen her."

"Her last video she posted was at this shed. We know because your car was in the video," Atlas asserts.

Enzo throws up his hands.

"Okay man. She came here, we got into an argument, and she left. That was it. I swear."

"You two seem to 'argue' a lot. Her grandmother told us about the bruises on her arms."

His friends awe at him.

"Oh come on. We sometimes fight. She hits me, so what? I ain't got nothing to do with her missing!" he protests.

"Aye," Goldilocks calls out to me, extending the vaping pen. "You want a hit?"

He and Banjo giggle as I ignore them. Whenever you're in an unfamiliar environment, you have to assess the situation. I've been doing that since I came in, and nothing feels right about this.

"Let me hit that," I say.

"That's what I'm talking about!" Goldilocks shrills, handing me the pen.

I take a hit of it. It's cherry. I haven't hit the pen since high school, but I have to show them I can handle my smoke. The smoke fills my lungs. The urge to cough it out is strong, but I deepen my inhale, allowing the smoke to stay longer. I blow out a ball of smoke in their faces.

"This girl knows what she's doing!" Banjo cheers as I hand them back the pen.

They continue vaping. That'll distract them as Atlas interrogates Enzo.

"I already told you everything," Enzo grunts.

I go down the hall, slightly opening doors, so I won't make a sound. In one room is a 3-d printer with an incomplete gun on the tray. I doubt these clowns have a license for that. In another room are numerous containers of chemicals on a table. Gas masks and hazmat suits are on the ground.

Whatever drugs they're cooking can land them big time in the reeducation camps, but this is Shed Court, nobody cares. The drugs and gun indicate these chumps are up to no good, but room after room I find nothing pointing to Cammy. This is just a drug addict's dirty shed. I start to go back to the living room when I stumble upon a dark room at the end of the hallway. It's the only one with the lights off.

"I think you're lying," Atlas accuses.

"I think I don't care," Enzo groans. "Wait a minute, where's the other girl?"

I turn on the lights. Cammy is on the floor with her eyes to the back of her head. She's pale, drenching in sweat.

"Atlas! She's back here!" I scream.

A loud ruckus comes from the living room. The walls shake as grunts shoot out. I race back, taking out my baton. As I come around the corner, arms wrap around my waist. Goldilocks lifts me off the ground.

"Where you think you're going?" he asks.

He rams me against the wall and throws me on the ground. He stalks towards me.

"You picked the wrong house," he laughs like a hyena.

My leg is right between his. I kick him straight in the crotch. He bends over, gasping for air. I jump to my feet and two piece him in the jaw, dropping him unconscious. I book it to the living room. Banjo crawls on the floor as blood leaks out of his head. Atlas wrestles Enzo over the gun.

Banjo takes out a knife as he staggers up. I kick him in the face. He drops back to the floor. A gun fires, halting me in my tracks. Trembling, I turn around, fearing the worst. My fear subsides.

Enzo's on the ground, holding his bloody leg. Atlas stands over him with the gun.

"You shot me!" he screams.

"Enzo, you're under arrest!" Atlas declares.

I run back to Cammy. As I pull her out, the light reveals her entire body. I freeze, seeing what's in her. A usb drive sticks out the port of her neck. It's electronic dope, labeled with 1000 gigs.

"Oh my god," I gasp.

I take her out, dragging her to the living room. She's a tiny girl, but dragging dead weight is a pain. I trudge through the hallway. By the time I get to the living room, I'm out of breath. Atlas handcuffs Enzo.

"You have the right to subscribe to an attorney. If you cannot afford one, a loan will be given in which-."

"Atlas! Forget him! She needs a hospital!" I scream.

He rushes over and helps me with Cammy.

"Don't I get a doctor too?" Enzo calls out.

"Shut up!" I yell, kicking him in the face.

The car zooms down the street, flying well over 80 miles per hour. Atlas jerks the steering wheel, trying to control it. Luckily the sirens are on. Cars disperse as we fly by. My heart pounds as cars become flashes of light.

"Have you ever driven before?" I tremble.

"Not over the speed limit."

At this speed, autopilot will not come on. You only drive this fast manually when you're a racer or have a death wish. Cammy leans on me. Her head is cold.

"What's wrong with her?" Atlas asks.

"She overdosed on e-dope. Over 1000 gigs."

"God."

Smoking is one thing, but nothing is as addictive and damaging as e-dope, not even liquid cocaine. It's digital drugs. All someone has to do is get a usb port implanted, and they can download unlimited gigs of sensations into their body.

I knew a girl back in high school who got on e-dope. Portia Tower. She was an all A's student and decided to try it one time. That's all it took. Once she felt that 1 gig of high, she never got off. She got addicted and went brain dead.

Now her parents can barely afford to keep her mind alive in a virtual reality. They hope one day she will wake up. It's crazy it's not regulated. It's as legal as candy.

We fly into the hospital's parking lot, barely missing a few cars. We rush to the front desk.

"She needs help! She had an overdose on e-dope!" I yell.

Atlas holds Cammy as a worker scans her. The scanner beeps with a red flash.

"I'm sorry, but she does not have-."

"Put it on my card!" Atlas demands.

They scan his card which gives a green light.

"Doctor!" a worker calls out.

The doctors rush over with a medical bed and take Cammy away. We have to wait in the lobby. When they call us back, Ms.

Kader is with us. Cammy is awake with a normal heart rate. Her grandmother cries. Atlas hands her a tissue.

"Ms. Kader, I know you've been through a lot, but so has Cammy. Just take it easy on her," Atlas says.

She nods and goes into the room. She and Cammy hug each other.

CHAPTER 5

The lights to Shed Court are off when we pull up.

"There are cops back at the shed arresting Enzo and his friends. They'll be put in holding," Atlas informs.

"Your buddies forgave you that quick?" I stammer.

"Not all of them are clowns like Dirk and his clique. We have some good ones in the department who finally answered the call tonight. You could join us."

"Sike."

"I'm serious. You did good work. We need more people like you."

The glass shatters, causing me to cover my face. Hands yank Atlas out the car.

"Atlas!" I scream.

My door swings open. Huge arms toss me to the ground. I try to get up, but a knee thrusts into my back, pinning me. Dirk and Boone attack Atlas. Atlas fights back, punching Dirk in the mouth, but Boone hits him from behind. Atlas falls to the ground, and they beat him. I try to push up from the ground, but the weight of the knee is too strong.

"Let go of me!" I scream.

"Shut up!" Verner barks.

He is big and strong. My efforts are futile as I watch Atlas get beat.

"You don't ever go against the boys!" Dirk barks.

43

Atlas is groggy as Boone yanks him up. Dirk pummels Atlas' face.

"You think you too good for your homies now?! Is that it?!"

Dirk stops. Thank God, no more. He takes out his baton and swings it in the air.

"This is what you get for breaking the code!" Dirk snarls.

He swings, but Atlas ducks. The baton crashes on top of Boone's head, knocking him out. Atlas grabs the baton and rams it into Dirk's face, breaking his nose. With the distraction, Verner doesn't see me grab a glass shard. I stab Verner's hand, twisting the shard in his flesh. He howls, launching himself off of me.

As he rolls on the ground, I grab my baton from the car. I smack Verner across the chin with the baton, sending his teeth flying. Atlas is on top of Dirk, pounding his face in. Dirk is not fighting back, helpless and groggy as his nose bleeds.

"Where is your dignity?!" Atlas demands.

"Atlas!" I yell.

The punches stop. Atlas trembles at the blood on his hands.

"It's over," I say.

He yanks Dirk to his feet.

"Get out of here!" Atlas orders.

Dirk helps his boys up. They skedaddle off. I put my hands on my mouth, seeing Atlas' busted mouth and cut cheek. I rush over and caress his battered face. The last time I saw him bleed was when he got beat up for trying to stop a purse snatcher. Stupid boy needs to protect himself better.

"God, are you alright?" I ask.

"It's just the job," he chuckles.

"What's so funny? You took a beating."

"You should see the other guy."

I grin. I try to stop it, but I can't help it. It's hard to stay upset whenever Atlas smiles. Pollux and Castor pull up on their bikes.

"Yo what happened?" Pollux asks.

"Nothing. Don't tell dad. Go inside and give me some ice please."

They stand there, amazed at his bruises.

"¡Ve ahora!" he screams.

They instantly book it.

"Kids don't listen," Atlas says.

"Tell me about it."

***

We sit on top of the laundromat, drinking Mr. Archer's liquor. It came from the stash he gets from retirement. The shed is taller than the other sheds, letting us see the entire neighborhood of Shed Court. It's made up of countless compacted sheds, stretching for miles. The San Francisco skyline and the bay are in sight.

There are no hills. They were destroyed a century ago, to make way for the sheds. The land doesn't get much rain fall. There's an underground tunnel that pumps water from the mountains in Oregon into the land, to keep crops alive and prevent fires. We have running water to drink and bathe in, but we don't use it on the crops. The tunnel doesn't give us as much water as the more affluent communities. That's why Ms. Blackford travels to Neo Silicon Valley to purchase more.

"It's beautiful," Atlas remarks, eyes glossing over the city.

"It's just buildings."

"I'm talking about our neighborhood."

I almost spit out the alcohol.

"You like this dump?" I ask.

Atlas frowns.

"It may be a dump, but it's our home. I have enough respect to appreciate it."

"Appreciate what? The losers, dogs going to the bathroom everywhere, hobos shooting up drugs?" My tone grows cynical. "People can't even take their children for walks without seeing needles on the ground. That's what you're so proud of?"

"You're right. Shed Court isn't perfect. We're not even from here, and it's a gutter," he admits. This catches me by surprise. "But what about Ms. Blackford, the little kids, the old couple who looks for recyclables every morning, Errol who works maintenance even on holidays? Those are the people I appreciate. People like you."

He gazes at me with his hazel eyes. A person can get lost staring into his dreamy eyes. They are a field of gold. I turn away, drinking.

"Can Pollux and Castor speak Spanish well?" I ask.

"They were only little kids when mom died, so she never taught them much. And dad, well……..." He looks away and sighs. "He's just tired. So they just pick up a little bit here and there when we talk."

"I remember when your mom use to make sweet potato pie," I chirp.

The taste of it comes back. I haven't tasted something so delicious in years.

"Those were the best! They were better than the ones at the grocery store!" he gushes.

We drink a few more bottles as we look out to the stars.

"Beautiful," Atlas speaks.

This again. Touching my hand, he smiles at me. Where did this come from?

"What are you doing?" I gasp.

His eyes grow wide.

"Nothing," he quivers. He backs far away from me, and drops his head. "Nothing at all."

He rotates his empty bottle as an awkward silence erupts between us. Why did I do that? He's my friend, and I made him feel stupid. Now, I feel stupid for what I did. He deserves more than my insecurities.

"Atlas," I say.

We stare at each other. Forget this. I rush in and kiss him. This doesn't surprise him because he cups my chin as we kiss. My mind is void of any thoughts, only set on what I want. I had a long day, I deserve some kind of peace. I want to stay in this moment forever.

I open my eyes. Wait a minute, what am I doing? I can't go through this again, the hurt and pain. No, never again. I break off the kiss, shooting back from him.

"I'm sorry, did I-," he begins.

"No, it wasn't you," I stumble. "It was-."

I say nothing as we look away from each other.

"I have to go," I say, getting up.

"Nova, please," he calls out.

I push his hand down.

"I'll talk to you later?" I guess.

I rush away without looking back. I pace back and forth inside the shed as everyone sleeps. What was I thinking? I wasn't, only caught up in the moment. That's what I get when I lower my guard. It was Dirk and his boys' fault. I was caught up in my feelings. The attack left me emotional, in need of comfort.

I can't let Atlas distract me anymore. He's still in my mind, but why? God, please take him away. I don't want to think about him anymore. I have no time for romance. I have so much to do. I need to find a job, one that beats being a cop. I have to get my mom's pills. Wait, her pills. My mouth drops.

"No," I utter.

I don't believe it. I really forgot her medicine again. How many hours was I out? Why did I even hang out with Atlas in the first place? I could've grabbed her medicine then. Man, I'm an idiot, forgetting twice. It's an hour before the pharmacy closes. I can ask Atlas for a ride. Forget it. It would be an awkward ride. I can walk fast, get on the bus, and make it in time. That's a good plan. I have this all under control.

**

I walk out the pharmacy with the medicine. Thank God, I didn't forget this time. It's approaching midnight. Buses don't run this late, so I'll order a Quickie Car. A light flares in the corner of my eye, catching my attention. It comes from the alley. Looking out, I see what's reflecting the light.

The bag falls from my hand, but I catch it before it hits the ground. My eyes stare at the source of the light. It's a gold heart necklace, dangling in someone's hand. My necklace. The perp shows it off to someone.

"100. I took this from some chick," the perp says.

The other person shakes their head and walks off. The perp stands alone in the alley, lighting a cigarette. I lurch into the alley, tiptoeing behind them. The lights are dim in the alley, giving me cover in the darkness.

"Hey! I'll buy it!" I call out.

He turns around. I kick him in the crotch. He drops to his knees, gasping as he looks at me.

"Remember me?"

I grab his head and ram it against my knee. He rolls on the ground, groaning in pain. I snatch my necklace. To have my necklace back is a blessing. Millions in this city, and I stumbled upon this alley at this time. This is more than just a blessing, it's fate.

Next time, I'm not wearing this to work. I know the words on the back, but I want to read them for good fortune. 'For my dear Wyn, I'll always have you in my heart.' My smile vanishes. Are you kidding me? It looks exactly like my necklace. I throw the necklace at the perp's face.

"Maybe you should give it back," I whisper to him.

The alley is clear. I stroll out, but slow down. A group of individuals wait at the end of the alley. It's too dark to see what they look like. They walk in my direction. Something isn't right. They walk in unison, not wandering like goons hanging out, but with purpose like they're gunning for someone – me.

It's better to be safe than sorry. I turn around, going the other way. Playing it cool, my normal pace resumes with my eyes to the side. Their speed increases. I pick up my feet. The footsteps grow louder, picking up with speed. I turn to see them running in full sprint. I dash off.

The end of the alley gets closer. I have no intention to stop once I'm out. I will run in the middle of the street and scream my head off. I'm close now. See you later creeps. A black van pulls up at the end of the alley, blocking my exit. Two individuals in black tactical gear jump out the van with cattle prongs. Screaming, I punch one in the face.

The hit does nothing as they grab my arms. I try to pull away, but they yank me back. A huge surge of electricity pours into my body. I hit the ground, unable to move. My entire body is numb as my face is married to the pavement.

I can't move my mouth to scream as the shock paralyzes me. All I can do is watch as they throw me in the van. A syringe dangles over me. My eyes fade, putting me to sleep.

CHAPTER 6

I spring up from the ground in sweat, gasping for air. White walls surround me in a square room. My phone is gone. I wear a white jumpsuit.

"Hello?" I call out.

No reply. This is no time to think. I've been kidnapped by God knows who. I have to get out of here. I pound on the wall.

"Help! Someone help me! Can anyone hear me?!" I scream.

My fists grow sore, but I keep pounding.

"Let me out!" I yell.

I run from wall to wall, pounding and screaming, but I get nothing. My hands bleed from hitting the concrete. My punches weaken. I fall back on the ground, mentally drained.

Okay think Nova. It's impossible to know where I'm at. That leaves who and why? I don't have any enemies. Jax was angry at me, but she doesn't have the power to organize this. This can't be personal.

The only thing I can think of is trafficking. My heart stops at the thought. Thousands of girls go missing every year without a trace. Many point to trafficking. I saw on the news about a rich girl who was kidnapped. Her parents paid the ransom, but never got her. She was found on the other side of the world. Her flesh was burned to the bone, and her organs were gone. I put my hands on my face, dreading a familiar fate. Oh no, I'm going to be sold into slavery or worse.

A loud exhaust comes from the wall as it slides open, leaving a partial exit. I wander out into a dark hallway. Over 100 women in white jumpsuits walk through the hallway.

"Hey," I call out.

Nobody answers. They focus on the light at the end of the hall, walking towards it hesitantly. I grab one girl by the arm.

"What's going on?" I ask.

"How should I know?" she whimpers.

I follow them. Exiting out the hall, we stumble into a huge auditorium. There has to be well over 100 people here, all women. Some have bruises on their faces. Many panic, crying out.

'Where are we?'

'How did we get here?'

'Help!'

A huge metal door swings open. Individuals dressed like the ones who kidnapped me march onto the stage. They have assault rifles. A short woman with a black pony tail strolls in behind them. She gets on the mic, glaring at us with disgust.

"Excuse me," she says.

People keep chattering.

"I said excuse me!" she barks.

The place falls silent.

"My name is Irma. Welcome to the trials."

"Trials?" someone whispers.

"For the next few days you will be tested physically and mentally to see if you have what it takes. There are 150 of you in this room. By the end of this, there will be 32. As for the 118 who fail, you will not go home, nor will you stay here." Her face flexes with a cold glare. "You'll just disappear. Any questions?"

"Is this some kind of prank?" a woman yells. "Let me guess a new tv show where people think they've been kidnapped."

She laughs, causing others around her to laugh. Irma reaches into her pea coat.

"Who do you think you are?" the woman mocks. "You think-."

Bullets light her chest up, propelling her back. Screams hit the auditorium as people back up from the bloody corpse. Irma holds a gun with smoke coming out of it.

"I'm the last person you saw," Irma declares. "Now it's 149. Does anyone want to make it 148 before we start?"

Whimpers fill the room.

"Good. Don't ask stupid questions. If you survive this, they'll be answered," Irma states.

Is this happening? It's so unreal. She expects us to go through with this like it's normal. She killed that girl like it was nothing. It's happening too fast for me to question it. I can only react, dreading what will come next.

The stage extends in the air. It reaches near the ceiling before stopping. It retracts back as the room expands mechanically. When everything stops, the stage is about a football field away from us.

"This is 100 yards. All you have to do is make it across, and you will pass this round," Irma says. "Begin."

Nobody moves as we are confused. A girl steps up, tiptoeing out. She takes one more step. An arrow flies from the side and hits her in her neck, killing her before she hits the floor. Screams are cut short when an arrow hits another girl in the chest. Arrows fly rapidly from one side of the wall. Everyone runs towards the stage screaming.

Flying arrows fill the room. As I run, women drop like flies. Blood splatters in the air. The sound of bones and flesh being torn is in the atmosphere. My eyes shift around. It's a bloodbath as arrows slaughter the women. My feet splash in a pool of blood. This is a nightmare.

I focus on the wall, allowing me to dodge the incoming arrows. The arrows torpedo out, ripping through the air. I duck, barely missing them. Many make the mistake of running straight, not paying attention to the wall. They're killed instantly. Some dodge, only to be hit by the next row of arrows.

If I want to survive, I have to dodge and not run so rigid. I have to maneuver around the others. It brings me no pleasure using humans as shields, but I have no choice.

We make it halfway as the numbers drop severely. Almost there. An arrow hits the girl in front of me, ripping through her skull. As she collapses, another arrow hits her from the other side. I see what's going on now.

Arrows fly in both directions, right and left now. Bodies hit the floor drastically. I jump over a body that's filled with arrows.

"Please!" a voice screams.

A girl crawls with an arrow in her leg. On instinct I want to help her, but that thought ends when an arrow hits her in the neck.

She dies choking on her own blood. The stage is a few yards away. Someone pushes me over. Falling to the ground, I gasp, knowing the danger that awaits there. As soon as I touch the ground, I jump back up in a slant.

The stage is right in front of me. I sprint straight ahead, not caring about technique, just praying I will make it. I collide face first into the stage, hugging it for dear life. The relief overwhelms me. More women are making it over as others are killed. One last woman races over, struggling as she wheezes. Everyone yells at her, begging her to make it over in time.

'Come on!'

'Hurry!'

She is inches away when an arrow strikes her in the head. She sinks to the floor. An alarm goes off as the stage lowers.

"Congratulations, you've survived. 51 of you didn't," Irma declares with monotone.

Cries continue. Some women throw up. I drop to my knees, trembling as I replay the horror. I think about all those poor women who didn't survive. Their eyes give us cold stares. The floor is a graveyard of bodies with arrows.

The wall opens up, revealing darkness. The floor rotates, moving the bodies into the opening in the wall. The wall closes. The new floor is spotless as if the carnage never happened. The room retracts, bringing it back to normal. There's a blood stain on my sleeve, but it is not mine.

"The number on the front of your jumpsuit represents the room you were in. You will now go back to your rooms and await further instructions," Irma orders.

We trudge back to the hall. One girl's on her knees, crying loudly.

"I can't do this! I want to go home!" she bawls.

A tall slender girl with an athletic build approaches her.

"It's okay. Come on, get up," the tall girl says.

She tries to pull the girl up, but the girl swats her hand away.

"I gotta get out of here!" she panics.

Irma and the guards notice the display. They march over. The tall girl books it.

"Why aren't you going to your room?" Irma barks.

Tears pour out of the girl's eyes as she stays on her knees.

"Please, I don't belong here. I want my mommy and daddy!" the girl begs.

"Get up and go to your room now!" Irma orders, unshaken by the girl's distress.

Come on get up. I gulp, fearing for the girl's life. She doesn't get up. Irma grows furious. She takes off her pea coat.

"Give me your baton," she orders.

A guard hands her a baton. It's not hallow like the one I had which was meant to sting. It's thick and hard all over its long frame.

"Please, I don't-."

Irma smashes the top of the girl's head with the baton. Blood pours out of her skull as she crawls. Irma drives her boot into the girl's jaw, dropping her flat on the ground. The girl whimpers. Irma unloads all over her body with the baton. The girl's bones crack on impact with the heavy steel. She puts her hands up to defend herself.

"Put your hands down!" Irma barks.

The baton hits the girl's arm. She screams as her arms break. We stand by as helpless spectators as the vicious beating continues. The girl's whimpers stop as she twitches. Irma pulls the girl's hair, revealing the swollen face. The girl's eyes show no consciousness.

Irma slams the baton across the girl's face and beats it to a pulp. The girl doesn't move as her face is unrecognizable. Irma finally stops as blood drenches the baton. Catching her breath, Irma puts back on her coat. She spots us watching.

"I swear, if you aren't in your rooms in the next 20 seconds, I'll send every last one of you to your ancestors!"

We hurry to our rooms as the guards rush us. Some women knock others down. I feel at any moment a bullet or baton will hit me. I leap into my room, planting face first. The walls shut behind me as I remain on the floor. As alien as this white room is, I am safe for now. All those dead bodies hinder this temporary safety. I rock back and forth in the fetal position, screaming as the images stick in my mind.

"Mommy!" I cry.

Please make them stop. My screams fade into whimpers. What will they have us do next? Will I ever get out of here? Why are they doing this? I just want to go home, but for now, and for however long they decide, this is my home.

A blue mist sprays out from the walls. Jumping to my feet, I put my face in my shirt. The mist covers the room. Surprisingly, the mist doesn't make me choke or cough as I breathe fine. My legs feel weak. I wobble, feeling woozy. My feet give out. I hit the ground. My eyes fade.

**

An alarm wakes me up. My jumpsuit is warm and clean, spotless of blood. I'm not sweaty anymore. My skin is smooth and moisturized. Energy flows through my body like I just ate a good breakfast.

Did that blue mist have something to do with how I feel? There are people who don't eat or drink. They have rooms in their homes that spray their bodies with nutrients. They don't even go to the bathroom, but they're rich.

For my kidnappers to have many rooms with this capability, they have to be extremely wealthy. It's obvious they have power. So rich and powerful, but not necessarily traffickers. I'm getting somewhere.

The walls open. I walk out, joining the others down the hallway. There's no hesitation or confusion this time. We all walk with direction, knowing another test is coming which means more people will die.

Irma and the guards are in the auditorium. The stage and mic is gone. There's a body opponent punching bag mounted on a pedestal.

"This next round will test your striking abilities," Irma informs. "You have 10 strikes to hit this bag. Each strike will be recorded, so the goal is to land the most effective blows to it. When you're done, a buzzer will sound, and you will be told which side to go to. Get in a line, and let's begin."

That's it? Just punch the bag, and onto the next round? Wow, I thought it would be hard, but thank God it's not. I'll pass this with flying colors. Only a sucker won't survive this part. Irma nods to the girl in the front of the line.

"Begin."

Letting out a huge breath, the girl marches to the bag. She brings her fist fully back and punches the dummy's face. Her fist cracks as her wrist snaps. She cries in pain, holding her dangling hand.

"You still have 9 more hits. Continue," Irma orders with no sympathy.

"I can't," the girl whimpers.

With a sigh, Irma takes a baton from the guard. We gasp. She raises the baton, but stops. She extends it to the second girl in line.

"Hit her," Irma directs.

The second girl trembles in fright.

"I can't," she stammers.

Irma's face twitches like she's suffering a malfunction. She takes out her gun and shoots both girls in the head. We scream briefly, getting use to death now. The guards hurry over and drag the two corpses away.

"Here's some advice," Irma declares. She taps the punching bag with the baton. A hard clicking noise sounds out as the bag remains still. "The bag is filled with concrete, so the most effective blows aren't the hardest ones. Be smart, if you want to survive this. That's the first and last tip I'll give out. Next one will be lead."

She nods to the next girl in front who hesitantly steps up. The girl feels on the surface. She lightly punches it in the chest. She groans, shaking her wrist, but punches it some more. The buzzer rings.

"Right," Irma states.

The next girl comes up. As I wait, Irma sends people right and left with no indication on what the lines mean. The buzzer sounds the same each time. In each line there are people with bruises on their knuckles.

There's no way to tell if someone passes or not. This feels forever as my stomach twists in knots. The only good thing about this wait is I get to watch other people. I see how they hit the dummy, the hits that cause the most pain, and the ones that don't. A strategy forms in my mind.

I reach the front of the line, staring into the dull eyes of the dummy like it's my opponent. In a sense, it's my judge and executioner. I strike the throat with my elbow, but I do not use all my strength, just enough for me to feel how hard it is. Grabbing its shoulders, I ram my knee into its stomach.

I strike quickly, not letting my fists stay on the concrete for too long. The force on my bones is hard, but not painful enough to make me stop. The buzzer sounds. I tremble, gulping at Irma. Please say something, or give me a nod to let me know I did good. Her face doesn't move.

"Left," she coldly states.

The wait kills me. I trudge to the line. My session replays in my mind. I should have taken breaks in between and allowed myself time to think. Why didn't I use my palms and the bottom of my feet to lessen the pain? This sucks. I wish I could go again.

I rub on my knuckles and elbows, feeling the scrapes and blood on them. This reminds me of that stupid game Bloody Knuckles I played back in middle school. Bullies forced us to play it for our lunches. I always won. They didn't like it, so we fought for real, and I won again. I can't believe the thought of it brings me joy as it briefly takes me away from this place. Someone taps me from behind.

"Aye," the girl behind me whispers.

"What?" I whisper back, keeping my eyes forward.

"We have to get out of here."

"You think I haven't thought of that? It's not going to happen. They have guns."

"We have the numbers. If we catch them by surprise and overrun them, more will join us. We just need a distraction."

"I don't think that's a good idea," I quiver.

"Neither is waiting to die. I served in the military, and I'm a cop. I can take these clowns, I just need some help. You with me?"

I gulp. My anxiety shoots up tremendously.

"I can't," I stammer.

"Suit yourself. I'm going to take these suckers to school."

She steps out of the line and approaches Irma.

"My head hurts. Do you have any aspirin?" she asks.

Irma nods at the guards. The guards march over to her.

"Perfect, thank you very much," she says.

The guards yank her by the arms.

"Wait, what's going on?" she shudders.

They escort her to a wall. They aim their guns at her.

"No!" she screams.

The bullets rip through her like paper, turning her into a cheese grater. Nobody in the lines react to her death. I glance at the corpse and turn my attention ahead, fearing I'll be next.

The last girl finishes. Everyone is nursing their bruises. The confidence I had at the beginning has left my body. After seeing the three girls get killed, I just want to finish this round alive. The guards march down the lines.

"Ready! Aim!" Irma orders.

They point their guns at my line. I swallow my stomach as my eyes expand. I throw my hands up, cowering back. Cries fill the air as many turn their backs.

"Aim!"

They turn their guns to the other line. Terror sweeps the girls on that side. The guards return to their original position. Cries are dying down. My heart still races as I am unsure of what's going on. I slowly put my hands back down. Is this some kind of psychological torture? Maybe nobody will die, and they just want to scare us to death. The guards turn to the other line and mow everyone down.

We jump back, panicking as the bullets tear the girls up. Bodies and blood flood the floor. The guards march behind Irma whose face doesn't move at the bodies.

"Back to your rooms," she orders.

We traipse back to our rooms. It brings me no joy that the round is over. My relief is brief, knowing the torment will continue. When will this nightmare end? Will I die before it's over?

***

For the next round, the auditorium's floor is a few feet below us with a pool of water.

"Today we're going to see how long you can breathe under water. It's pretty simple. Don't come up until the water goes down," Irma tells. "Any questions?"

Nobody says anything. We drop down into the pool. As soon as everyone is in, a red laser shoots out of the rim of the pool, covering the entire top. Someone sticks their hand out towards it. The laser slices her hand off. Bubbles shoot out of her mouth with screams as she clutches her bloody stump.

So that's what it does. What an idiot. Thanks for letting us know what not to do. She reaches out for help, but everyone swims away from her. She grabs my shoulder. I kick her in the stomach, sending her back. A girl behind her smashes her head against the wall until she stops screaming. Her corpse floats to the top where the laser slices her into many pieces.

I don't feel sorry for her. She was a liability for our survival in this round. However, I am in disbelief at how the other girl killed her with no remorse. We're becoming animals. Our only goal is survival.

With each second my muscles tense, my head hurts, and my eyes strain. I look at the lasers, praying they will cut off, but they remain. Some girls around me black out. Their unconscious bodies float to the top where the lasers cut them up. Others purposely swim up. They can no longer take the pain of not knowing when they'll come up again. The pool fills with blood and limbs. A leg floats by me. The smell of blood hits my nose.

The average person can hold their breath for 30 seconds to 2 minutes. This feels like hours. At any minute I will fade out. The urge to swim to the top is strong. I close my eyes and open them seconds later, but the lasers are still there. I close my eyes again, this time not opening them back up.

There's nothing left fueling my will. I have no hope. As soon as this is over, I'll be thrown into another pit. The only thing keeping me alive is my family. Not the promise of seeing them, for I don't know if I will ever see their faces again. It's the thought of them that keeps me from swimming up. I imagine many different memories: going to the beach, movies, and park. Atlas hits my mind.

My headache increases as my nose bleeds. I can no longer hold my breath. I open my mouth uncontrollably. Water pours into my lungs. My lungs feel like they're on fire with lava inside them. Either drown or get cut in half. There's no point in fighting. This is the end. These are my last thoughts before I black out.

I gasp heavily, coughing up huge amounts of water. The surface beneath me is hard as I can breathe again. Around me, girls are coughing and vomiting on the ground. The water in the pool is gone as pale corpses and limbs are inside.

"Couple more seconds later, we would have been ripped to shreds," a girl next to me coughs.

Irma stares at us with no emotion. I already know what's coming out of her mouth.

"To your rooms," she says.

**

I wake up. There's someone wearing a bull mask and a suit, sitting in a chair in the room.

"What is this now?" I ask.

"Sit," Bull Face speaks.

The male voice is crispy. I slouch in the other chair.

"I'm going to ask a series of questions, and you will answer them honestly," he says.

That's it, just questions? No physical torment or bullets? Impossible. It's never this easy with these tests. The calm atmosphere doesn't fool me. I must stay on my toes.

"Are you ready to begin?" he asks.

I nod with a sigh, grinding my teeth at the rhetorical question. Like he even cares. He presses the remote in his hands. The walls glow.

"How long have you lived at your current residence?" Bull Face asks.

"Twelve years."

A grocery store shows on the walls. It changes to a picture of women marching. Judging by the fashion and phones, it's from the early 21st century.

"What was the first thing you thought of today?" he asks immediately after the last question.

"Escaping," I sigh.

"If you had to choose between being a gorilla or tiger, what would you be?"

I turn to the changing images on the walls, seeing celebrities on the red carpet then a night show host laughing.

"A gorilla."

"Are you or have you ever been a member of the terrorist group known as Hades Hammer?"

"No."

"Do you think corporate warfare is staged by mega corporations for economical gain?"

"Maybe."

"Are you or have you ever been a member of the terrorist group known as Hades Hammer?"

I smirk.

"You asked me that already."

"Should everyone be given an affordable subscription to a functional police department?"

"I can barely pay my mom's medical bills. How can I afford to take care of everyone else?" I rant.

The interrogation continues with rapid questions. There is no structure. They're all random. He repeats many questions, asking, 'Are you or have you ever been a member of the terrorist group known as Hades Hammer.' This interrogation is a broken record.

As I answer, I look at the pictures on the walls: police fighting rioters, skyscrapers, moon colonies, peaceful protests, game shows, and much more random photos.

I lose track of time, answering so many questions. There is no point to any of this, to any of this torture. My life is a joke to them. They abuse us for no reason other than because they can. It doesn't matter who these people are: rich elitists, sadists, or some whack religious nuts.

What's the point of going on, if I'll be stuck in this rat race, chasing the next objective? I clench my fists. If they won't give me my freedom, I'll force them to kill me. I am about to stand up when the pictures stop, reverting the walls back to white.

The walls open. A woman in a white lab coat comes out, holding a jet injector. Inside of it is a syringe with green liquid.

"What is that?" I stammer.

"Hold still," Bull Face orders.

She injects my neck with the syringe.

"Ouch!" I yell.

I feel a speck of blood on my neck. The pain instantly goes away. Bull Face and the lady leave the room. Another test I imagine. Let me guess, they put something deadly inside me, and now I have a certain amount of minutes to get it out before it kills me. I saw that in a movie once. The walls open back up. There are less women in the hallway than before. We meet Irma and the guards in the auditorium. There's someone new with them.

It's a man wearing an aqua blue suit. His face is tan like he spent too many hours in a tanning machine. He ogles at us like we are dessert. He looks familiar, but I can't place his face.

"Congratulations, you remaining 32 have survived!" he cheers. "You've probably seen me before."

Yes, but where? He looks more familiar by the second as his white teeth shine. I still can't remember exactly. Suddenly, it hits me. The suit, tan face, and cherish attitude are all too familiar. My heart picks up fast at the realization. I saw this guy on the television every week when I was a kid.

"My name is Blaze Neroburn. It's my honor to officially welcome you as members on this season of Last Valkyrie."

"Oh no," I gasp.

CHAPTER 7

The room fills with gasps. The statement baffles everyone. Last Valkyrie? This is impossible. There's no way this is for Last Valkyrie. So many things aren't right. Women submit and volunteer to be on the show. Nobody forces them.

"But wait how can this be possible? What about those who sign up to be on the show?" Blaze mocks. He laughs. "There are millions who would kill their own mother to be here, but they're useless to us. If you were volunteers, you could quit at any time, not follow the rules, and make demands. That wouldn't be entertaining now would it?"

He's a fool, if he thinks we won't tell anyone what they've done to us. Once I get out of here, I'm snitching. I'm sure the others have the same idea. If this is Last Valkyrie, then I don't know why nobody in the past told. I refuse to let this sicko hold me against my will any longer.

"Oh, if any of you think about snitching, think again." He takes out a tablet. Glowing blue squares are on the screen. "You remember that syringe you took to the neck a while ago? We've implanted devices that can track you, listen in on your conversations, and also detonate at the touch of a button."

My heart drops as I put my hands on my neck. Our faces explode with fright.

"If you want to make it to your matches, don't snitch, or it'll be boom! Only if we had a demonstration." He grins devilishly. "It seems we have 34 people, and we only need 32. Let's start subtracting then!"

We scream in panic, but there's nothing we can do. A girl runs towards Blaze.

"No please, don't let it be me!" she shrieks.

Irma shoots her between the eyes.

"Wow!" Blaze cheers, eyes on the tablet.

I cradle in a corner, trying to ignore the screams and panic. God don't let it be me please. What would it feel like to have my head blown off? Would it be painful? Even if I don't feel anything, the idea scares me.

There's no way it'll be me, right? Out of 33 women, what are the odds Blaze will press my number? Come to think about it, the odds haven't been in my favor lately. Oh god, it might be me.

"Eeny, meeny, miny, moe," Blaze counts as his finger hovers over the tablet.

He presses a button. The room falls silent in anticipation. My heart pounds. Is this when I die? What will they tell mom and Luna? Maybe nothing, and I'll be reported missing. That's a better fate than my family having to look at my headless corpse.

"What is that?! My neck! It's getting hot!" someone screams.

A girl frets, putting her hands on her glowing red neck. Everyone backs up from her.

"Oh no!" she cries.

"I love this part!" Blaze laughs.

Her fear excites him. The girl's face swells with blisters and bubbles as her neck expands.

"Somebody help!" she muffles.

The increasing mass of her flesh clogs her throat, making it hard for her to speak. Her head explodes, raining blood and flesh everywhere. A drop of her blood gets into my mouth, souring my tongue with its aluminum taste. My insides twist. I throw up. It feels like my stomach is ripped out of my throat. Blaze laughs frantically.

"Momma always said, don't let your head get too big," Blaze teases. "Any questions?"

A girl timidly raises her hand.

"When do we go home?" she whimpers.

Irma shoots her a glare. Taking out her baton, Irma marches towards the girl. Irma towers over the girl.

"You go home when we say you go home! You fight when we say you fight! And you die when we say you die! You got that you prima donna!"

Irma strikes the girl in the stomach with the baton, dropping her to her knees.

"Get up now!" Irma orders.

"Get the picture now? We own you." Blaze declares. His grin stretches, revealing his bloody gums. "Most importantly, I own you. Don't worry, whoever wins, gets the detonator taken out."

Why don't the Valkyries tell after they win then? I stop dwelling on this question as I walk back to my cell. This is the truth. After all these years, this is what goes on behind the scenes. I can't believe it. Millions of people lied to. All those years staying up late to watch the show, believing in the spectacle.

All those Valkyries, those strong women I looked up to. I believed they signified greatness. It's a lie. The legend of Nokomis, the greatest warrior to have ever stepped into the ring, is all a fraud. She was larger than life to me. I had toys and posters of her. I idolized her. I loved her.

But none of it is true. She appeared strong, but in reality she wasn't. She was just another pawn who did what she was told even after she was free. It's good she died. That fake sellout got exactly what she deserved.

I don't know why I hate her since I'm in her shoes now. She did what she had to do to survive, but this doesn't stop my anger. Nokomis and the entire world have betrayed me.

***

I sit on the ground in my room, not moving. The door opens, bringing in a man and a woman. Their vibrant looks bring color to the bland room. The man with the red mullet wears a yellow suit and has a tattoo of a star on his face. The woman whose puffy hair is in the shape of a giant bow has powdered skin like she bathes in chalk.

She's more conspicuous than her counterpart. She wears a thin see through jumpsuit that reveals her skinny body. The plant sewing on her suit covers her private areas. A less flamboyant entourage, carrying briefcases, follows the two into my room.

"Aren't you looking good!" the woman praises. She circles around me with lust in her eyes. "Body like that, you're going to knock them dead!"

"What?" I mutter.

I clench my fists, wanting to knock this woman's lights out. The man steps up to me as the woman keeps ogling.

"Please excuse Venus. She has her own way of giving compliments," he explains.

Venus shoos him away with her hand.

"You have a body on you girl. The better you look, the more we get to work with," Venus says.

"That reminds me. Allow us to officially introduce ourselves," he mentions. "I'm Flavius, and she's Venus. We are your managers with skills in fashion, design, and public relations."

"We're going to make you as stunning as possible in and out of the ring. You'll stand out for the entire season!" Venus enthuses. "Or however long you survive. But don't worry dear, we'll do our part!"

Her lack of remorse and empathy stuns me. She's a prancing idiot. Is everyone brain dead or void of empathy? She claps her hands. The entourage opens the briefcases, revealing the cameras, makeup kits, and other beauty utensils.

"We're going to get you ready for your intro video, for the world to see you for the first time. Since it's just introductions, there's no pressure for you to look your absolute best. We just want you to look presentable," Flavius explains. "We'll CGI the dress and background."

"There will be time for us to do our absolute best work on you!" Venus promises. "Consider this as a scrimmage."

The introductions are brief videos introducing the Valkyries. Usually they talk about who they are, where they're from, and why they're on the show. I remember watching the introductions as a little kid. Valkyries did them someplace that was meaningful to them, or showed who they were. Knowing the intros are done in a locked room instead, haunts me. They give me a chair to sit in. They comb my hair and powder my face.

"Do you have a man, a special person back at home?" Venus pries. "I'm sure a girl like you has all the guys chasing after her."

Atlas comes to mind. Wait, why in the world am I thinking about him? No, get out of my mind ugly.

"Umm, no," I quiver.

Talking to strangers about my personal life makes me uncomfortable, but Venus talks like we've known each other our entire lives.

"No man?" Venus asks. "Let me guess, you don't have 1, you have many? You like to keep your options open, right? Why have one when you can have them all? They play games, so why can't we, am I right?" she raves.

Lady would you shut up? I don't know you. And even if I do have someone special, why would I tell you?

Flavius smirks. It's the first reaction he displays since I've met him.

"It's okay to be nervous. Doing introductions can be uneasy for Valkyries especially after what they go through," he says, painting my nails.

I realize I have been rubbing my sweaty hands on my pants.

"We've done this many times, all with confused and afraid girls. Trust us, we'll do our part in making sure you're at your best," Flavius promises, looking me in the eyes.

His gentle tone brings some kind of comfort to me.

"After we're done with you, you'll forget you have a bomb in your head," Venus giggles.

That reminder stresses me out. I need something to cut the tension and relieve me.

"How long you've been doing this?" I ask, ignoring her comment.

"This is our 20th season," Flavius says.

"How do you like your job?"

"Girl I love it! It's the best ever!" Venus cheers.

At least someone's having a good time. I figure Flavius feels the same way. They finish. I look a little bit more alive than usual given my current state. My face shines a little bit with the makeup, giving me some life. My hair is straight. I have to admit, I look good. The entourage sets up a camera in front of me.

"You've watched Last Valkyrie before, so you have an idea of how the introductions are done. Let's do a test run," Flavius informs.

How does he know I've watched the show before? Millions watch it, so it could be a good guess unless they know a lot more about me than I think.

From what I've watched in the past, the intros are simple and easy to do. Just a few lines. It's a job interview basically. Speak for thirty seconds. How hard is that?

"You don't have to say who you are and where you're from," Flavius says. "That's all standard, and we'll add that in later. Right now focus on what you want the world to know."

Venus shoots me two thumbs up with a huge grin.

"3,2,1," a camera crew member says. "Go."

"Ever since I was a kid, I always wanted to be on the show. To me, being a Valkyrie symbolizes what it means to be great. Now it's my turn to shine."

"Cut."

I feel like I did well. I'm not a pro, but for introductions, it's good enough. The room's silent. Not a word from Flavius or Venus as they observe me. The silence breaks when Flavius claps. Good, he's pleased by my speech. Suddenly, his claps turn sloppy as he looks bored.

"Congratulations. You've inspired nobody," Flavius states.

"I don't think you could have bored me more if you read my botox disclaimer," Venus insults.

"But the intros are about who we are. We tell people why we're here," I stammer.

"And who are you Nova? Not who you think people want you to be, but what makes you unique?" Flavius asks.

"I'm a girl with a bomb in her head!" I yell.

I kick the seat, sending it across the room. The camera crew steps back, trembling at me as if I'm an uncaged tiger ready to strike. There's no reason for them to be afraid. I'm the powerless one.

"This one has some fire in her! We can use that," Venus charms.

Bowing his head, Flavius sighs. When I didn't know my fate, it was scary. Now that I know what lies ahead, it terrifies me even more. This isn't helping at all.

"I'm sorry," Flavius says. "I mean before you were brought here. There's something about you that makes you unique. You have to see it in yourself first before the world sees it. Can you see it?"

For a moment, I am not the helpless girl who was kidnapped. I am Nova from Shed Court: a sister, daughter, and friend to many. Nokomis appears in my mind. I imagine I am her, stuck in this room.

"Yes," I declare.

"Let's run it again," Flavius directs.

I take a deep breath as they count down.

"Action."

"I'm not here to make friends or trends. I'm here to make corpses out of those so-called warriors who stand in my way. After I'm done leaving a blood bath, I will be the last Valkyrie standing," I declare.

My words are lies. I don't believe them. I just think that's what a Valkyrie would say. The room's silent again as I await their reaction. Venus claps, jumping up and down.

"Excellent Nova! As far as intros go, that was splendid!" Venus cheers.

"You did good," Flavius congratulates modestly.

We film the other part of the intro. I say my name, where I'm from, and what I do for a living. Well, what I did for a living.

"Too-da-loo Nova! We'll see each other again when the show starts. That's when the fun begins!" Venus exclaims.

"See you soon," Flavius says.

The wall opens.

"Nova? That's an interesting name. I think we can do something with it," Venus babbles on her way out.

It's funny. These two strangers are the closest ones to friends I have right now. I don't know if it's some kind of trick to relax me, or it's part of their jobs. I was stripped of my dignity and treated less than human yet these two, despite how outlandish they are, show me compassion. Mist sprays out the walls. Here we go again.

CHAPTER 8

I wake up with the sun hitting my eyes. My eyes are so depraved of sunlight, I shield them with my hands. It's brighter than ever. Blinking rapidly, my eyes adjust to the light. I see without discomfort.

I'm in a hover car high in the air. A flock of doves fly nearby outside the window. The clothes I wear are the same ones I wore when I was kidnapped, but they're clean and warm. My keys are in my pocket. I've never been in a hover car before. It was a childhood dream to ride in one.

The automated pilot steers the car towards the ground, descending us from the air. The screen up front glows with the words, 'Press Here.' I tap the screen, and a recording plays.

"You will be arriving soon to your residence," the robotic voice says. "You do not have to bring any clothes or hygiene ornaments to the island. They will be provided. In your pocket is a new id with your current address. It has been updated with a code that will void you of any misdemeanors, if you are arrested. You have also been given a debit card for expenses. The car will be back at your house in two days at 8am. Do not be late."

My new id card is gold with my photo from the intros on it. In bold letters it says '**Official Valkyrie of Last Valkyrie**.' There's a paragraph of tiny words on the back that I don't bother to read.

Sitting back in the chair, I focus on seeing my family again. I pick my nails. The anxiety consumes me. I still have no idea how long I was gone. The car drops me off at Shed Court.

The atmosphere is quiet as I walk in my neighborhood. There are no kids or dogs out. This is very unusual. I hurry to my shed, dying to see my family. I put my keys in to unlock the door. Before I can lift it, the door lifts from the other side.

I smile dimly. It's the best I can do with all I have been through. The door is completely up. Luna meets me with her mouth hanging, astonished to see me.

"Luna," I gasp as my smile widens.

The joy from seeing her erases my worries.

"Nova? They said you would come," she speaks softly.

My eyes water at the word 'they.' The ones who kidnapped me.

"I only have two days, but I want to spend time with you and mom," I say.

"You want to spend time with us?" she questions. "Now you want to be a member of this family?"

"I had-." I halt, remembering to stay in line. "I went off, it was meant to be a surprise. You know how much mom loves that show. I have a good chance to uplift our family when I win."

"What makes you think you can show up after what you pulled?" she asks.

"I told you about the show-."

"I don't care about the show!"

"You're not making any sense," I stammer.

I rush into the house.

"Mom! It's me Nova, I'm home!

79

No response, leaving me dumbfounded.

"Where's mom?" I ask.

Luna shakes her head with tears.

"You should have thought about mom before," she whimpers. "You really are a character. You deserve to be on tv."

"What are you talking about?" I interrogate. My voice grows loud. "Where's our mom?"

"Why did you forget her medicine?" Luna weeps.

My mouth drops with gasps. Her pills. No, I couldn't have. I forgot that I had forgotten them in the first place. Her chair isn't in the living room. It's always with her, and she's always here. I slap my hands on my head. A huge weight hits my chest. It's hard to breathe as my body fills with panic.

"Where's mom?" I quiver.

"Why," she says, shaking her head.

"Mom!" I yell.

I rush straight into her room.

"Mom, I-."

I freeze. My eyes are dead set on the obituary on the desk. The world stops around me. No sound, feeling, or life; just the empty chair and the picture of my mom when she was younger. The words read 'In Loving Remembrance of Atira.'

I collapse. My face hits the floor. A river of tears pour out of my eyes as I pull on the carpet, screaming.

"No!" I cry.

I am just a little girl, alone and afraid in this big world. I now see how Valkyries are able to kill each other with no remorse. The show turns them into shells without souls. I have become a shell. I plod back to the living room. Luna glares at me.

"You see what you've done," Luna whimpers.

"Luna, I-."

She runs up and punches me in the face, knocking my head sideways. My cheek stings with a burning sensation. The only pain I feel is from the loss of our mom. I stand still. I keep my hands down, ready for her to turn my face into a punching bag. I deserve my sister's rage.

"I hate you!" she screams.

Her punches continue. She's no fighter; it's not her nature. I have been hit harder, but I act like her punches hurt as I put my arms up to defend. She needs to believe she's hurting me as I have hurt her.

She raises her fist again, but stops. She marches away in tears. Trudging through the court with my bags, my mind is lost. No more thoughts come through my mind. I am a husk of depression.

"Nova," a voice calls out.

Atlas approaches me timidly. He looks at me as if I'm an alien.

"Why? I get that you don't like it here, but did you really have to leave like this?" he asks.

"How did it happen?" I respond.

Six days - that's how many days after I left, my mom died, Atlas tells me. A day after my disappearance, she had a fever of over 120 degrees. She threw up constantly for two days until she was

81

rushed to the hospital. Over the course of the next few days, she slipped in and out of consciousness before she had to be put on a ventilator.

For 2 more days, Luna, Atlas, his dad, Ms. Blackford, and more friends watched as my mom breathed through a tube. I was nowhere to be found. On the 6th day, that was when my mom breathed for the last time. At that point, they never bothered to ask where I was. Then they saw me on television as a Valkyrie, a lucky girl out of millions, who got to live a dream.

"I'll be back in two days," I state.

I want to tell everyone the truth especially Atlas. Unlike Luna's rage towards me, Atlas' sullen eyes show disappointment. His heart is broken as if he expected more from me. Luna didn't put me on a pedestal, but I have broken whatever perfect image Atlas had of me. This breaks my heart even more. I wish I can tell him, not only about the show, but how sorry and stupid I am. It's all my fault, but none of it matters now. I leave my home behind.

***

My mother is thin like always, but now she has peace. My tears drop on her naked body as she's on the tray in the morgue. Countless surgical scars paint her thin breasts. In the end, all those surgeries were useless.

I remember going with her to the hospital for the operations. At first, she held my hand going in, but soon I had to help her before she became limited to a chair. I fall to my knees, wrapping my arms around her. I want to hear her heart beat so bad, to hear her reply, but nothing comes out. The only sounds I hear are my own cries.

I roam the streets, ignoring the busy sidewalks containing arguments, conversations of joy, and poverty. I rest on a bench in the business area, blending in with the night life. People ignore me, walking by with their faces in their phones. Tired, but unable to rest, I force my eyes shut, drowning myself in darkness.

Something hard hits my foot. I open my eyes. A police officer glares at me. The words on his vest reads the name of a company I don't even care about.

"You're loitering," he states.

I get up.

"I'm leaving," I mumble.

He sticks his baton in front of me. This takes me back to the past. I see the corpses again, Irma standing over them with a bloody baton. 'Back to your room,' Irma orders. I snap out of the nightmare.

"It's an automatic fine. 200 dollars," the officer declares.

"I don't have any money!" I snap back.

He gets in my face.

"You got some attitude on you, don't you girl? I'm going to need to see some identification," he rants.

As I reach into my pocket, he puts his baton on my hand.

"Slowly," he orders.

He snatches my id out of my hand. He reads it. His eyebrows shoot up as he gulps. He knows who I am now, but this dummy is in too deep to back out now. Go ahead, do your job idiot. He scans my id. The scanner beeps. His eyes stretch more as he trembles at me.

"I…..I..," he quivers. He swallows his throat, straightening himself out. "I'm sorry, I had no idea you're a Valkyrie."

He quickly hands over my id, shaking.

"Forgive me Ms. Nova. My family are big fans of the show. Can I get an autograph and a picture for them?"

I step into his face, glaring at him.

"They don't care about you either," I snarl.

I stroll off. I play with my id card, caressing its thickness. The gold on its smooth texture rubs against my fingers. The edges are sharp enough to cut someone's throat. I could slice my own wrist with it. Why not? It would end this suffering. How would Luna feel about it? Perhaps she wouldn't care, already lost so much to even feel sorrow anymore.

I could run to a random person and tell them I was abducted, and Last Valkyrie is a lie. That would be the quickest way to end things. I wonder if any of the other Valkyries ever killed themselves or got killed before the show started.

That reminds me of Jetta, a Valkyrie from a past season. I didn't think much about her intro video out of all the others, but after that, she was never on the show. When Rae, who didn't have an intro video, appeared, I knew Jetta had been replaced. Nobody noticed, but I did. I thought Jetta had cold feet which was odd, but now I know the truth. The edge of the card presses against my wrist. It would be easy. I put the id back in my pocket. Not today. It would be too easy.

CHAPTER 9

I book a room at a hotel on the debit card the show gave us. I want to stay close to Shed Court, so I go with a cheap one nearby rather than a fancy hotel in the city. These 2 days before I leave are for family and friends, but I have none. I have nothing to do, but to get drunk and stare at the holes in the walls of my hotel room. I stare at the holes for hours, ignoring the obnoxious music and yells in nearby rooms. My life replays in my head.

What if I went to the pharmacy a minute earlier? What if I didn't see the necklace? What if I just left my necklace at home? Mom would be alive, and I wouldn't be here. I go to the future, and what's in store for me. I have no idea what I will find on the show or who.

What will the other Valkyries be like? Will they be mean, friendly, or scared? There are different personalities on the show, but nobody knows what they're like off camera.

The battles come into my mind. Watching them as a kid was fun, but having to be in them scares me completely. This is too much to think about. I don't want to think about it anymore during these days.

Occasionally, I go back to Shed Court. I stand near a tree in the child cemetery. It's weird, but it's the only place I can watch peacefully without being seen. Not many people come here, only whenever they have to bury a love one.

The headstones have dates, but no names. Parents of Shed Court typically don't name their children until they're five years old. That's due to the low survival rate for kids born here. The protein blocks are to thank for that.

I watch the people of my neighborhood. Atlas goes to work, his father smokes his cigarette, Ms. Blackford feeds residents, kids play together, and cars go in and out. Sometimes I spend hours chilling, waiting to see familiar faces to make me feel at home. I wait to see Luna, but she never comes.

She finally comes out. She wears mom's planter gloves and hat. She plants. That was mom's job before she got sick, then it was mine. It's the time of the month for the tunnel to give us water. Hopefully it will be enough. There are talks about reducing water due to another drought. They want to preserve more for the richer communities.

Luna's hair is tied, and she wears no makeup. It's rare to see her not dolled up. She digs into the soil, sweating. I never took her to be a laborer, but she goes to work. I want to call out to her, and tell her how sorry I am, but it's no use. I keep watching her until she finishes and leaves.

Entering into the club, neon strobe lights strike my eyes. Soaking up the music, I stroll to the bar and order a drink. Before I know it, rows of empty glasses are in front of me with no sign of slowing down. Suddenly the music stops. The beat drops. The ceiling opens and dancers drift down on levitating poles to the stage.

The club roars with excitement. Paying no attention to the dancers, I immerse myself in the clubbing experience. This is the time of my life. My problems and worries can wait because for now, this is my atmosphere.

"Hey bartender! Give me another one please!" I yell.

The bartender chuckles and fills another glass.

"You must have won the lottery, or lost your job," the bartender says.

"Why not both?" I ask.

He laughs. A man with rainbow hair marches up to the bar as he vapes.

"Yo, me and my boys been waiting for a long time for our drinks," Rainbow-Head tells. "What's the holdup?"

"There is no holdup. You're going to have to wait," the bartender grumbles.

Rainbow-Head groans then blows smoke into the air. The fruity smell fills my nose, intriguing me to ask for some. In times like these, past habits of mine are thrown out the window. We glance at each other.

"Man these cats be tripping," he complains.

I shrug. Someone shoves my shoulder lightly. A muscular man staggers over me, checking me out with a grin.

"Wow you looking fine!" he hollers in my ear. "What's your name girl?"

His breath reeks of alcohol.

"Cleopatra," I retort, turning back to my drink.

"I can be your Alexander," he giggles, pressing into me.

"Alexander was hundreds of years before Cleopatra. I'm not interested."

I shove him back. He yanks my arm, causing me to spill my drink.

"I just want to have some fun," he grumbles, voice growing intense. "What's your problem?"

Rainbow-Head steps up to the meathead. He lets go of my arm.

"Aye brody, get off her. She said she ain't messing with you."

"What are you going to do about it?" Meathead snarls, getting in his face.

Two buff individuals stagger behind Meathead simultaneously. They have the same cheap crew cut hair on their dazed faces, looking like Tweedledee and Tweedledum.

"We got a problem?!" Dee yells wasted.

"Looks like someone wants to be a white knight!" Dum calls out in the same hammered voice.

Two guy step next to Rainbow-Head. All three rocking tattoos across their bodies. One is tall with a metal arm. The short one wears an orange visor that drops to his mouth.

"Aye Tyrel, you got a problem?" Metal-Arm asks.

"Look what we got here! Pony boy got some friends!" Dum cheers.

"How about I beat the steroids out of your mouth huh?" Metal-Arm threatens.

"How about you get out my face?!" Meathead demands.

Meathead shoves Metal-Arm. Bouncing back, Metal-Arm punches Meathead in the mouth with his real hand. Dum takes out a gun and a badge.

"Protocom Police! That's an assault on an officer! You're all under arrest!"

Tyrel and his crew freeze in their tracks.

"That ain't right. Yo boy started it!" Tyrel protests.

"We can do whatever we want!" Meathead yells, rubbing his bloody mouth. "Now get outside!"

The cops shove them outside.

"You can't do this to us!" Tyrel argues.

"Shut up!" Dee barks.

I feel bad for them. Technically it was self-defense, but laws don't mean anything if you lack money or power. Assaulting a cop is what they call a political crime. That's a guaranteed trip to the reeducation camps.

As an inmate there, you spend 12 hours a day doing manual labor, and the rest locked in a room, watching corporate videos on being a good customer. The videos aren't the bad part; watching them over and over again until bed is the real torture.

My mom had a friend who lost his corporate job, and in the heat of the moment threatened to blow up the building. They sent him to one of those camps. When he got out, he was never the same. He recited the corporate anthem in his sleep, complaining he couldn't get it out of his head. He ended up hanging himself.

The disruption messes up my taste for more drinks. I pay my tab and book it. I go outside only to see a disgusting sight. The cops have Tyrel and the others handcuffed on the ground, kicking the mess out of them.

"You thought you were tough?!"

"You getting whooped tonight boy!"

I have to do something, not because the cops are abusing their power. On any other day I would mind my own business like a smart person, but Tyrel stood up for me. It's only right to pay him back. I march over.

"Hey leave them alone!" I yell.

Meathead smirks at me.

"Did you come to say sorry?" he asks. "I'll show you how a real man takes care of his woman."

He rubs my arm. I shove my id in his face.

"Take care of this!" I snarl.

He inspects the card. He drops the smirk. He tries to remain confident, but his face cracks with uncertainty.

"Is that a threat?" he mumbles.

"If you want it to remain just a threat, you'll leave them alone."

I keep my scorn on him as he ponders. I am sweating, but the night hides it. I have no idea if my threat is convincing enough.

"Aye boys, let's leave these clowns here. We got other things to do," he tells.

The other cops groan.

"I said let's go!" he snaps.

The cops take off the handcuffs and march away. As Meathead passes me, he thrusts his shoulder into mine.

"I hope you get your head cut off," he mutters.

I let out a huge breath of relief as they leave. Tyrel helps his friends up. They have bruises.

"Those pigs ruined my shades!" the short one growls, holding his cracked visor.

"Work your magic Hawk," Tyrel suggests.

Hawk taps his visor, changing the color to black, hiding the cracks.

"You guys alright?" I ask.

"No we ain't alright! Do we look alright?" Metal-Arm yells.

"Aye, Xander be cool. She just helped us out, and you ready to take her head off like she was beating us up," Tyrel intervenes. He turns to me. "Thank you."

"You did stick up for me back in the club."

"What was that you showed them anyways? You made them back up like you had the plague," Tyrel chuckles.

"Oh, it's nothing," I say, flashing my id card.

"Woah! Is that for real, you really a Valkyrie?" Tyrel chirps.

"Oh yeah."

They exchange grins at each other. This is not what I wanted when I saved them. I don't want people to worship me and treat me differently. Please no, I'm just a Valkyrie. I want to scream that it's all a lie.

"Wow, that's incredible! We got saved by a Valkyrie!" Tyrel praises. "Aye there's a party going on tonight. You want to come?"

"No thank you, I appreciate it though."

"Come on," he continues. "Me having your back ain't nothing to what you did. We were heading to the camps, if it wasn't for you."

They give me pleading grins. Although I don't know them, I have no reason to suspect they will hurt me. They're aware of my status. Any harm done to me will bring them more trouble than the cops. There's nothing to fear from them. I can use a distraction to get my mind off of things.

"Oh why not?" I agree.

They cheer.

"That's what I'm talking about!" Tyrel shouts.

They lead me to the parking lot where their bikes are. They press the buttons. The bikes levitate in the air.

"You ever rode one of these?" Tyrel ask.

I shake my head.

"First time for everything," he says with a grin.

I rest back on the motorcycle chair, holding onto the seat.

"Don't be shy. I won't bite."

I put on a helmet. Motorcycles scare me, but I am learning to throw away my fears little by little. This is my first time on a motorcycle, but I still notice when the motorcycle speeds above normal.

"Yall ready for some fun?!" Tyrel screams through the intercom in his helmet.

They give him thumbs up. We jump on the freeway. He turns up the gas. I clutch on the back of the seat harder. Tyrel laughs.

"Aye man, the speed limit is 50, you're at 75!" I call out.

"Oh wow, you're right. We're going too slow!"

He cranks up the speed. We zoom down the road. A gust of wind hits my face. Cars honk at us as we race past them, maneuvering around them with ease. Tyrel rides like a pro. My heart races as cars disappear only seconds after coming in sight.

"Dude slow it down! You're going to pick up the police again!" I scream.

"That's why we have you!" he laughs.

Sirens go off. A floating police drone pursues us.

"Hey coppers, you want me?!" he screams with delight. He flips the drone off. "Come and get me!"

"Please reduce your speed now!" the police drone orders.

He laughs. The drone scans our faces. The light goes from red to green when it hits my face. I've never seen that before.

"Have a good day," the drone says politely, flying away.

"What?" I stammer.

"It scanned your id and knew not to mess with us. What I tell you? We're above the law!" Tyrel declares.

We continue to fly down the freeway as his enthusiasm increases with the speed. He has no regard for life or death. We arrive to a lone shed on the beach. I jump off the motorcycle and rush to Tyrel.

"What was that? You could have killed us!" I bark.

"Relax. We've been riding for years. I wasn't going to let anything happen. Besides we have you," he chuckles.

He gives me a playful shove. I slap his hand down.

"I'm not some get out of jail free card!" I protest.

93

"It was just some speeding. It wasn't-."

"No!" I scream. "You can't commit crimes because you can get away with it. People get thrown in jail because cops falsify reports yet you're asking for trouble. What if I wasn't there to protect you?"

Tyrel's jolly attitude is gone as he looks down in silence.

"My bad. We good?" he mutters.

"Sure," I reply.

His face lights up.

"Party's still on!" he cheers.

It irritates me how he saw my status as an opportunity for his childish ways. Yet I am jealous of his rebel spirit. Thinking back to the motorcycle ride, there was a brief moment when I was mesmerized by his fearlessness. The way he toyed with death with no care for the rules captivated me. I thought my life sucked, but ever since becoming a Valkyrie, I realize how much freedom I had. To live in this world with no care or restriction is a dream I can only live through him now.

A woman with metal braids comes out the shed. Her eyes, nose, and mouth share resemblance to Tyrel.

"Oh my god, what happened to your face?" she shrieks.

She yanks Tyrel's chin, inspecting his face.

"It's fine," he says, putting her hand down. "We ran into some cops who thought they were hard."

"Cops?!"

"Tessa, I said it's fine. Nova helped us out."

He points to me.

"How?" Tessa stumbles.

"She's an upcoming Valkyrie. The cops know better not to mess with her."

"Wow!" Tessa exclaims. "Thank you for saving my idiot brother."

"Hey!" Tyrel calls out.

"The cops started it," I say, shrugging.

"What did I tell you about getting in trouble?" Tessa snaps at Tyrel.

"Didn't you hear her? They started it," he defends.

"I don't care. You're always in some mess." She looks to me. "What are your plans now?"

"Tyrel said there's a party tonight. I don't have anything going on, so I accepted the invitation."

"Party huh? Well, let me get you something inside."

Tessa squints at Tyrel who looks away. The shed contains dozens of computers connected to each other. Dangling wires are in the air. I have to constantly duck underneath them to get by.

"So, Nova. I'm sure your family must be excited that you're on Last Valkyrie. Where are they at?" Tessa asks, hesitantly.

She doesn't want to sound rude or nosey.

"It's a long story."

She catches my drift and leaves it alone. She comes back from the fridge with some water for me.

"Thank you," I say.

"Tyrel, can I speak to you please?" Tessa asks.

"Wassup?"

"In the kitchen," Tessa mumbles. She smiles at me. "Make yourself at home."

They walk off. I sit down on the couch next to Xander. He hands me a drive of e-dope.

"No thanks," I politely refuse, not that I could physically take it if I wanted to.

He shrugs and plugs it into his bulging biceps. The siblings speak quietly, making it hard for me to hear anything. I peek into the kitchen. Tessa barks at Tyrel in a sharp whisper, getting in his face. She catches me looking and smiles at me. Hawk is at a table in the living room, fixing his shades.

"Hey Hawk what'chu doing?"

Ignoring me, he continues working.

"You really like those glasses, huh?"

He turns around. I scream. His eyes are entirely red lights, shining at me. His sclera is completely metal.

"Aye Hawk, what we tell you?! Nobody wants to see your ugly face!" Xander barks.

"It's okay. It just surprised me that's all," I stammer.

Hawk stares at me with a mute face as I inspect his eyes. It's like he's use to the stares. I forget I'm prying as I step closer. What happened to him?

Realizing how rude I am, I snap out of my gaze. Hawk goes back to work like nothing ever happened. The siblings come back. Tyrel keeps his head to the floor as Tessa shoves him.

"Tell her," Tessa demands.

"Tell me what?"

Tyrel sighs, scratching his head.

"There is no party. I invited you because we're going to do a job," he reveals timidly.

"Job?" I ask.

"What he means is we're about to do something illegal, and he thought it would be fun to bring you along," Tessa tells.

"Why?"

"Extra hands?" he guesses.

"You see what you did dummy? You got this little girl in trouble," Tessa berates.

"I can handle myself."

"We don't want you to get hurt messing around with us. It's best if you leave."

I shake my head at Tyrel who can't look me in the eyes. I want to knock his lights out. How dare he trick me after all I did for him? This is the problem with helping people. They always take advantage of your kindness, and you end up in a worse spot. Part of me wish I left him at the bar. I head for the exit when Tyrel objects.

"Come on Tess, you know how long we've been planning this. We need all the help we can get!"

"We know the risks, we'll do it as we planned."

I stop at the door. Just walk out stupid girl. You don't owe them anything anymore. It's true, but my feet remain put. If I leave, the rest of my life is out of my hands: Last Valkyrie, fight to the death, and if I win, which is slim, I'll be told what to do for the rest of my life. But taking a chance with them, although it would be short, I get to experience freedom a little bit longer. I let go of the door knob.

"What is the job?" I ask.

They look at me like I'm crazy.

"You don't owe us anything," Tessa says.

"I don't care."

Tyrel and Tessa exchange nervous looks.

"Follow us," Tessa instructs.

We go into the kitchen. The table projects a holographic train with the words Nano Foods.

"This automated train leaves headquarters each morning to downtown San Francisco where it delivers foods to stores. We're stealing what's inside," Tessa tells. "I'm going to hack the rail system to make it believe the train is at a light. That will stop the train and allow us to go inside.

"When the train stops, we'll have limited amount of time before the rails move again. We have to be quick. You sure you want to do this, Nova?"

I think about the risks. What if Blaze is hearing this conversation and decides to blow my head off at any moment? Would he really waste a Valkyrie over theft? Like he said, we can do anything as long as we don't tell on them. Still, what if I'm caught? This is a felony, so flashing my id card isn't going to be an option like last time. Will the show come to my aid if I get arrested, or will they just press the button and find another Valkyrie like they did with Jetta?

I imagine being in the interrogation room when suddenly bam! My head explodes. Then the cover-ups, and everyone believes the story. A Valkyrie commits theft and blows her brains out with a police gun to prevent jail time. With all the scenarios running through my head, I realize it doesn't matter. My life fell out of my hands the day I was kidnapped. It may never be in my hands again. After a long thought, I finally speak.

"What are we waiting for?"

CHAPTER 10

This isn't my first robbery. In fact, I've done it many times in the past. When I was a little girl, I stole from grocery stores. It was when I was first introduced to protein blocks. I couldn't stand the taste. I wanted to eat real food again. I traveled almost an hour to the nearest grocery store that sold food and took what I wanted.

At first, I was cautious. I took only essential foods such as milk, grains, plants, and meats. I took it for my family, lying to my mom that it was part of a school program that gave food to families in need. I started off nervous, but after getting away so many times, I got bold and stole more than just essentials. I took candy and other sweets, and saved them for myself.

My reign came to an end when I was finally caught. My mom didn't have the money to get me out. Even though I was just a little girl, they were going to send me away to a junior reeducation camp for five years. Fortunately Deidre, Atlas' mom, paid for me to get out. My mom beat me so bad, I couldn't sit down without feeling the burn for 2 weeks. She told me, 'I don't care how bad things get, you never steal.' In a way, stealing from the train isn't much different than stealing from grocery stores. As long as we're fast, and nobody sees us, we'll be fine.

Tyrel drives the van down a ditch. We stop at the side of the railroad. Homeless encampments and tents are everywhere. He hands us black ski masks to go with the black pants and sweaters we have on. We wear all black.

It's quiet until I hear the loud engine of the train. It's nowhere in sight, but its engine roars loud like it's near us. Tessa types fast on a laptop with focus. I take a peek. Hundreds of numbers are on the screen, none of which I understand.

"As soon as this train stops, move out," Tessa tells.

The train approaches, wind picks up around us with a gust. Tessa hits a button, and the train stops immediately.

"Now!" she orders.

We jump out. Xander gets to the train first. With his metal hand, he crushes the handle on the train's door.

When I step inside, the air turns cold. Containers of dairies and meats surround us. The entire room is a fridge. I pause as my eyes feast on the delicious looking meats and cheeses. It's been so long since I've seen real food. I'm tempted to reach into the containers and devour it all. The thought of salami waters my mouth. Xander shoves me from behind, forcing me to remember why we are here.

"Move!" Xander yells.

I run to the crates. They are about the size of medium mail packages, around 25 pounds, I estimate. I pick up several and hurry to the van. I run back and forth, picking up what I can as Xander opens up the other train cars.

"Thirty more seconds!" Tessa screams as she carries loaves of bread. "That's it! Let's get out now before they come!"

Putting the crates in the van, I look back at the train.

"Nova, get in!" Tyrel yells.

My eyes stay on the train, seeing all the food left behind. I can grab some more. It's not that far from me. I still got time. I run back to the train.

"Nova!" they call out.

101

Ignoring them, I run into an open car and pick up the first crate I find. The train starts moving. I jump out with the crate. It tumbles in my hand. I catch it before it hits the ground. I sprint back to the van as they yell my name. A loud siren goes off. A police drone flies towards us. I hop in the moving van.

"Pull over now!" the police drone demands.

The bumpy ride causes everything and one to bounce inside the van. Crates hit the walls. My bottom leaves my seat.

"Homie, drive faster!" Xander yells.

"We're in a van, what do you expect?!" Tyrel barks.

Tessa gets on her computer and types. I pray whatever she's doing will save us.

"Final warning!" the drone orders.

I look in the mirror, and my heart drops, seeing a gun barrel come out of the drone.

"Tessa. Do something!" Xander screams.

Sweat covers her face, wetting her keyboard as she rapidly types. The drone lowers behind us. I stare down the barrel of its gun. This is how I'm going to die. It could have been in front of a crowd of millions, in front of the entire world, but no. I will die in a ditch with nobody to watch it.

It makes no difference now. I stand still. As everyone panics, I do nothing. It scares me to know I will die, but I'm wise enough to not resist. The drone crashes to the ground. It bursts in flames. I gasp in disbelief, clutching my chest. The rest of the ride is silent as we ponder our escape. Tessa glares at me.

"Pull over," she orders, mugging me.

The van stops. Tessa grabs me and throws me out. She slams me against the van. I can take her, but my arms remain down. There's no reason for me to protect myself. She has every right to be mad.

"What is your problem? You almost got us killed!"

"I know," I utter.

"How did the drone even know we were there?" Xander asks.

"It was alerted when the train moved with her inside," Tessa tells. "What do you have to say for yourself?"

"Nothing. If you want to waste me, go ahead. I did what I did."

She raises her eyebrows. Her forehead scrunches up as confusion takes over her anger. Tyrel laughs.

"You think this is funny?" she scorns.

"Lighten up Tess! Did you see how many crates Nova took? She was faster than all of us and had enough time to get more. She got balls!"

"She almost killed us. Did you get hit on your head and forget that?!"

"Because of her we got a lot more crates than we expected. We're going to make more money. The reward was worth the risk. We stay escaping the boys today. Man that was exciting!"

Tessa releases me, backing up in disbelief. She's in a foreign world, unable to recognize us.

"What is wrong with you people?" she gasps shaking her head.

Everyone goes back in the van besides Tyrel and I.

"Never mind Tessa, she can be a prude," Tyrel laughs. "This time we're really going to have a party tonight. You wanna come after we sell some of this stuff?"

The sun is beginning to set. My heart still pumps with the adrenaline from the hectic chase. I have to admit I love the energy these folks bring out.

"Sure why not?" I say.

***

We change the van's plates and spray paint it a different color. We drive to local sheds in Shed Court to sell some of the food. Tyrel puts speakers on the top of the van and plays loud music, alerting the residents. Residents come out of their houses and run to us like we're selling ice cream.

People of all ages, from elderly to little kids, gather around like we're Santa Clause. Even some members of Shed Court's police buy food from us. None of them are from Atlas' immediate circle.

The residents' sullen faces explode in delight as they hold real food in their hands. An old lady cries as she thanks us. She says she would drop to her knees, if she had enough calcium in her brittle bones.

"How come I never see you in my neighborhood?" I ask them.

"We have a mutual agreement with that fat lady to keep our businesses away from each other," Xander grumbles.

"Ms. Blackford!" Tessa and I shout at the same time.

We smile at each other.

"She says she doesn't want the trouble we would bring in her area, but in reality, she doesn't want the competition," Tessa says.

By night we're at the beach, chilling at a bonfire with drinks. Hawk stares off at the sky. Xander plays basketball, dunking on people while yelling insults. Tyrel tries to pick up a few girls.

"What's your favorite color? I got one for each of yall," Tyrel boasts.

The girls laugh in pity, walking away.

"Oh come on! Where there's a rainbow, there's gold!"

"Idiot," Tessa chuckles.

Her laughs fade as she stares into the fire. From her calm gaze, I can tell she is at peace in this moment. There is no worry of the dangerous jobs they will have to do over and over again, and the cops on their tail. This beautiful moment gives her solace. This is what I don't understand. She can have this moment forever until death, but she chooses to jump into the fray.

"Tell me Tessa, why do you risk your life and freedom to help people you don't know or owe?" I ask. "There are jobs that don't require committing felonies."

Keeping her gaze at the fire, she shrugs.

"We don't make the smartest decisions, but if it's just for ourselves, what's the point?"

"You'd have less cops on your tail, more peace."

"Can't be at peace, if I don't help those around me who struggle." She tosses her empty bottle into a recycling robot nearby and hands me a drink. "My turn. Tell me about yourself Nova."

"What do you want to know?"

"I don't understand you. It's like you have a death wish."

"What's wrong with that?" I ask, shrugging. "It's not like I'll be missing anything."

"That's why you're going on the show? You want to die?"

I bite my tongue. No you idiot, that's not why. My impulse is to scream at her, but my mind slows me down, forcing me to think.

"If I did, can you blame me? A good death beats living in a terrible world like this, wouldn't you say?" I state.

She grins.

"Can't say I disagree, but is life so bad that the only solution is death?"

This is not a question that she needs an answer to. She already knows how she feels about it. This is a way for her to understand my thinking.

"Look around. You tell me," I say.

"I'm not talking about the world, I'm talking about your individual life. What you have to offer."

"And what is that? My parents are gone, and my sister hates me. I might as well be dead. I have nothing," I gripe, raising my voice.

"Why are you on the show?"

"What other choice do I have?"

I think about the hidden double meaning of my words.

My comment stuns her as she pauses. She faces the beach and sits back, relaxing. The water calmly moves tonight.

"You see Hawk over there. He was sent to the reeducation camps for a crime he didn't commit. They ripped his eyes out. Xander lost his arm when the Sons of Hades blew up the police station he worked at. He's addicted to e-dope to kill the pain. Tyrel and I have been on our feet ever since our orphanage burned down."

"I'm sorry, I didn't –. "

"I don't want your pity," she interrupts. "It's up to you to make something out of your pain even if you die." Our eyes meet. She has my full attention. "Even if you win, bring home the money, and your sister hates you; live or die, you still have a choice on how you go out."

The shore traps my eyes as I get lost in a daze. What was I doing with my life before I was kidnapped? Nothing, I realize, nothing at all. Now it may be too late to appreciate what I have.

CHAPTER 11

They drop me off at Shed Court the next morning.

"You are a bad woman! Drop them dead. Literally," Tyrel praises.

We slap hands, chuckling.

"Aye," Xander calls out. He hesitates to speak more. "Thank you."

I nod at him. Hawk takes off his glasses, gazing at me. My first reaction is to step back and look away, but I control the fear by looking at him. There's a silent pause then he smiles. His smile is joyful like he sees happy days ahead of him. I smile back.

"Good luck," Tessa says.

It's quiet as I walk through my neighborhood. Since my departure, a new atmosphere sweeps Shed Court. No play, laughter, or fun. My mom's death woke people up to the dark reality of our lives. They cannot hide from it anymore.

Hopefully I can make it home, say goodbye to close friends and a few others without the entire neighborhood seeing me. The twins speed past me on their bikes. Pollux bangs a metal pot with a stick in his hand. How he manages to do so while riding, I do not know.

"Nova's here! Nova has returned!" Pollux calls out.

"Shut up!" I snap in a whisper.

They keep yelling, circling the block. I continue towards my shed. The doors to the other sheds lift. People come out in disbelief.

"It's Nova," a voice says.

Chatter fills the air as everyone sees me. I can no longer keep my presence hidden. I ignore the dozens, keeping my eyes on my home. Once I make it inside, I'll be fine. The residents will grow tired and go back home, seeing I will not come out. I hope Luna is still inside, so we can talk.

My efforts to avoid people become futile as a large crowd forms around me. I scan the crowd, being on guard. There's no telling how they will react to me. They can throw heckles or objects.

A lot of people were friends with my mom. I doubt they forgive me. I hope they will not hurt Atira's daughter, but you never know from these people. Once a man butchered his family with an axe. This was during the Shed Court Police Strike, so there were no cops to arrest him. The residents took justice into their own hands and hanged the man.

I stop as the crowd engulfs me, blocking my way. They completely surround me with intrigue on their faces. Silence fills the air. I gulp, waiting to see what will happen next. The hanged man hits my mind. If they decide to take action, I will be at the mercy of the mob.

A little girl runs through the crowd. She hugs my legs, planting her face into my stomach. It's Saylor, Phoebe's daughter. She gives me her innocent eyes.

"Nova, will you win?" she asks naively.

"I, uh," I stutter.

Phoebe grabs her hand.

"Come on," Phoebe says.

"Please win. I don't want you to die. Kill them all!" Saylor rants.

"Saylor!" Phoebe snaps.

"It's okay, Phoebe." I drop to my knees and exhale, facing Saylor. "Yes, I'm going to win."

Her face lights up, smiling with missing teeth. I try my best to sound confident.

"Can I come play at your mansion when you do?" she asks.

I close my eyes, holding back my tears. I hesitate.

"You can bring all your friends with you."

"Yah!" she cheers.

She hugs me. Phoebe burst in tears with a smile and takes her daughter away. Ms. Blackford steps from the crowd. Her round cheeks lift as her eyes water.

"Nova, why?" she asks.

"I don't know," I mumble.

She raises her eyebrows at me as if she's trying to figure something out. Whatever suspicion she has goes away as she hands me a bag of plums.

"I can't," I plead shaking my head. "You need all the food you can get."

"No, it's my wish, please."

I accept the fruit. She hurries off before crying. I spot Atlas and his father in the crowd.

"Nova, I get it," Mr. Archer states. He takes a puff of his cigarette. "This is a bad place, and you want to get out."

"I can explain-."

He put his hand up.

"Our families go way back even before you were born. If your parents were alive, they wouldn't agree, but they'd understand. No matter how people look at you, we'll always love you."

We hug for the first time in years. I feel like a kid again as he wraps me in his huge arms. He becomes that man again, comforting a little girl, letting her know there's light at the end of the tunnel. It feels like my dad is hugging me. I look up at Mr. Archer, picturing it's my dad again.

"Take care of yourself kid," he says, patting me on the head.

He fades into the crowd, leaving me and Atlas. Our eyes meet only for a few seconds before separating.

"So you're really out of here huh?" Atlas says.

"Yeah."

"Can I call you?" he asks.

I blush, hiding my smile. Thankfully it's impossible for him to see me blushing.

"Atlas, you know we don't get to have our phones on the island?"

"Oh!" he blurts in embarrassment. "I can use a hologram."

"Are you serious? That's going to put a hole in your pocket."

"You make it sound like you don't want me to contact you."

I laugh. It's impossible not to admire his persistence. It's part of his charm, and it's what I like about him.

"We'll be in touch," I say.

He scratches his head.

"About that night on top of the shed," he falters.

I throw my arms around him, and he hugs me back.

"You did nothing wrong," I whisper.

I give him a quick kiss on the cheek. He gasps with a smile. I want to say more. I wish I have more time to spend with him, but it's best to leave it like this. I don't want him to get too attached, and now I fear he will. But I'm glad I got to say this much.

I meet with other residents in the crowd, receiving their wishes. Some are people I never spoke to, but only saw over the years. They wish me good luck. There are others who I am more familiar with; we share longer conversations, talking about how much we'll miss each other. I take pictures with the little kids. They ask me questions, wondering what weapon I will use, how many kids I will have with the Chosen One when I win. The little girls even ask when can they be on the show.

"Uh, you can-," I falter.

What am I supposed to tell them? I've been lying since I got out, and lying to them breaks my heart even more. I just turn to the parents with confusion. The parents shoo them away.

"Focus on going to school first!" a parent barks at her daughter.

Last Valkyrie is a dream come true for people, but the people of Shed Court understand it's a one in a million chance. They don't put their hopes and dreams on a lottery like this show. The daily struggles of their lives force them to succumb to reality.

Camden, the daughter of the landlord, who I had beef with in high school but later settled it, gives me a hug. I haven't seen her cry since her boyfriend dumped her. The old couple who recycles cans and waves at me in the morning, wishes me luck. After all these years, this is the first time I hear them speak.

Not everyone is sincere in their goodbyes. Ms. Lien, a friend of my mom who use to come over for talk and tea, tells me I ruined my family and ought to be ashamed. She still wishes me the best, saying that my mother would want me to survive. Even Dirk and his boys are here. They nod at me.

For a decade this has been my home. On any given day, I would disparage it as a dump. As I leave, the things I hate about here are finding a place in my heart— the sounds of barking dogs, loud music, annoying kids, and the entire rut. All I want is one more day. I should have been more appreciative. Oh my god, I don't believe it. I'm really going to miss this place.

"Goodbye," I say, waving to the crowd.

They leave as I make it over to my house. The shed is quiet. I go to Luna's room, but it's locked.

"Luna, please," I say.

I wait, but the door remains shut. I hear nothing. This isn't how I want this to go. I want to see her face to face. I check my phone. The arrival of the hover car approaches. No, I can't wait any longer. It's now or never.

"There's nothing I can say to make you forgive me. It's my fault for what happened to mom and dad. I haven't been a good sister. You deserve to hate me. But I want you to know that no matter what, I will always love you. I will come back."

I hear sniffles on the other side of the door. I walk away, already knowing she's not coming out. The hover car meets me outside.

"Please put your eye to the scanner to verify," the virtual assistant says.

Ascending in the air, I look down at the shed, hoping it will open. The shed grows further as I get higher in the air. In a matter of seconds, I am out of the city. San Francisco becomes a speck in the distance as I'm over the ocean. I burst out in cries, plowing my face into the seat.

"Are you okay?" the virtual assistant asks.

"Shut up!" I scream.

I hate this car already. One hour until my arrival. I use this time to let my tears out. Fifteen minutes go by, and I am still crying on the floor as a mess. I stare at the ceiling. When did my world fall apart?

CHAPTER 12: Nova's Story

"Dad, do I have to go to work with you?" I asked.

"Do you want to watch your mom and her friends pot plants?"

"No," I sighed.

He rubbed my hair.

"We'll get ice cream afterwards."

I smiled, tasting my favorite cookie dough ice cream already in my mouth.

"Atlas' dad is bringing him today," my dad snickered.

"And?"

"I see how you act when he's around."

"Wha-what? I do not like him," I stammered.

"I never said you liked him," he chuckled.

We walked into a multistory building. His luggage rolled on the conveyer belt through the scanner. The monitor glowed, displaying an assault rifle and pistol. The machine beeped.

My eyes met the LED face on the robot standing in the booth. This was new. It had been a human guard at the booth before. Although it had no eyes, I felt like it was staring at me, gazing directly into my soul. The robot locked me in a trance, hypnotizing me with its red screen face. This gave me a weird feeling. It was like it had a mind of its own. The scanner beeped, snapping me out of my daze. The panel doors opened.

"Welcome in Mr. Orion and miss," the robot said.

"Oh she's not that old," my dad joked.

A beefy man with large arms walked towards us. My dad's eyes grew wide as he smiled.

"Wassup, Archer!" my father greeted.

They slapped hands. Their biceps bulged from their strong handshake. They held the handshake as their veins popped out in a friendly competition to see who was stronger. They always did this.

"How's classes going Nova?" Mr. Archer asked.

"I got all A's, sir," I boasted proudly, standing up tall.

"That's what I'm talking about!"

We slapped hands front and back and saluted each other. It was our special handshake.

"How's security?" my dad asked.

"On edge, and that's sugar coating it. Augustus needs to send more arms down here," Mr. Archer grunted.

"You know he would if he could."

"Yeah right. He's just trying to protect himself at that stupid summit."

"This is Hyperion Industries. Who's going to get through them turrets?" my dad boasted.

"Does that mean we won't get to see Augustus Hyperion today?" I worried.

"Sorry Nova, but he's busy today. Maybe next time."

"Okay," I sighed.

"Yeah busy having his ego stroked," Mr. Archer laughed.

Having your dad work for one of the most powerful and richest people in the world, but never seeing Augustus was irritating. I had done a presentation on Augustus, bragging that my dad was cooler than the others because he knew him. They had challenged me to bring him down to the school, but my dad said he was very busy like always. Augustus was more than just a famous CEO. He was an icon, a genius solving the world's biggest problems, making life better for us. That was what my dad always told me, and I believed it.

We entered a room. I was excited to see the boy at the other end. He wore virtual reality goggles as he struck the air.

"Atlas!" I blurted out.

He took off the goggles and smiled.

"Nova!" he cheered.

"Perfect couple," my dad joked.

They laughed, leaving us.

"What are you playing?" I asked.

"Some fighting games. How about you join, so I can whoop you."

"No you won't!"

After the match was over, he jumped in the air with his hands up, parading around.

"That's not fair. You always pick him. He's overpowered," I complained.

"A win is a win."

I groaned.

"Aye I got a better idea than playing video games. I'm talking about some real fun."

"Like what?" I asked.

"How about we get out of here and explore this place?"

"What?"

"Come on. Don't you want to see the cool stuff they make here?"

I backed up timidly.

"I don't know," I faltered.

"Come on," he persisted, tugging my arm. "We're not prisoners. We're 10 years old. We can have a little adventure."

My tongue was tied, but that didn't stop him from pressing on.

"You have all A's, you deserve to have some fun. Am I right?"

My eyes hit the floor. Every instinct told me to stay put and obey my dad. He would kill me, if he caught me messing around his workplace. On the other hand, I was dying to get out of this typical routine. All these years without seeing what they made here. If I couldn't see Augustus then at least some cool gadgets. I was 10 years old, a big kid. I didn't need my dad to hold my hand. I made decisions without him all the time. I dropped the vr goggles.

"Let's go," I said.

"Yes!" he exclaimed. "It'll be our little date."

"Ugh, no!" I giggled, giving him a light shove.

We peeked out the room, looking both ways. The hallways were clear. We tiptoed down the hall with our backs against the wall.

118

"Where exactly are we supposed to go?" I asked.

"My dad has a map of this place back at home. I remembered some of it. Let's just keep moving, and we'll come across some stuff," he explained.

His uncertainty wasn't assuring. Part of me thought about going back, but then my curiosity would be left intrigued. It was time to fully commit. I had seen commercials about Hyperion Industries, and I was close to seeing its wonders. We made it to an intersection. A man came out the door down the hall. We jumped back.

"Woah!" Atlas whispered.

Peeking out a little bit around the corner, we saw a man in a white lab coat and glasses. He paced back and forth, sweating profusely. It was hot, but the air conditioning in the building was fine yet this man sweated an ocean.

"Come on babe, what do you mean it's not working?!"

"Relationship troubles," Atlas giggled.

The man slammed his phone at the floor. It shattered.

"Great!" he complained, going over to pick up the pieces.

I kept moving. I turned around, and Atlas was not behind me. He came out from the intersection.

"What were you doing?" I asked.

"Nothing. I was just trying to see where that man went. There was nothing there," he muttered.

He placed something in his back pocket.

"What is that?" I asked.

"Nothing. Let's keep going," he declared.

Everything looked the same the more we walked, just plain walls and regular doors, nothing of interest. This became a maze. I regretted coming with him now. This entire day was a waste.

"Are you sure there are things here to check out?" I sighed, growing impatient.

"Don't worry, this is just the main floor, trust me. We'll see a lot of cool stuff once we get deep inside."

It felt like a goose chase until we came to a big metal door. The big red words printed across it said, 'TOP PERSONNEL ONLY.'

"Well, it was fun while it lasted," I sighed.

"It just begun," Atlas snickered.

He revealed an identification card from his pocket. My mouth dropped at the picture on it – the sweaty man.

"You took his card?!" I whispered sharply. "Are you serious?"

He shushed me.

"He dropped it. What else was I going to do?"

"Leave it. We don't even know if it will work. It could trigger an alarm if it-."

The door unlocked with the card.

"You were saying?" he chuckled.

My heart dropped. I jumped in front of him.

"We should stop. We don't know what's behind that door. There's a reason it needed a key," I cautioned.

"What do you want to do? Give the guy his card back? We're going to be dead if we get caught. Might as well make the whooping worth it."

The doors tempted me to go inside and uncover whatever was behind them. I was nervous as my heart raced. If I was in my right mind, I would have known my pounding heart was a clear sign to go back. But I was ignorant and took it as a challenge. I put my hands on the door.

"You're a crazy boy," I laughed.

We pushed the doors. We froze, mouths gaping in awe at what was in front of us. Machines were building machines, weapons, automobiles, and brand new home appliances yet to hit the market.

Scientists were in other rooms looking through microscopes. It looked like a bigger and more advanced science lab than the one at school. Getting noticed wasn't in my mind anymore. I was too focused on the environment, absorbed in the atmosphere. Creativity and innovation sparked the entire place, introducing us to the impossible.

A holographic screen popped up in the air, displaying the logo of Hyperion Industries.

"Here at Hyperion Industries, we understand how dangerous the world can be," the elegant female voice spoke. Pictures of riots, Hyperion's corporate flag burning, and bombings showed. "That is why we are dedicated to building a safer and better world for you and your family."

The video ended with a family smiling at the camera while a heavily armed robot watched from a distance.

"The world's first fully automated combat robot is coming soon to a city near you."

We walked through the assembling line where cars were being put together. We were like kids in the candy store. In the other room, a man pressed buttons on a metal belt he was wearing. He disappeared and reappeared at the other side of the room.

"Wow!" Atlas gasped.

"I'm glad I came here," I enthused.

This was worth dozens of whoopings and being grounded for life.

"Look," I pointed out.

A heavy gun floated above a blue light in a room. It didn't have a barrel like normal guns. It had a huge ring glowing with red. It was something out of a science fiction movie. We glanced at each other, already catching our drifts. Rushing into the room, we ogled at the gun.

"This thing is so dope!" Atlas admired, reaching towards it.

"Wait don't touch it," I warned.

He gave me his childish smile, making me more nervous. I knew what he was thinking. I grabbed his hand.

"We saw what we wanted to see. This is cool, but it's time to go," I cautioned.

"This is so dope! Don't you want to test it out?" he cheered.

"It's a gun, not a toy."

He laughed, taking my hand off his. I was powerless as he approached the gun that entrapped his eyes. He was possessed by the allure of it. Something about boys and danger, feeling like they're invincible, caused them to seek thrills in danger.

He grabbed the gun. He stumbled backwards, trying to muster the strength to hold its heavy weight. It was too strong for him as he struggled. He couldn't hold it correctly, only able to bring it to his waist, pointing it at the wall.

"I can handle this," he boasted. This was a lie, but he was fully convinced of it. "There's nothing to worry about."

He dropped the gun. It hit the ground and glowed.

"Oh no," he fretted.

A loud hum came from the gun.

"Atlas, get away!" I screamed.

I ran towards him as the sound grew louder. A blast emitted from the gun, sending us into the wall. My head smacked the wall. Before I hit the ground, everything turned black.

I opened my eyes. The room flashed with red lights as an alarm repeatedly went off. Drywall covered my face. It got into my nose, forcing me to sneeze. Atlas groaned as he staggered to his feet.

"Oh no," I uttered.

Smoke came out of a giant hole in the wall. The alarm went off throughout the entire laboratory as people ran out.

"We have to go," I ordered.

We rushed out the room. Running through the laboratory, we went unnoticed by everyone else. Panic consumed their faces.

"Why is everyone running out? The damage was back there," Atlas said.

"I don't think it's about what we did," I gulped.

I was such an idiot. I wished I was with mom. I begged to be back with her, watching her pot plants. That boredom was better than the terror I was going through. We made it out to the hallway where people were still running.

"This is bad, this is bad!" a worker quivered.

"Let's get back to the room before our dads notice," Atlas said.

"What are we supposed to tell them?"

"Not the truth."

I gulped, not knowing if I was able to lie to my dad. It wasn't out of fear, but out of respect. I had never lied to him. He was honorable and loving, and even if it worked, I would be haunted by guilt.

"Nova!" my dad screamed.

Our dads ran down the hall towards us. I shook. At least I didn't have to lie anymore.

"Oh no, we're in trouble," Atlas quaked.

"What are you two doing? We told you to stay in the room!" Mr. Archer screamed.

"We were looking for the bathroom," Atlas shivered.

"The bathroom isn't over here. You already know where it's at!"

My dad shook his head at me.

"Dad, I'm sorry," I whimpered.

"We'll talk about it when we get home," he sighed.

They snatched our hands, marching us down the hall.

"Dad what's going on? Why are people running?"

He said nothing, looking ahead. Both our dads sweated rivers. My dad had always been calm, but now he looked like his soul was snatched away.

"Dad!"

"I'll explain later," he said.

"We have to get them to safety first," Mr. Archer whispered.

A scientist ran up to them holding a tablet.

"Sir it's worse than we expected. The destruction in the testing room knocked out our defenses completely," the scientist squealed.

"How long will it take to get them back up?" my dad asked.

"About thirty minutes. It's already rebooting now."

"We don't have thirty minutes! Contact headquarters for more people!" Mr. Archer demanded.

"They said they will not move them until the summit is over."

"Try everything you can to speed up the reboot. We need those turrets back on line," my dad ordered.

The scientist ran forward. The walls exploded in front of us with a ball of fire, incinerating dozens of people. Crisp bodies laid on the ground. Fully armored soldiers with rifles jumped through the opening.

"Get back!" my dad yelled.

Our dads shoved us behind a wall. The soldiers fired, killing workers. Hyperion Industries' security ran to the scene, trading bullets with the soldiers.

The sound of gun fire filled the air as bullet shells hit the ground rapidly. I peeked around the corner to see the action. Bullets bounced off the soldiers' armor with no effect as the soldiers tore the security to shreds.

Taking cover by a pillar, our dads reloaded as the soldiers advanced. Scientists were shot in the back as they tried to flee. A worker got shot and dropped right next to me. His dead eyes stared at me as his blood filled the floor. Covering my ears, I rocked back and forth on the ground.

"Oh my god, oh my god!" I cried.

"Nova," Atlas said, pulling on my arm.

I ignored him, stuck in my trance.

"I can't do this," I wept.

"Nova! We have to go!" he screamed, grabbing my attention.

He pulled me to my feet. We ran down the hall where a wide metal door was at. Our dads and the rest of the survivors ran behind us. There was no telling what was behind this door. Instinct propelled me to run straight.

I rammed my shoulder into the door. It remained still. My dad swiped his card through the door. Exhaust shot out as the door slowly opened. We barged in, not waiting for it to fully open. A few scientists ran behind as the soldiers pursued.

"Wait!" a scientist cried.

The soldiers mowed down the scientists before they could make it. A few people yanked the door shut. The room had shelves of weapons. The security guards ran over and traded their pistols for assault rifles. They took body armor from the shelves. The armor wasn't as fortified as what the soldiers had. The scientists freaked out as they paced back and forth, crying. One got on his knees and prayed.

"Dear father please protect us," the scientist whimpered.

Mr. Archer got on his phone. A massive holographic face popped up - Augustus Hyperion. I gasped in delight upon seeing his face. At last the great Augustus Hyperion was going to save us. There was nothing he couldn't do.

"Sir, we are being attacked. Forces have overwhelmed us, they're everywhere," Mr. Archer told.

"I am aware of this," Augustus responded calmly.

His voice echoed throughout the entire room.

"Then please send reinforcements now sir," my dad fretted.

"All remaining forces are protecting the summit. You must hold your position until it's over, or until the defenses get back on."

"There won't be enough time!" Mr. Archer yelled.

"None of this would have been a problem had your defenses been online. I cannot sacrifice company resources for your failure."

"Resources? They're going to steal all the tech and files here. Surely you care about that?"

127

"I activated a fail switch that deletes all the data and destroys the technology here. They won't be getting anything."

"You're leaving us here to die? What about the children?" my dad begged.

Augustus turned his calm gaze to me and Atlas. His projection was literally larger than life. His holographic image took my breath away. I had never seen him this close. A mix of excitement and fear swept over me. I was eccentric to finally meet him and scared of the soldiers, but there was also the fear of the unknown. The way he looked at us with apathetic eyes, gave him an impartial aura. I had neither confidence nor doubt he would do the right thing. All I could do was pray.

"Please save us," I whispered, hoping the terror in my eyes persuaded him.

"I am sorry," he said in his calm voice with an unflinching face.

The feed cut off.

"No!" Mr. Archer screamed.

He slammed his phone at the ground. I stood still, shocked. How was this possible that Augustus Hyperion turned his back on us? He had donated millions to charity, gave gifts to sick children in hospitals, and volunteered in homeless shelters. A man as noble as him became heartless all of a sudden. It was unimaginable.

Harlan who had survived the hallway attack shook as he typed fast on the tablet.

"How's the reboot going?" my dad asked.

"I'm trying to speed it up, I was able to get it down to fifteen minutes. I'm doing everything I can," Harlan trembled, pressing on the tablet.

Sparks came from the middle of the door. The metal started to melt. The scientist screamed as the guards stepped up. Mr. Archer handed a rifle to a quaking scientist.

"If you can press a button, you can pull a trigger," Mr. Archer declared.

The scientists cowered back.

"We protect this place with our lives, and now you're too afraid to fight for yours?" Mr. Archer yelled at the scientists.

"Leave them. It's not their job to fight," my dad said.

"We need all the help we can get!"

"You want to give guns to our kids too?"

Mr. Archer paused as his anger dropped.

"That's not what I meant," Mr. Archer hesitantly said.

"If we can't stop them, a few more scientists won't help. This is our job."

Mr. Archer glared at the scientists and threw the rifle down.

"Cowards," he scorned.

"Everyone else take cover!" my dad ordered.

The security guards approached the door. I ran up to my dad and tugged on his pants.

"Dad," I stammered.

"Nova listen to me."

"Please don't go."

"I said go now!"

"I can't! This is my fault! I was in the testing room and made the gun go off! I caused all of this!" I cried.

He lowered his gun. Getting on a knee, he caressed my cheek.

"It's okay," he comforted.

"No it's not. I-."

"You did nothing that will make me stop loving you."

"But people died. I don't want to lose you dad."

"As long as you have me in your heart, I'll always be with you." He took me in his arms. I felt his heart. It was beating fast. "Right now I need you to hide because they need me. Can you do that for me?"

"I think," I guessed.

"We'll get ice cream after this. It'll be cookie dough, your favorite. We'll even get sprinkles."

We smiled. He kissed my head.

"Now go my child."

I hurried into a small storage room where everyone hid behind shelves. They shut the door. The scientists hurried me to the back, behind a shelf where Atlas was at. I sat next to him and squeezed his hand. We looked at each other with terror in our eyes.

"It's going to be alright," he trembled.

Neither of us believed it. We both sweated profusely, breathing hard. Taking a deep breath, I closed my eyes and counted. I prayed that when I opened them, my dad would be in front of me, telling me it was over.

Bullets fired. I jerked back, clenching harder on Atlas' hand. Yells came from outside the room as the bullets continued. It was impossible to tell who the yells came from.

I covered my ears, but the gunshots were still loud. The scientists cried more. Each agonizing second felt like hours. I wished it stopped already. I didn't care what the odds looked like, my dad would make it, no matter what. He was the toughest person I knew.

The bullets stopped. I opened my eyes. Nobody moved a muscle. Maybe it was all over, and we won. The door opened. Please let it be my dad, coming to the rescue.

"Come on out!" a voice yelled.

Nobody moved. The gun cocked.

"We can do this the easy way, or the hard way." the voice continued.

"Stay here," a scientist whispered to Atlas and me.

With their hands up, the scientists came from behind the shelves, crying.

"Is there anyone else?" the voice asked.

"No, it's just us," a scientist replied.

Bullets fired, ripping the scientists apart. Their bodies hit the ground with blood. Atlas and I jumped up against the wall, placing our hands over our mouths to silence our cries. Through the shelves, I saw a pair of boots marching towards us, splashing in the pool of blood. A soldier came around the corner. Their blood-stained visor blocked out their face, giving them the presence of something not human. Atlas and I held onto each other in absolute fear, looking at death itself. The soldier raised their rifle at us.

"Don't worry kids. Close your eyes, it'll all be over," the soldier stated.

I had never thought about dying before. It had always seemed normal, watching people get killed on television. I had watched it, and didn't think twice about it. That was how customary I was to it.

Staring down this barrel as the hand of fate touched me, I realized death was horrifying. I was petrified and frozen in fear, surrendering my life to this soldier.

"Please," I cried.

"What are you doing? They're just kids!" another soldier yelled.

"You know what the bosses said, no survivors."

The soldier focused his aim back on us. Blood spurted out of Harlan's mouth as he gasped. He murmured something.

"Oh, four eyes has something to say," the soldier taunted.

"I said…… it's back online," Harlan coughed.

He pressed his tablet. He stopped breathing. The room beeped. Gun barrels emitted from the walls, pointing lasers at the soldiers.

"Intruder alert, you are not welcome. Prepare to be removed," a robotic voice announced.

"No!" the soldier screamed.

The turrets fired a brigade of bullets, blasting the soldiers. I covered my ears, screaming until my lungs got sore. I opened my eyes. Nobody was left standing. Atlas and I tiptoed out, walking over the dead bodies. Blood painted the walls. Corpses were stacked on each other. It was like walking through a cemetery. Mr. Archer crawled on the floor, missing a leg.

"My leg," he groaned.

Atlas sprinted over to him.

"Dad!" he cried.

I ignored them, looking at my father who laid in a puddle of blood. His chest barely moved. I ran over with tears.

"Dad," I wept.

"Nova?" he wheezed.

I dropped to my knees.

"Dad, please," I cried.

"I guess I'm going to have to take a rain check on that ice cream," he said.

He chuckled then coughed in pain, clutching his chest. A calm look manifested on his face. He was steady despite the pain. He put his bloody hand on my face.

"Dad please don't leave me," I whimpered.

"Nova, be strong."

His hands fell from my face as his eyes rolled to the ceiling and stayed there.

"Dad!" I uttered.

There was no response, only lifeless eyes. I gripped his shirt.

"Please dad wake up!" I whimpered.

I held onto his body. Planting my face into his bloody chest, I sobbed a river of tears. Crying so hard, I wheezed as his blood filled my nose and mouth. I felt numb. I wished I had never been born. I wished I was the one who died.

CHAPTER 13

The ocean stretches out endlessly. The water is peaceful, allowing my mind to let go of stress. An island comes into sight. Tropical mountains clothed in green pierce the clouds. As I get closer, I see a smaller island nearby. A luxurious mansion is on it. Tiny islands are scattered across the ocean.

The hover car drops me down in front of the mansion. I join the rest of the women. We walk to the golden gate that surrounds the mansion. The gate opens. A robot on wheels strolls over to us.

"Hello, everyone, I am S.E.D.! Welcome to the Siclades Islands!" it greets cheerfully with immense animation. "Just follow me, and I'll get you to Mr. Blaze Neroburn."

The mansion's huge double doors open. As I step in, fresh air breezes into my nose. It's unlike the polluted air of the industrial city I'm familiar with. The sensation is alluring. The floor is marble. The decorated interior sparkles. Elegant classical music plays as we walk down a hallway.

The hall is filled with gold statues of former winners of the show. This is the famous Hall of Valkyries, stretching for about 50 yards. It's like being in a museum, so much rich history. Each statue catches my eye. I stop at, of course, Nokomis' statue. It has the design of her armor. Even though I know the dark truth, this hall captivates me. I cannot resist its magnificence. It's like I'm a kid again, looking up to these legends. Someone bumps into me.

"Watch it!" a short girl barks as she marches forward.

I ignore her, looking back at the statue, but its allure is gone. The shove reminds me of the harsh reality of this place. There is no wonder, just death. I continue ahead, not paying any more attention to the statues.

The robot takes us to the end of the hall where there's a balcony. At the top stands Blaze Neroburn, ogling at us. I don't understand why people love his smile. From my standpoint, it's creepy like he wants to eat us.

"Aren't you all looking beautiful?!" he cheers. "Your image is the name of the game. The more appealing you are, the more the fans will love you. You'll have more bettors behind you. That means patrons!"

Patrons are the people who throw their support in for a Valkyrie. They can be anyone. If they like what they see from her personality, interviews, and fights, they'll send all kinds of gifts. Special training equipment, weapons, armor, and many other things beyond what the show provides.

That's why it's so important for us to keep the audience engage through our personas. Sure, you can rely solely on your own physical ability to survive, but don't complain when you're given a knife to fight against someone who has a sword, shield, and stab proof armor.

"Tonight we're on the Felix Neptune show for the world to see you live. That's when you'll meet the Chosen One. Your managers will be here to get you ready," Blaze continues. "Fortunately cameras don't start rolling until then, so you have the entire day to get yourself ready. From there, it's open season. You never know where or when the cameras are on."

Except for in our suites. There are no cameras in the Valkyries' living quarters. After all the years I watched the show, not once did they air inside there. It's the show's way of giving Valkyries a break from the fans. Although I won't have to worry about the audience 24/7, this sense of privacy is only an illusion. With the detonators in our heads, someone's always watching us. Blaze points to the wall. Plates with our names are on the wall.

"Please drop your phones in those slots, and you will be given a new phone. You'll get your phones back when this is over. Oops. I mean one of you," he giggles.

We drop our phones in the slots. Chrome phones with the show's logo come out of the slots.

"You won't be able to contact your families with the phones, but you'll be able to stay up to date with everything that's happening on the show," Blaze says.

He claps his hands. A door opens. A bunch of people in gray tunics come out. They wear metal face masks.

"These are your personal servers. They'll show you around. They're at your service at all times."

The servers find Valkyries to stand by as if they know exactly who to go to. A young girl, about the age of Luna, approaches me. We make eye contact briefly. She instantly bows her head, cowering in fear.

"Only the people in this room, your managers, trainers, and the Chosen One know about the golden rule. If you mention it to them when cameras are rolling, you're dead. If the location is of interest, the cameras are on. Cameras or otherwise, we hear everything."

Shivers run down my spine, imagining my head exploding like that poor girl. There's a map on our phones, showing locations of no interest. Pretty much the entire island glows with red, showing all the hot spots where cameras are at. Only a few are not of interest in the eyes of the viewers such as our rooms, the wilderness on the other islands, and a nearby church. Yes this show has that. Oh how sweet and considerate of them. I get to make confessions without the world watching.

The Valkyries dip out, following their servers. The servers' necks have barcodes on them. Every single one of them. What in the world?

"Nova may I speak with you please?" Blaze calls out.

My heart sinks. What can he possibly want with me? He slides down the rail. As he approaches, he softens his voice.

"That was quite the show you and your pals put on with the Nano Foods train."

"Wait?" I gasp trembling. "I....don't...... know what you're talking about?"

"Oh come on now. Didn't I just say we hear everything?" he laughs.

I gulp, standing their helpless and speechless. He gives me a playful shoo with his hands.

"Don't worry. Your secret is safe with us."

He struts away laughing. Getting my breath back under normal, I wipe the sweat off my head and follow my server. The way to my suite is silent. I want to say something to her, but she avoids eye contact with me. As we're in the elevator, I glance at her, but she keeps her eyes to the floor.

"What's your name?" I ask.

She says nothing. Forget it. We get to my floor. I step onto the velvet carpet in the wide hallway. The housing quarters are simpler than the lavishness of the rest of the mansion. The retinal scanner at my door scans me. Seeing my room, leaves me breathless.

It's not just a room, it's a house. The room is bigger than my entire shed. Dropping my bags on the floor, I take a tour of the entire place. It has its own living room, kitchen, and bathroom. The marble of the kitchen shines bright at my eyes.

My eyes light up at the food inside the refrigerator. It feels like I'm back in the Nano Foods train, only difference is I can eat whatever I want now. I feel the round texture of the green apple in my hand and bite into it. After all these years, I forgot the taste as the sweet and sour juices fill my mouth. I stretch out on the couch, paying no attention to the large television in the living room. The gold chandelier meets my eyes as I get comfortable on the couch. It's been so long since I've been able to extend my body completely on a comfortable couch.

The bedroom alone is bigger than our rooms combined back at home. You can run sprints in it and break a sweat. I launch myself onto the bed, waiting to see if my back will meet a hard surface like with my bed at home. Instead, the memory foam absorbs my body.

This is going to be sweet. The bathroom is huge, but its size isn't the best feature. I put my hand under the bath faucet. Water automatically drizzles out. It's not lukewarm like back at home, but actual hot water that relaxes me. For the first time in years, I bathe in hot water, giving myself a real shower. There is no timer I have to abide by in order to conserve water. I can fall asleep and spend an eternity in this soothing shower. This sensation is overwhelming. I'm in heaven.

It's time for a bath to fully relax myself. I haven't had a bath since dad died. We only take showers back at home since we can't waste water for baths. Only if Luna and Atlas were here. I would love to see the look on their faces.

Is it wrong to enjoy this place while they're back at home in the real world? I was kidnapped and forced to be here. Why should I feel bad? I deserve to have some peace.

I gaze at the water. Inhaling deeply, I drop beneath the water. I could end it right here. It would be easy; just open my mouth and let all this water fill my lungs. It would be like that pool of death I was in. I would actually look forward to blacking out.

Why am I still thinking about these kinds of things? I get out of the water, gasping for air. These depressing thoughts aren't as frequent, but they still come. They're not going anywhere. I have to learn to deal with them.

I can't believe this entire place is all mine. That's when I see the server is still here, standing in the corner of the living room. Her mask blocks her full face, but I can see the void in her eyes. She's emotionless like she has no soul, just occupying a shell.

A knock comes on the door. So that's what a door not made out of metal sounds like. It's actually pleasant unlike the banging of a shed door. Venus barges right in with the entourage following her and Flavius. My managers wear their flamboyant clothes.

"Oh, Nova!" Venus cheers.

She gives me a hug, kissing the air around my cheeks.

"Hello, Nova," Flavius greets.

"I never get tired of walking in these suites! So fantastic!" Venus enthuses. "How you loving it so far?"

"I-."

"How do you like your server?"

"She's fine?" I guess.

"You mean it?" Venus answers in a snobbish way. She snaps her fingers at the server. "You girl, make me a Bloody Mary. On the hop!"

"Don't talk to her like that," I intervene.

Venus raises her eyebrows.

"Nova, it's fine. They don't mind," Venus chuckles in amusement. "See."

She waves her hand at the server, bringing her over. Venus claps in the server's face. The server doesn't blink.

"The mask injects them with a serum that makes them obedient," Flavius reveals.

Venus laughs at the shock on my face.

"Don't be sad. It's perfectly legal," Venus charms. "That's what they get for aiding Hades Hammer. They're lucky they didn't hang like the rest of those sympathizers."

"But how do they eat?"

"They don't. The masks give them nutrients," Flavius says.

"At least they don't have to worry about what to eat, am I right? They should be thankful," Venus laughs.

"I think we should get ready now," Flavius interrupts.

"Nova you're going to love how you look!"

For the next few hours, they go to work on me. I watch the clock, but it doesn't do any good, so I keep my eyes on the big mirror. They do my makeup first, making my dark skin gloss with dewy. My eyelids and cheeks sparkle with gold makeup. Lipstick as shining as chocolate paints my lips.

They give me a manicure, perfecting my nails before coating them with gold. Flavius does my hair, braiding the sides. They curl the rest of my afro, running it through the center of my braids on top. They spray my entire body with an oil, illuminating my naked body. Flavius brings over his briefcase.

"Close your eyes," he softly speaks.

As I close them, the silk on the dress incases me. Without my sight, I slip into the shoes. Its plush comforts my feet. I fidget in my new outfit, standing a few inches taller. A cold weight of metal wraps around my neck, settling on my collarbone. It is light, only a few ounces. The temporary coldness goes away as my neck warms itself against the smooth texture.

"You can open them," Flavius says.

What I see in the mirror is unlike anything I have ever seen before. My skin and eyes sparkle with the purple dress. Gold, pink, and blue star-shaped gems cover the dress. My neck wears a gold necklace composing of several rings. With each step, the gems light up the dress, giving me the presence of an exploding star. What they did for me back at the trials pales in comparison to this now. I don't look gorgeous. I shine like a supernova.

"Nova the Star," Flavius compliments, looking at me in the mirror.

"Thank you," I say.

My hands sweat again. On instinct, I go to wipe them on my dress, but Venus swats my hands down.

"No, don't ruin it," she says. She hands me a handkerchief. "Carry this with you."

"When you're answering questions. Imagine you're talking to a best friend. You have one don't you?" Flavius asks.

"Atlas," I reply without thinking.

Imagining a conversation with Atlas won't be easy when he already knows so much about me. But it's the best way to calm myself down.

"Don't worry, I'll be in the front row. If anything goes wrong, look at me and pretend I'm asking you the questions," Flavius says.

His voice calms my nerves. Flavius has been so helpful in this short time we've known each other. He's the only person I've met on this show that seems to have a heart, or at least acts like it. Before anyone realizes it, night is here, signaling we have to leave. In less than an hour I will be in front of the entire world.

**

The interviews are set in the city known as Delos, one of the islands part of the Siclades. We arrive to an underground parking lot that has my name on it. The more I experience conveniences like this, having my own parking spot when I don't even own a car, the more different I feel. I'm not myself anymore. It's not bad or good. It's like I'm a new person with no familiarity around me. Before we go our separate ways, Flavius grabs my hands.

"Be yourself and let the world see you for who you are."

Flavius heads out of the parking lot as Venus and I go to the elevator. As we're in the elevator, Venus takes out a silver capsule and pours out a line of powder on her hand. She snorts it loudly. She checks her face in the mirror, wiping off the residue.

"Are you nervous?" she asks.

"Yeah," I timidly say.

"I remember my first time being on television. I was quaking like a baby. You'll get use to it after a while."

She fans the air around her, breathing heavily.

"Are you okay?" I ask.

"Of course! Why wouldn't I be?!" she exclaims, overly excited.

She paces back and forth. Wow, the drugs has her bouncing off the walls. She hands me the capsule.

"It'll calm your nerves," she offers.

"I'm fine."

"Drug free? Yeah say no to drugs. They're bad," she laughs.

How long is this elevator going to take? Even for a skyscraper it feels long. The elevator dings.

"Smile and look pretty." For a moment she dozes off as her smile fades. Her voice goes into a whimper. "They love it when we smile."

The elevator opens. The other Valkyries are behind the stage in a line. A member of the camera crew leads me to my spot in line. I stand on a number. I am twenty three.

I hate being in the middle. On one hand, I don't have to go out first. I can relax and watch the other Valkyries. However, the longer I have to wait, the more I will be anxious. By the time it's my turn, the crowd will be bored after listening to everyone else.

We walk on stage in a single file line, heading to our seats. The audience claps. My heart pounds. My feet are somewhat use to walking in high heels, but with stage fright, I fear falling. I am relieved to sit down. The audience is a rainbow with their bright colorful attires lighting up the place. Above the main section of seats are the elevated seats and the balconies. Every seat is filled tonight.

Felix Neptune, the host of a late night talk show, parades on stage as the audience cheers. Every year a show gets the honor to do the interviews, and this year for the 12th time, it's Felix's turn. His face looks unreal in person because of all the cybernetic implants.

The glowing blue eyes, sparkling gold plated jaw, and metal scalp allowing him to change the color and length of his hair at will. This year, it's a silver Mohawk. Normally people have implants to improve their efficiency, but the wealthy do it for style. Delos is filled with people who are as machine as they are human. He does his usual shtick of throwing out jokes, entertaining the crowd then he gets to the point.

"Let's introduce this year's Valkyries!"

I recognize the first girl, Hera, from the trials- the slender athletic girl who tried to help the one who was beaten to death by Irma. She walks on stage in her crimson dress, wearing flame eye shadow. Her green eyes bloom in the light, looking beautiful. Hera says she aims to bring back honor to her family who lost everything during the Crash of 73.

Each interview is 3 minutes. An alarm goes off, the Valkyrie leaves, and the next one goes up. With each one, my time nears, and my anxiety grows. Each Valkyrie works some kind of story. Bellona, the muscular girl who killed the girl in the pool, promises to cut the heads off of her opponents, only after beating them so bad she will find out what god they pray to. This gets a nervous laugh from Felix.

"You might hurt them so bad, they'll forget who their god is!" Felix jokes.

The crowd laughs. He's good at lightening the mood.

Athena, the small girl from the Bronx, who bumped into me earlier, with an intense scowl on her face, struts to the stage. Her aggressive posture makes up for her lack of size. I doubt anyone will underestimate her, after all she made it this far. She promises she is full of surprises.

There's one girl who sticks out. Elpis, with her dimples and puppy eyes. Rather than a boastful presentation, she's appreciative and humble. Felix asks her why she wants to be on the show.

"To give hope to the people out there who are suffering and don't believe they can achieve their dreams," she gracefully says. "I had a father who passed away recently. His death inspired me to reach out and become something more. Even if I join him before the show ends, I know I will have made a difference. "

The crowd awes as Felix holds back tears. Elpis must've been an actor because her speech is captivating. If I didn't know any better, I would believe it too. Valkyrie after Valkyrie they come out until my seat glows. They call my name. Time slows down as I approach the grinning Felix, stepping into the spotlight with him. He bows before me.

"Nova, I understand you are from Shed Court. So it must be a big change coming to the island. What is the biggest difference so far?" he asks.

I take a moment to think, trying to figure out the best answer as well as the most appealing one.

"The size?" I guess.

146

"Well this place is big," he chuckles.

The crowd eats it up. Good, that means I'm not boring them yet. I force a chuckle.

"You're a moon miner. That's a dangerous job. Would you say your job has made you physically and mentally tough for this show?"

"People die every month from my job, and I had a few close calls. I am use to danger and being under pressure. Nothing can prepare me for this, but I have some readiness."

"And about this dress. You are stunning in it!" he admires, causing the audience to clap. "What are those gems made out of?"

I turn to Flavius in the front row, remembering our previous conversation.

"Gemstones straight from Mars."

"Look at you. You're named Nova, work on the moon, and wear rocks from Mars. You were made for space!"

This is what I like about Felix. He does his best to make the Valkyries stand out.

"There are trainers in the audience tonight." The big screen shows the trainers sitting in the balcony section. Looking serious, they wear black tunics. "Do you have a certain trainer you're interested in?"

"Which ever one keeps me alive," I state.

Everyone laughs, but the trainers.

"Now I want to talk about something more serious." Felix's tone changes. "Your parents."

"What about my parents?" I ask, taken by surprise.

"Your father, who worked for Hyperion Industries, died while serving for them, correct?"

"Yeah."

'Served' isn't the correct word, more like murdered, but if that's what makes them sleep at night.

"Ladies and gentleman, let's take a moment to honor those who serve the Conclave. If not for them where would we be?" Felix announces formally.

The audience claps. I have to give Felix credit for turning my tragedy into support, but man. These people really believe their own lies.

"And your mom recently passed away didn't she?"

My heart drops as my chest tightens.

"Yes," I calmly reply.

"Now Nova, I say this with all due respect, but we checked the morgue reports. Your mom died around 2 weeks ago. That's around the same time Valkyries came to Delos for auditions. Is there some kind of coincidence?"

The entire place is silent. Is this some kind of set up, or do they actually believe this lie? My answer has to preserve my innocence while keeping my head connected to my body.

"My mom's death was unfortunate, but if I didn't leave at the time I did, I would have missed the auditions."

"But why were you so quick to leave home? Regardless if your mom died before or after you left, why did you continue with the auditions? There's always next year."

I can feel the makeup on my forehead sliding down due to my sweat. My eyes turns to Flavius for help, but he keeps a calm face, nodding as is he expects me to know the answer.

Why is Felix doing this? All of a sudden he wants to get serious. His tone isn't accusing. I assume he figures I have a good reason, and it will make the audience like me more. Now his style is becoming a disadvantage for me.

"I had to get away as soon as possible. Ever since my loss, I couldn't stay," I tremble.

"Your loss? You mean other than a parent? What could have been more devastating than losing your own mother?"

Oh no. Why didn't he move onto the next question? I take a deep breath.

"The loss of my unborn child."

CHAPTER 14

My words settle in with the crowd as the camera sets on my frown. I see the stunned faces of the audience. Did I really say that? I lower my head, closing my eyes in embarrassment, not knowing how they'll react. This could be the end of my run before it even starts. The crowd might see me as weak and turn on me.

"You had a miscarriage?" Felix asks sincerely.

Looking at him, I nod.

"A couple months ago. Ever since then, I've been looking for a way out to leave the pain behind. I saw Last Valkyrie as my ticket out."

"How does the baby's father feel about your reason for coming on the show?"

"I never told him about his child."

The crowd gasps.

"He doesn't know he could have been a father?" Felix sputters.

"No."

Felix is speechless as he blinks rapidly. He puts his arm over me. I don't even know if he's allowed to touch me.

"I want you to know that you're a brave woman," he sympathizes.

The buzzer goes off. The entire audience stands up and claps, including the trainers. That's a first.

"Ladies and gentlemen, Nova!"

I traipse back to my seat. I stare at the ground the entire time as Felix introduces the others. I drown out the speeches. A cold chill sweeps over my body. Thankfully the cameras are on the interviews, and nobody sees my dejected face. As time goes on, I slowly drift out of my gloomy mood, focusing back on the stage. I cross my legs, relax my shoulders, and smile, thinking back to what Venus told me. The grief still races inside me. The final interview ends.

"Now ladies and gentlemen, it is time to reveal this year's Chosen One!"

The drums roll. Who will it be this year? Then again, I don't care. I doubt the Valkyries do. The only ones who care are the viewers, dying to see who the Chosen One will be, like they're opening Christmas presents. For the last several years, the Chosen One has been a member of the Conclave, or someone with connections to them. The drums stop.

"Everyone welcome Octavian Hyperion!" Felix announces.

Wait who? The audience and Valkyries clap as the curtains open. A tall young man with broad shoulders strut out. As he waves at everyone, I stare at his sharp jaw. That striking feature sticks out, looking very familiar. It's like I've met him before, but I've never met a Hyperion in person. Where in the world would someone like me have met someone from the Hyperion family?

He goes down the rows, shaking the Valkyries' hands. I scan the rest of his features: the eyes, perfect smile, and smooth hair. Is he a distant relative or part of the immediate family? They have so many members in the family, it's hard to tell which one he looks like.

Out of all the Hyperions I have seen on tv, there's one that's coming back to me, the one Octavian looks like the most. It's the one I was face to face with, but through a hologram, that day at Hyperion Industries. A face I will never forget. My god, he's the son of Augustus Hyperion.

The world stops around me. There are no lights, no crowd, and no show. It's just me alone once again in the void, the same void I felt when I held my dying dad in my arms. I can't believe it. I have to put my life on the line for that wretched Hyperion family.

Why can't it be the other families of the Conclave: Belenus, Moneta, Fortuna, or Feronia? Why not at least a cousin or a friend of the family, not the child of Augustus himself? Octavian looks exactly like his dad.

"Nova," a voice says.

I look up. Octavian towers over me. He takes my hand with his enormous hands. They're big, but also soft and comforting to my hands. His hands feel like silk. Looking me in the eyes, he takes a knee as if he's getting ready to propose.

"I'm sorry about your loss," he whispers.

"Thank you."

He continues down the line, greeting the others until he makes it back to Felix. They shake hands and hug.

"Welcome Octavian!" Felix greets. "Your family and I go way back. How does it feel to put a Hyperion back in Last Valkyrie?"

"Well first off Felix, I'm sure we can all agree that Hyperion fever is off the charts tonight!" he declares.

The crowd chants his name.

"After college, I didn't know what I wanted to do in life. When I was offered the job as the Chosen One, I knew where my future was.

"So all I have to say is I accept this honor. Because when it's all said and done, there will be a new member of the Hyperion family. And when you're a Hyperion, Felix, you're a Hyperion for life!"

The crowd explodes in more cheers. Despite my disdain for Octavian, I have to admit, he radiates confidence, knowing how to work the crowd unlike any other. He's poised in the spotlight, born for this. It must be a trait the people of Delos all share: Blaze, Felix, and Octavian.

"Thank you, thank you!" Felix excites. "Now after all the interviews, who will you be taking tonight?"

Octavian looks up and takes a deep breath.

"This is going to be a hard decision," he says, turning to us. "You're all amazing beautiful women with great stories to tell."

This is all going too fast for me to process, from the interview to Octavian. I'm not ready to go on a date with him. If I'm chosen, I will make a fool out of myself, and it'll make things worse. Please don't pick me, out of all the people and nights, not now.

"Elpis," he announces.

Relief hits me as the spotlight shines on Elpis. She pulls up her dress and walks over to Octavian. They speak a few words then walk off, holding hands.

"There you have it folks. What a beautiful couple! For all of you watching at home, stay tune for the reception!" Felix says.

Venus runs over to me backstage.

"Nova, I had no idea about the baby, but that was excellent!" she boasts. "You were funny, and the audience liked you. You weren't chosen tonight, but don't worry. You got a lot of people's attention."

I'm quiet in the elevator as she keeps talking about impressing people, ignoring my obvious dejected state. Everything settles in. The baby – how will people treat me now? Will they show me sympathy or look at me as weak and pathetic? Venus said I was impressive, so hopefully it works in getting patrons. Then there's Octavian. Now I have to double my efforts in pretending to adore him. Can things be any worse?

***

The reception is in the ballroom on the top floor. Managers chauffeur their Valkyries around, introducing them to potential patrons. I am told about the unsaid rule between the managers. No manager intrudes on another when they're introducing their Valkyrie to patrons. This is to limit competition at the reception- a peaceful time for mingling. Yet this never stopped a manager from trying to one up another, forcing everyone to focus on their Valkyrie.

The attendants are the elite from around the country and the world: bankers, executives, movie producers, judges, and all kinds of wealthy people. They're the ones we want to impress. Some I recognize such as Adric Tyrell, a famous actor. Majority of them, I have no idea who they are, but I don't need to. The powdered faces, lavish bright clothes, and cybernetics speak for themselves.

"Nova, I want to introduce you to some friends of ours," Venus says, grabbing my arm. "Just smile and look pretty."

I turn to Flavius for help, but he just nods. I gulp, seeing the group of strangers she leads me to.

"Hey!" Venus greets.

"Venus!" one of them cheers.

The group exchanges greetings with my managers, hugging them as I stand by.

"Everyone, I would like you to meet our Valkyrie, Nova," Venus boasts.

"So this beautiful thing is yours?" praises the woman with diamonds implanted all over her face. The diamonds project a shining ray that changes colors as she speaks. She eyes me up and down with thrilled eyes. "It's amazing you look so beautiful even after losing a child."

Her cherish tone unsettles me. Empathy isn't her strong suit.

"It's such a shame," the older gentleman sympathizes. He wears a vintage astronaut helmet. "The impoverished have always reproduced even when it's not in their best financial interest."

"It's not too bad. At least she gets to be on the show now she doesn't have a child," the man with the pet fox says as if I'm not here.

They all agree, nodding their heads except for Flavius and I.

"If Nova wins, she can do a feature for your magazine," Venus suggests. "It's been a while since there was a winner from California. That would make some headlines."

"Let's not get ahead of ourselves," Astro-Helmet chuckles. "We have to see her in the ring first."

"Then you will be her patron?" Venus pushes.

155

"As long as she smashes some heads!" Diamond-Face enthuses. "She makes it rain with blood, we'll make it rain on her!"

This gets more laughs from everyone except for Flavius and I once again. With each person I meet, the absurdity and obnoxious conversations grow.

Wolf Amano, a real estate tycoon and the owner of Los Angeles, complains about losing real estate on Mars due to attacks by Hades Hammer. He says I could do a fundraiser for him if I make it to the 4th round. He will invest in me then. The only problem is, if I make it to the 3rd round, I doubt I'll still need his help.

Daron and Trinity Nylund, the dual owners of EraseMe want me to go bald to stand out more. Their logic is it will catch everyone by surprise and make me the hottest trend. If I win, they say, I could always come to them to have my memory wiped of the hairstyle.

This receives desperate applauses from Venus. Kona Frakes, a famous singer who has her consciousness stored in an android, offers to sing during my entrances. In return, she will lend me her arm as a weapon. As I keep meeting new people, it seems they are more interested in what I can do for them than actually helping me.

Venus seems to not care about this as she constantly laughs with her companions. The laughs feel manufactured and fake. It's an attempt to make themselves feel friendly with people they have no other reason to associate with. These people are idiots. The more Venus shows me around like a trophy, the more removed I feel. Her praises sound like exaggerated reminders of ordinary things about me.

'Nova worked on the moon.'

'Her dress has gems from Mars.'

'This girl is from Shed Court, so you know she's tough.'

We're on this show to fight, that's what it's all about. Who cares about all this glamor and politics? Through it all, Flavius stands by, not saying much. I wonder if he shares my discontent for this charade.

Venus' head shifts in all directions looking for more people to engage with. She stops in her tracks. Her eyes are glued on a group consisting of an older woman, a manager, and his Valkyrie. A grin plasters on Venus' face like she sees gold.

"Nova, dear. Do you know who that lady is?" Venus asks with excitement, pointing to the older lady.

I examine the unfamiliar lady. I have no idea who she is, but I pretend to try to figure it out in order to not seem rude.

"I don't think so," I guess.

She sighs at my ignorance.

"That's Freya Ogun! Her family makes many of the weapons used for the games! An endorsement from her will give you access to a lot of weaponry," she cheers.

"Venus, don't. She's already talking to a manager. Remember the rules," Flavius cautions.

"Rules are meant to be broken. You want Nova to win this or not?" Venus says carelessly.

Flavius shakes his head as Venus struts over. The manager talking to Freya shows off his Valkyrie Lyssa. Lyssa didn't say much during the interviews. She was soft-spoken, and from the looks of it, a little timid. Ignoring the manager, Venus jumps right in front of him to face Freya.

"Hey Freya, how's business?!"

Freya shrugs.

"The usual,"' she yawns.

"Did I show you my Valkyrie, Nova? The girl who lost her baby," Venus boasts.

Freya's unamused face sparkles at me. Ignoring everyone else, she marches up to me and takes my hand.

"Sweetheart, I am so sorry for your loss," she mourns.

"It's fine, Ms. Ogun," I reply.

"Please, call me Freya."

Lyssa's manager's nostrils flare.

"Oh please will everyone stop feeling sorry for her. It's not a big deal. Get over it," the manager snorts.

Venus gasps in offense.

"How dare you say that Yavin?! Nova's been through a lot, and you have the audacity to demean her struggle? You should be ashamed!" Venus scolds.

"How dare you interrupt me when I was speaking, Venus? You want to talk about hardships? Nobody has gone through what Lyssa has, and that's what people are going to love about her!" Yavin snaps back.

Venus smirks.

"What is there to love about her? She's as dull as your wood," Venus insults.

They step up to each other, slanging insults about their attires and references to their love lives. It causes a scene as people gather around. Flavius steps in.

"Easy everyone. There's no need to get all moody. We're all friends here," Flavius consoles.

"Apparently not! Friends don't show each other up!" Yavin barks.

"I apologize. We'll be leaving. Tell the kids I said hi."

Venus stomps away. Lyssa's eyes cower to the floor as a haunted look remains on her face. She's been like this since the interviews. Of course the Valkyries are suffering, but unlike everyone else, Lyssa makes no effort to hide it. She has nothing to show that she is alive inside. Why is that? My wonder fades as I follow my managers.

"I think we should stop chaperoning Nova. Let her find her own way around here," Flavius suggests.

Venus' eyelids stretch.

"And miss out on the opportunity of making a good impression?" Venus objects.

"Trying to impress people never impresses them. It's best for her to be herself and let it come naturally."

"Alright," Venus sighs. "But if you need us, don't be scared to come get us. Come on Flavius, let's see what our friends are up to!"

They skip off, allowing me to breathe for once. Finally, I have some space, and I'm not too eager to give it up by trying to impress the next person I see. After that fiasco, the only desire I have is to be alone. I take a seat at the bar, not wanting a drink.

The bar's a great cover, so I won't look awkward standing by myself.

"You look like you need a drink," a woman says.

She sits next to me. She's not a Valkyrie. She doesn't wear flamboyant clothing like everyone else. Her black dress is simple with no decorations, and she barely has any makeup on. Her face has no cybernetics. In fact, unlike most people here, she looks human.

"Thanks, but no thanks."

"I get it. Your managers are forcing you to meet people, and everyone in this city is an obnoxious clown."

"Yeah, that's exactly how it is," I marvel, turning to her.

"They did the same thing to me. It's a shame, this show never changes," she sighs.

"You too? Who are you?" I baffle.

She chuckles in amusement at my lack of knowledge. She takes the glove off her hand, revealing burn marks on it. As I shake her hand, I feel on the scars. Her face becomes more familiar then it hits me. I realize who she is.

"Minerva Metis," she introduces.

"Oh god," I gasp.

Minerva Metis. The former winner of Last Valkyrie 15 years ago. This was back before the Conclave got a monopoly over being the Chosen One each year. Nobody expected her to win that year. She was small, looked weak, and was unappealing. Yet, she used her brains to outsmart everyone. With no patrons, she made her own weapons and even traps in the ring.

One of her tricks was a hallucinogen that spread from her breath. When her opponents inhaled it, they went crazy with hallucinations. Before they could find out it was all in their heads, Minerva killed them.

"Here's some advice. The only support you need is from the everyday fans. Forget the elites who do the betting. They're going to throw their money at whoever the fans choose, so focus on the viewers," she explains.

"And how do I do that?"

"Same way you do with any fan base. Give them what they want."

"I think I'd take a drink," I say with a smile.

"Bartender, get us two Martian Martinis," she calls.

The bartender pours our drinks.

"I was thinking of something simpler," I suggest.

"There's no need to stay on guard. There will be time for that later," she laughs.

From the first sip of the drink, we talk. She intrigues me about her humanitarian work such as building libraries, orphanages, and hospitals in underprivileged areas. Unlike most winners, she stays out of the spotlight which fascinates me even more.

"Not like some of these newer winners who have to tell the world every time they do some good," she groans.

"They can't hold a door open for someone or feed the homeless without taking a video."

"Next, they'll post about cutting their showers by 30 seconds to save water, and everyone will clap for them," she laughs.

We joke with each other, making fun of Delos' society. The cybernetics and makeup make people look like robot clowns. The managers are crazy for patrons. They're obsessed with everything.

We theorize the managers weren't born, but grown from test tubes. They've been programmed with limited emotions that causes them to act like they're on crack. Maybe Flavius is the exception, being the only natural born one.

Then the trainers, oh my. We don't understand why they act like they have sticks up their behinds and never smile. Perhaps they were made in the same lab as the managers, but the scientists forgot to give them any emotions.

Our table fills with more empty glasses. Not enough to make us overly drunk, but enough to get us in the mood to have a good time. This allows me to still be cognitive.

The conversation is one of the most genuine conversations I have had in a while. There's no angle to impress her, or get knowledge on the ins and outs of the show. I'm only interested in knowing about who she is as a person, and so is she. She never asks me about the baby. It's a huge relief. She's more interested in where I come from and life at Shed Court.

"What about your family? Do you still keep in contact with them?" I ask.

"Not after the divorce. His family really hated me for not giving him kids. I don't care about them," she gloats.

"No, I mean your original family."

She lowers her glass as the smile vanishes. Her eyes lower with a gloomy look.

"My family?" she repeats.

"I'm sorry, I didn't mean-."

"I haven't seen them since-." she begins. Her mouth freezes as her eyes get lost on the attendants. Suddenly confidence shoots into her voice with a smile. "Since I decided to audition! Life really has been good since then!"

Man, I shouldn't have asked. I feel ashamed, forcing her to relive the tragedies of losing her real family. This must be how all the winners feel. I can't continue this conversation, now that it is spoiled. Her use of the word 'audition' tells me she's in character now. It's time to go.

"I think I had enough to drink. It was nice meeting you," I say as an excuse to end the conversation.

"Oh the pleasure is mine," she enthuses.

We shake hands. As I walk away, she calls out.

"Nova, just one thing," she says. She smiles, but not like before. This smile looks fake, giving me a weird vibe. "It's all a game."

I bump into someone, face smacking right into their chest. I see the sword pin on the button of the tunic. Looking up, my eyes meet with the trainer glaring at me.

"Sorry," I blurt.

"Can you clowns be any more careful? Reflexes like that, you're sure to get your head cut off," he groans.

"Excuse me?" I utter.

He marches past me without saying anything. Wow, maybe they really were created in a lab with those sticks. How much longer do I have to be here? The bathroom is a great place to relax my mind.

The bathroom is empty which is good. My reflection stares back at me in the mirror. Throughout all the anxiety and nonsense I faced tonight, I still look great. Venus and Flavius did a wonderful job. Tears and sniffling break my attention away from the mirror. The soft cries come from a stall. Opening the door slightly, I find Lyssa on her knees in tears.

"Lyssa," I utter.

Her tears ruin her mascara. She bawls louder. I kneel down.

"Lyssa, you can't let anyone see you like this," I caution.

"Who cares?! We can't act like this is normal! I can't do this!" she screams.

She trembles, cradling back and forth in the fetal position.

"I just can't," she whimpers.

I should leave her and be done with this problem. Lyssa is competition. An unstable Lyssa is no threat to me, but she is innocent and doesn't deserve this, none of us do. I can't resist the need to help her even if it won't benefit me. I cover her face with a towel.

"Let's get to the roof. There should be nobody there," I say.

We pass a few people on our way out of the bathroom.

"This one had too much to drink!" I laugh.

They giggle as we move past them on our way to the elevator. A party on the roof surprises me.

"What?" I stutter.

Dozens are scattered, playing loud music, doing drugs, and making out. The vulgar party lacks the sophistication and elegance of the one in the ballroom. Judging from the formal clothes they wear, I figure they have nothing to do with the show. A group of people stagger near us. One of them reaches out with e-dope.

"Hey you want a hit?" he mumbles.

They all reek of drugs and alcohol. I shake my head, and they go away. I lead Lyssa to an empty spot near a rail. Nobody bothers us. They're too busy with the party. I remove the towel from Lyssa.

"Just breathe, everything is going to be alright," I assure.

"Stop saying that! Does anything look 'alright' to you?!" she grumbles.

"No. But crying won't make anything better. This is our life now," I sigh.

I sound like my mom when I was too scared to go to school after dad died.

"I'm not like any of you," she whimpers. "You all went out there tonight with confidence. When the Valkyries fight, they have no fear. There's something that makes you all unique, but I'm just afraid and weak."

By the sound of defeat in her voice, she isn't going to last long. It surprises me she made it this far.

"We're all afraid, Lyssa. Afraid we won't see our families, afraid of death, and the unknown. But it hasn't stopped us now, and that's why we've made it this far. All of us, including you."

"Maybe, but only one of us can survive," she calmly speaks.

With that vile reminder, a heavy feeling hits my gut. Her words shatter the false reality I created for comfort. I still don't know if I have what it takes to be the Last Valkyrie.

It remains quiet between us as I turn my gaze to the city. The sky has a shade of purple and pink from Hurricane Ragnarök that hit a few weeks earlier. The islands were left untouched by it, thanks to the defense system that encased the islands in a massive dome.

I never had a view of an entire city like this before. Traffic, sirens, and the other islands are in my sight and ears. Questions of what kind of people live in this city come to mind. Are they all morons who embody the insanity of Last Valkyrie, or are they something else? Do the people of Delos have love for each other, worries of the future, and dreams beyond their lives like everyone else?

What's going on back home? I wonder what Luna and Atlas think about my interview, if they're even watching. The longer I'm away, the more lost I am. In this mega city of millions, I am alone.

Lyssa stares at the ground exhausted. Is she thinking about home as well? What was home like for her? Yavin said she went through loss. I can't imagine what she went through that made her this way. What did Lyssa lose?

CHAPTER 15

Venus' voice irritates me on the ride back. Hearing her talk nonstop this close to midnight cannot be any more painful. My eyes are weary, being up so late, but she rambles like she just drank barrels of coffee. She gives me a rundown of all the people she convinced to be a patron.

Morgana Wkye, a partner at a law firm, loved my dress and got on board. Corvin Markell, an executive at Nano Foods, ironically, agreed to support me. There are many more people who Venus got for me. I'm thankful for how far she went for me, but I don't need to know every single detail. She even reads off hundreds of comments on social media from fans who like me. When will this torture end? Looking out the window, if I have to hear 'strong woman' or 'the baby' one more time, I swear I will jump out.

"I think Nova is tired," Flavius says.

"Well, enjoy your rest because tomorrow is when the training starts!" Venus cheers.

Whoever my trainer will be, I'm sure they'll be a jerk. At least, I'll have momentum with the support I'm getting. We say goodnight at the mansion. My suite rings when I enter in.

"You have a hologram from Atlas," the virtual assistant speaks.

"Atlas!"

I run to the disk on the floor and step on it. It glows, digitizing a hologram of Atlas in front of me.

"Atlas," I gasp.

His face brings me so much joy even though it's a hologram. He's the one person I can be myself with tonight.

"I've been trying to contact you since the interviews. I didn't know about the baby. I'm sorry," he mourns.

I rub the goosebumps on my arm.

"It's fine," I mutter.

"No, it's not. I was being selfish when we broke up. I thought it was about me, and that only pushed you further away. If I had been more considerate, you could have told me about the baby, our baby. You wouldn't have left. It's my fault you're here," he defends.

"Don't blame yourself. This was my choice, and that's why Luna hates me."

"That's not true. You have to stop putting everything on your shoulders. Luna should forgive you. She doesn't know what you lost," he argues.

"She lost her mom, Atlas!" I shoot back.

He goes quiet.

"I'm sorry, that's not what I mean. You have to stop treating yourself like you're a bad person."

"Maybe I am."

"Nova-."

"I'll talk to you later."

I step off the disk. His image vanishes. I drop to my knees, wetting the floor with tears. I don't deserve any forgiveness. I don't deserve the patrons and fans who love me. The truth is, it's all fake. There was no baby. I'm just a liar.

***

An alarm ruins my sleep. Unlike the ringing of the hologram, this one is constant and louder. Scanning my suite, I find nothing. The door to the hallway is locked. This is irritating. It's 1 in the morning, and I have a headache from the interruption to my sleep. Enough of these games already. The floor next to me slides open, revealing stairs leading to the dark.

Interesting. This is no accident. It's designed by the show. Another gimmick I figure. The steps glow as I walk on them, lighting my path. I get to the bottom. I'm in a hallway with a door at the end. The door automatically slides open, letting me inside a concrete room.

My mind flashes with images of the trials as I remember the white room I was trapped in. I traipse inside the room like I'm stepping into a prison. The door behind me slides shut, echoing a loud sound. Goosebumps cover my arms from the coldness in the room, making me nervous.

"What's going on?!" I yell.

The wall on the other side slides open. Out from the dark comes a figure. It steps into the light.

"Lyssa?" I gasp.

The wall shuts behind her. We exchange puzzled expressions.

"Nova, what is this?" she worries.

"I don't know. I don't understand."

"You're not supposed to understand," a female voice speaks from the loudspeaker on the wall. "It's simple – 2 of you came in, one of you is leaving alive."

The voice sounds familiar. I gasp as my heart drops, recognizing the brutal voice of Irma.

"What?" Lyssa stammers.

"What are you talking about?!" I yell.

"What I said. You two are fighting to the death. Now you can debate on how you want to do it, but no one is leaving until one of you is dead."

The speaker cuts off.

"Irma!" I scream.

I rush to the wall, ignoring Lyssa who doesn't move. I bang on the wall.

"Let us out you monster!" I yell.

I keep banging. I stop hitting as the irony settles in. I am trapped in a room, and they won't let us out until they get what they want. There is no escape. I whimper, feeling defeated.

"Lyssa. We just-."

My eyes shoot open as Lyssa lunges towards me, hands clawing for my throat. Jumping out the way, I back up to the wall.

"What are you doing?!" I yell in shock.

She shakes her head with tears.

"This is what we came here to do," she whimpers.

"No, this can't be! We aren't supposed to fight like this! The fights happen in the arena with cameras!" I protest.

"It doesn't matter," she argues, stalking towards me with desperation on her face. "Only one of us can survive."

"Lyssa, please," I beg.

She charges at me. I step back and hit the wall. Her hands wrap around my throat. On instinct, I punch her in the nose, getting her off of me. With the separation, I flee to the other side of the room. She glares at me as blood gushes out of her nose.

"Lyssa," I whimper.

Screaming, she races towards me. Fear and disbelief paralyzes me as she gets in my face before I can react.

She yanks on my hair. We tussle, pulling on hair. Her rage overpowers me. She wrestles me to the ground. Her hands find a home on my throat. She squeezes the air out of it. I gasp faintly, kicking the floor hard.

A flick of her blood drops into my mouth. The sour taste of her blood ignites my fire, giving me the will to fight back. Adrenaline pours into me. I elbow her in the eye, penetrating the soft tissue with my bone. She flies off me. I spring to my feet as Lyssa crawls. I ram my foot into her jaw. A loud pop rings out as her jaw ruptures against my foot.

"Die!" I scream.

I jump on top of her and bash her head against the concrete nonstop. She throws weak punches. My anger numbs me to the hits. Her hands fall. Blood pours out the back of her head, wetting my hands, but I don't care. I bash her head in more, feeling the inside of her skull. Her eyes go still, ending my rage. I stop.

"Lyssa?" I gasp.

Seeing the blood on my hands, I tremble. The unmoving eyes stare at me, causing me to jump off her body with a pounding heart. The blood is sickening. I throw up. The discomfort in my stomach is nothing compared to the guilt and terror I feel.

"No, what did I do?!" I cry.

I clap my face and cry, smothering myself in her blood. I think back to the innocent girl who I helped. I've met many people on the show, all seem like aliens to me. Lyssa was the only one who reminded me of me. Like Lyssa, those memories are now dead.

The walls open, leading to a different hallway that's part of the mansion. Moping out of the room, I see other women with their battle scars. Bruises and blood cover everyone as they're in dismay. Some cry and others stand still, speechless at the blood on them. Nobody says a word as we walk down the hall to the living room.

Bellona stands out. She has no bruises or cuts. I don't think the blood is even hers. She shows no emotion, not bothered by anything. She struts through the hall, shoving people out of the way. I tremble, imagining how she killed her opponent. We arrive to the living room where Blaze and Irma are at. A huge grin is on Blaze's face as Irma looks unsympathetic.

"Congratulations! You've all made it through the 1st round," Blaze cheers, clapping his hands.

We gasp in confusion.

"For the 75th anniversary, we did the 1st round different as a surprise. Your fights were all live streamed," Blaze praises.

"You mean this was planned?" Elpis asked.

"That's right! The only people who knew about it beforehand were bettors and patrons!" he cheers.

His eyes flare with enthusiasm as none of us are responsive. Athena laughs as blood leaks out her mouth.

"That's brilliant! You're a genius Blaze!" Athena applauses.

Blaze's grin stretches as he nods rapidly.

"What can I say?" Blaze charms, taking a bow.

"You should win an award for this!" Athena laughs. Her smile vanishes. A glare appears on her face. "You monster! I'ma rip your throat out!"

Athena charges at Blaze. Irma steps up, shielding him. Hera grabs Athena and holds her back.

"Who do you think you are?! You think this is funny?! How about we go rounds in a room?! We'll see how much you're laughing after that!" Athena rants.

Blaze laughs, enthralled by Athena.

"Wow, that's what I'm talking about Athena! My woman!" Blaze cheers with excitement, bouncing up and down. "Yall seeing this right here? This is how you get fans and patrons!"

Athena keeps yelling, throwing out threats to Blaze's amusement. He dips out, laughing as Irma follows him.

"Keep that up, Athena. You're going to knock them dead literally!" Blaze exclaims.

I can still hear him laughing down the hall until the main door closes. Athena shoves Hera off of her.

"Get off me!" Athena barks.

"You need to calm down. You could have put us all in danger going after him. You don't know what would have happened," Hera argues.

"Actually I do. I was going to kill him, but if you have any doubt," Athena steps into Hera's face, "we can start round 2 early and find out."

"That tough girl attitude worked for the cameras, but it doesn't scare me," Hera declares.

"It's not an act," Athena retorts, clenching her fists.

Someone laughs, cutting the tension. It comes from Ira. Her grin is so wide with sharp teeth, it's as if her cheeks were ripped off. She has the smile of a demon.

"What's so funny?" Athena scorns.

"Look at you, all emotional. What did you expect? We're going to die one way or the other. Might as well enjoy it!" Ira laughs.

Athena huffs and puffs, marching towards Ira.

"You think this is funny?!" Athena yells.

Athena punches Ira in the nose. The room falls dead silent, awaiting what will happen next. Ira slowly turns to Athena with a grin.

"You're going to have to do better than that if you want to survive, little girl," Ira giggles.

Athena screams in anger. Yanking Ira by the hair, Athena unloads on her face. With each punch, Ira laughs more, unaffected by the hits. Athena, now panting, drops her arms.

Blood gushes out of Ira's nose. Her frantic eyes don't blink once as she laughs. Athena's jaw drops as she slowly backs up. Her look of surprise changes to disgust.

"Freak!" Athena scorns.

She spits on the ground and marches off. We slowly disperse to our rooms. As I head to my room, I lock eyes with Elpis. She is pale with a busted mouth. The joyful Elpis from the interviews is gone. It's not an act; she truly is terrified.

When I told Lyssa we were all afraid, I didn't know what fear was. I never killed anyone. I know what fear is now. It's like what Blaze said. He owns us. Realizing I have absolutely no freedom, scares me completely.

I trudge to my room with a defeated spirit. I must've accidently hit the call button on the wall because my server comes in. Where did she just come from? She just pops out of nowhere, ready to serve. I wonder what she does on her free time, if the show even allows that. Is she locked in a room, doing nothing all day, waiting to be called? She looks at me with docile eyes, attentive to whatever I need.

"Just go away. It was an accident. I don't need you right now," I mutter.

She doesn't move, and this makes me angry.

"I said go away! I don't ever need you!" I scream.

I throw a vase at the wall. Startled, she presses the button and runs back into the opening of the wall. My hate towards her isn't personal. I despise everything about Last Valkyrie including myself.

I feel bad for being angry at her. She did nothing wrong. She's innocent. Does she hate me too? I imagine what she thinks of me. 'What do you have to cry about you privileged baby? They give you a show for your oppression, and everyone else gets nothing for theirs. Think about that when you die in front of millions of fans.' It's amazing how they fool the world into loving us.

CHAPTER 16

Loud knocks wake me up. My eyes meet the morning sunlight. Who can this be? I can't handle another trick by the show. I'll lose my mind. It could be my trainer. When I open the door, Venus throws her arms around me.

"Are you alright?" she whimpers.

"Venus," I wheeze.

She squeezes the air out of my lungs with her hug.

"Oh, I'm sorry," she murmurs, releasing her hold.

"Nova, we didn't know Blaze would have done something like that!" Flavius declares, clenching his teeth.

"That monster!" Venus barks. Her voice softens as tears run down her face. She caresses the scrape on my head I suffered from last night. "Nova, our dear. You didn't deserve to fight in the middle of the night without preparation. It was cruel."

Something is different about them. I have never seen Venus anxious, or Flavius agitated, but it's something else. Oh my. They're not wearing any makeup or flashy clothes. Flavius' face is dull. Venus' is pale with bags around her eyes. The stress is hitting her the worst.

"Are you alright?" I ask Venus.

"Of course not. How can I be? You could have been killed. I almost collapsed seeing you get beat. You poor girl," she weeps.

I feel sorry for her, seeing her cry. I didn't know she is capable of tears.

"On the bright side, I won. My patrons must be happy," I mention, in hopes of cheering her up.

They glance at each other.

"What is it?" I ask.

"Every patron we got for you last night dropped their support after seeing your match," Flavius reveals.

"What?!" I gasp. "Every single one of them? How? I won the fight. Wasn't that good enough?"

"When you cried after the match, they saw it as weakness and didn't think you were a right fit."

I jump right into Flavius' face.

"I killed someone! Was that weak?! Excuse me for being a human being!" I yell.

"Nova, please. It's their choice," he murmurs, recoiling back.

I'm taking my anger out on someone who has no control over the matter. I feel bad for yelling at Flavius. I don't want to push him away when he's only trying to help. My anger subsides, taking my voice back to normal.

"I'm sorry. It's not your fault. At least the fans still like me," I chuckle.

Flavius drops his face in his hands, and I know the answer isn't good. Venus turns on the television which only plays Moment of Blaze. It's Blaze's talk show where he talks about Last Valkyrie – the matches, rankings, updates, and everything else a fan or

Valkyrie wants to know. He talks about last night's fights, praising the winners' grit to survive.

"We're turning up the heat!" he announces. "Viewership of last night's episode hit a new record, more than any premiere. Keep it up ladies!"

The rankings are shown in a circle filled with the survivors' names. The closer you are to the center, the higher your rank is. Everyone is somewhere near the center, or at least in a good spot. Everyone, but me. My name is alone near the rim of the circle.

"I don't understand. Why don't they like me?" I groan.

"It's the algorithm," Flavius reveals hesitantly. "It takes your fights, trending rate, number of patrons, and their influence, and it creates a rank from them. Your fight set off a chain reaction, influencing the other variables."

"Am I really so bad?" I whimper.

He hesitates, not wanting to offend me. Venus steps in.

"Nova, don't be too hard on yourself. People don't expect Valkyries to care for each other. Next time, wait until you're alone to cry," she offers with a smile. "They're not people, they're your enemies."

"But I won! I did everything they wanted and this is how they treat me?!" I yell.

I sink to the floor. My chest is heavy. I feel the walls are caving in, trapping and squeezing me.

"I thought all I had to do was fight, but that's not good enough. I don't think I'll ever be," I whimper.

Flavius kneels next to me, grabbing my hand.

"It's not the end of the world because a few people don't like you," he says, slightly chuckling. "You're still alive which means we can still make a difference."

"What about the patrons I lost?"

"Forget them!" Venus scorns. "They're not the only game in town. I didn't like those robotic clowns anyway."

Flavius and I laugh.

"Don't worry about how people view you. You train hard and destroy your opponents, the crowd will have no other choice, but to love you. You are a good fighter. I saw that hook," Flavius compliments.

"Well, I did box," I chuckle.

This is what I like about Flavius. His ability to get me to drown out the chaos, so I can focus. Now I have to concentrate on my training coming up soon. No one knows who my trainer will be. I don't know how they will treat me. I doubt any trainer will be pleased with being paired with the girl who had a nervous breakdown. There's nothing that can prepare me for my training, but then again I wasn't prepared for any of this.

***

I leave the house, wearing the one piece training garment I got from my closet. When I see the fishpond out front, I stop. My eyes are glued on the baby angel sculptures that are pouring out water. They're magnificent with shiny granite, but it's something else that has my attention.

Ira stands naked in the pond, bathing in the water. There are scars on her back. Missing flesh, her back is painted with thick welts. These aren't fresh scars. They lack blood. She must've had them for years, but her back horrifies me.

She turns to me. Her scars keep me in a trance, unable to move as we lock eyes. Her face is expressionless, non-reactive to my presence. Ignoring me, she turns away as the water pours over her.

I've seen that face before. The lifeless face the Valkyries had during the trials. But Ira's is slightly different. There is no shock to hers, just an indifference to the pain like she's use to it.

The light rail takes me around the island to the training complex. Gazing out towards the island beneath me, my mind goes back to Ira's scars. How did she get them? Was she sent to the reeducation camps?

I imagine she was tied down and whipped, crying as the lash ripped her flesh apart. It's hard to picture her crying. She's the type to laugh, begging the torturer to hit her harder. Hawk comes into my mind. I see his black eye sockets. I see Lyssa now. Her brains are all over the floor, and her blood is on my hands. Stop no more! I snap out of my trance. I have to stay focus.

I use the phone they gave us to see what people are saying about me. Scrolling on the internet can be peaceful.

    'Nova can't fight for her life.'

    'My dying grandfather's going to last longer than Nova's next fight. Absolutely terrible.'

    'She cried over Lyssa like someone spat on her mother's grave. But don't worry, you're going to get a front row seat next to your old lady soon enough!'

    "What?!" I scream.

I throw the phone at the floor. It bounces right back into my lap undamaged. These shatter proof phones come from child labor in different countries that lack the infrastructure to afford an adult working force. They pay children pennies to mine, and corporations pay less to make them.

I don't care about the rankings and comments. I don't need some stupid numbering system and backers to get through this. As long as I can fight, I'll be fine. I doubt any of the other Valkyries have a background in fighting. I may be lacking in patrons and equipment, but money cannot beat pure skill. Forget the patrons.

Inside the training complex, I walk down to an elevator. The elevator scans my eyes and lets me in. As the elevator goes up, I look through the glass and see other Valkyries training. Each Valkyrie has their own floor for training.

They strike dummies with weapons, climb up walls with rope, hit moving targets, and do other exercises that focus on a feat. We have different schedules, so not everyone is here. The schedule on my phone gives me my trainer's name.

My floor, like the others, is about half the size of a football field in length and width. There are racks of weapons and practice dummies. In the center, stands a man with his back facing me.

I traipse over there, wondering how to introduce myself. Everyone and thing is surreal; I struggle with talking to people on this show. I'm still not completely use to my managers yet. My footsteps make noises yet he doesn't turn around. He's average height, muscular, and bald. I gulp.

    "Maximus?" I ask.

He turns around, revealing the sparkling gray beard that covers his entire face. My eyelids expand as the surprise hits me. Oh god. It's the trainer I bumped into last night. Anger takes over my shock. Anger of always being in spots that do more harm than good. My kidnapping, Lyssa, and now this.

"I'm-." I mummer.

"The worst student I ever had who won't make it to the 2nd round," he insults with no emotion.

He circles around me, inspecting me with snobbish eyes. It makes me feel small, but my anger absorbs my insecurity.

"I don't care about patrons. I can win by fighting," I groan, tired of being judged.

"How can you fight when your opponent has better weapons and armor? You think experience will defeat that?"

"Isn't that why you're here to train me? Wars have been won by people who were less advanced than their enemies."

He stops right in front of me. Nodding, he slightly smirks.

"Interesting," he admires. "But skill means nothing without direction. Punch me."

"You're serious?" I stutter.

Before I can blink, he moves with lightning speed. He punches me in the chest with the weight of a dumbbell. The punch takes me off my feet. I lose my air. I land on the ground, trying to catch my breath.

"Why did you do that?" I wheeze.

"I wanted you to hit me, you didn't. So I encouraged you," he replies.

I jump to my feet with a rush of air and adrenaline. I square up with him. This man is going down.

I swing at him. He's fast, moving out the way before I realize it. He remains calm, nonchalant about my strikes. He steps to the side as I swing. I lose my balance, tripping over myself from my own force. I catch my balance.

"Again," he states from behind me.

I'm really angry now. I charge with a brigade of punches, one after the other. He dodges with ease. I keep swinging. My punches are hectic without structure, all over the place as I hope they'll land. Striking the air, I lose complete control of my balance, sending me to the floor.

"You're all emotion. No technique."

"I'm sure I'm not the only Valkyrie who is emotional about being here."

"And you won't be the only one who gets killed."

I slam my fist in the mat and bounce up, glaring at his unapologetic face. I wish I could knock that self-righteous look off his face, but he's too quick for me. Where did they get him from? Are all the other Valkyries having a hard time with their trainers or is it just me? Is he jiving me because of last night at the reception? Is he taking his frustration out on me? If only I could-.

My thoughts are cut off as he jumps right in front of me. He punches me in the stomach, dropping me to my knees.

"Focus," he instructs.

"Why are you such a jerk?" I groan, staggering back up.

"Did you come here for a trainer or a friend? Because if you want someone to hold your hand through everything, you're in the wrong place," he asserts.

There's no reason to be surprise by his lack of sympathy. He's aware of my kidnapping, he's part of this whole game too. He doesn't try to convince me with smiles like Blaze and my managers. He's brutally honest. A part of me appreciate that. I spit on the ground.

We spar with kendo sticks. I never used one before, but it's not rocket science. Just attack and defend. I aim for his head. He blocks it. Next thing I know, the tip of his kendo stick pokes my stomach lightly.

I go for another strike. He blocks and taps me on the shoulder with the stick. Each strike I deliver, Maximus blocks easily, not breaking a sweat. My blood boils at my weak attempts.

My rage fuels my attacks as Maximus remains calm, easily defending himself. I start to gas out as my punches slow down. He doesn't have to try anymore. He grabs my stick and yanks me forward, tossing me to the ground. He drops a bottle of water next to me.

"Tired already?" he says.

For the next exercise, I wear weighted ankle bracelets while climbing up a rope that dangles from the ceiling. It's a struggle to climb up as I constantly fight against the pull of the weights. I reach the top. I jump to the next rope nearby. The rope slips from my hands. I fall down to the mat. The mat absorbs my fall like trash bags. It still knocks the wind out of me.

"You can't jump and reach at the same time," Maximus says.

Sprinting back and forth, I wear a blindfold while avoiding punching bags. I smack into them repeatedly, getting knocked down. I can't run for 10 seconds without running into them. It's over. My face is completely sore.

"Listen to the sound of the bags moving across. Hear them coming towards you," Maximus tells.

There's one drill that doesn't involve complex movements. It's with a grappling dummy. I practice punches, kicks, and takedowns on it. The only hassle is the weight of it. Due to the lack of breaks, I throw up a few times.

After a few hours, training finishes. I rest on the mat, soaking in sweat. I came in around 9, but it's 12:30. Maximus hands me a metal card. A hologram pops up on it, showing my location and a map.

"What is this?"

"It's from your patron."

On the back of it is a signature that reads MM - Minerva Metis. I shoot up from the floor in surprise.

"But I lost all my patrons," I gasp.

"Apparently not."

"What am I supposed to find with this?"

"Go and see." He walks away. "Same time tomorrow."

The idea that I still have a patron after my crazy show boggles me. I am happy Minerva liked our conversation so much that she didn't turn on me. But why send a map and not whatever I'm supposed to find? Patrons send weapons and armor, not maps. I hope I find a secret armory. I like the idea of that. Only one way to find out.

***

A hover car is outside the training complex. The door opens, with nobody inside. I'm above Delos' skyline shortly. The car flies past the skyscrapers. The city becomes distant as the outskirts come into view. Miles of solar power plants stretch across the land – the fuel source of this immerse society. Thousands of solar panels on the ground reflect the gray sky.

I continue past the solar farms, and that's when I see a structure off to the distance. The structure's true form comes into sight. It's an enormous black cube surrounded by bare land. It stands many stories in the air and is as wide as numerous blocks. I have never seen anything like this before. The monolith's perfect symmetry resembles something cut and forged by the hand of God.

I walk hesitantly towards the structure, gazing upon its massive size. Blocking out the sun with its frame, it casts a huge shadow around me. The weird feeling inside me grows. I reach out to touch the monolith. Its surface is sleek metal, smooth on my hands. My amazement goes from curiosity to confusion as I am stuck with no idea on what to do next. I take out the silver card and poke at the walls with it. Nothing happens.

"Come on! What am I supposed to do now?" I bark.

Minerva is too smart for her own good. I should have known a genius like her would make a gift too complicated. Doesn't she know not everyone is Einstein?

I slam the card on the wall. Air releases out the monolith. The wall slides open, making an opening the size of my height. I stare at the darkness inside the monolith.

As I cower back, fear hits me. The little Nova who was afraid of the dark, relying on her father to tell her monsters weren't real, is back. Looking into the abyss, goosebumps radiate on my skin. I feel like something from the shadows will snatch me.

What if it's not a gift, but a trap? Minerva's way of killing me off, so she won't be associated with a loser like me? Is this even from her? Stop being afraid girl. What else do I have to lose? I take a long stride into the dark. The light from outside fades as the wall closes.

Streaks of blue light run through the concrete walls, glowing dimly. The light provides a dim path to the middle where a medical chair is at. There's a metal headband on the chair.

"Welcome Nova," a female voice says.

I jump back startled. A transparent purple woman digitizes in front of me.

"Who are you?" I ask, getting my racing heart under control.

"I am Library. Information. Android. LIA for short. Minerva cannot be here due to business, so I am here to assist you."

"Minerva gave me a library? I don't see any books."

"This place is the book. An entire database filled with millions of gigabytes of information running through the walls."

My fingers ravage my hair, pressing on my scalp. This surprise hurts my head.

"What am I supposed to do with a library? I'm here to fight, not learn," I groan.

"You can learn how to fight."

I didn't think about that. This place can be of some use.

"Okay. LIA show me books on fighting. Let's start with martial arts, hand to hand combat, and sword fighting," I say.

"There's a limit to what your brain can process. If you go overboard, you may suffer severe brain damage which is why I'll put in a limit."

Sitting back, I put the headband on my head. The metal is cold around my skull. I don't feel anything. Suddenly a shock surges through me. My body clenches. What happens next is what I can only describe as the craziest acid trip.

I fall through space, passing by enormous planets I have never seen. Bright colors such as green, yellow, and red paint the cosmos, flowing like water. Disfigured creatures, melting clocks, floating heads, and other surreal figures surround me on my fall. The more I descend down, the further the bottom grows from me. My skin vibrates, shifting around my bones.

"What is this mess?!" I yell.

A large shark is at the bottom. Out from its mouth is a gigantic version of me. My clone opens its mouth and swallows me, taking me into the dark. Springing up, I gasp heavily. I feel the chair underneath me as LIA stands to the side. Sweat rains on my face as I shake.

"You have just completed your first synch," LIA informs, unbothered by my frantic state.

Stupid android. I could be on fire, and this potato would show no emotion. If she was real, I would throat chop her in the trachea. Wait a minute, how do I know chopping someone in the throat is the best way to cut their oxygen?

I realize I know things that I didn't know before. The exact length of certain swords, how to wield them effectively, vital parts of the body, and much more. It's all new yet it feels like I've known this info for years like the alphabet. It comes in rapidly like learning hundreds of words from a new language, but it doesn't overwhelm my mind. In fact it soothes it, rejuvenates my spirit.

"More of your knowledge will come over the next few days. But this doesn't mean you are physically skilled in what you have learned. You will still need to train your body for muscle memory," she explains.

And here I thought I would wake up as a complete warrior, able to destroy my opponents without any training.

"To prevent overload, come back no sooner than 6 months."

"Six months? To be safe, let's meet next decade, 2pm on a Friday?" I laugh.

She doesn't register my sarcasm as she digitizes into thin air. In the hover car, the high I felt after the synch is gone. I now have a massive headache as fatigue settles in.

I'm glad training's over as I throw up plenty of times on the way back. When I arrive back to the mansion, I wipe my sweat off and put a towel over my head to hide my face. If the cameras catch a glimpse of my face, Venus will lose it. She will make me wear makeup even for training, just so the cameras won't see me as a mess. The coast is clear as I walk down the hallway.

"Boo!" Ira shouts, jumping in front of me.

I jump back, swallowing my heart as the towel flies off my head. I put my fists up, staggering in a stance. The synch still has me lethargic, but if she wants to fight, I'm down.

"Nova you can relax. I won't bite," she laughs.

"What do you want?" I demand.

"I just want to say hi to my fellow Valkyrie. Can't you be friendly for a second?"

"Not with your kind."

She gasps, putting her hands on her chest.

"My kind? What's the matter? I never did anything wrong to you. I just want to be friends," she mocks with fake tears.

"You're a freak. You take misery as a joke," I snarl.

"All of this is a joke. No matter how far we climb, life will always laugh at us." Her playful voice remains the same. "All that stress is probably what killed your baby."

I am stuck. For a second, I clench my fists, but I remember I never had a baby. If I don't react in a believable manner, everyone will know it was a lie.

"I can't wait to see you die!" I bark.

It's not too excessive nor underwhelming. In fact it's how I really feel about her. I stomp past her as she giggles.

"See you later," she calls out.

Dreams of battle visit me at night. I am in the coliseum of ancient Rome, fighting against gladiators as thousands cheer. I block the warrior's sword with my dagger and slice his heels. I didn't know how to use a blade before, but in this dream it becomes second nature.

The arena transforms into villages. I race towards them as if I'm on autopilot. My body has a mind of its own. I'm the passenger. A bearded man lunges towards me, yelling some foreign language. It sounds Germanic. I block with my shield and slice his throat with my axe. His blood paints my face which delights me. Even my mind acts on its own, making me crave battle.

I close my eyes and reopen them. A crimson robe clothes me as I wield a katana, fighting ninjas on top of a mountain. I cut them across the chest, painting the snow in their blood. They rain down from the sky endlessly, coming out of thin air.

Everything shifts. I'm in an MMA cage. My opponent's face is blurred. My anger provokes me to charge. I take her down and bash her face in. Each punch feels light as if I'm striking the air. The blur around my opponent's face clears. I freeze, seeing the face. It's Lyssa. Her eyes are completely black. Blood pours down her skull and mouth as she stares at me. I jump off her. The entire crowd has the same pitch black eyes. Blood covers their faces.

I shoot up from my bed, sweating in a panic. The ocean outside my window serves as a clear indicator that I'm back in reality. The headaches and physical fatigue is gone, but I'm mentally drained. I drop my face in my hands. Even when she's dead, Lyssa haunts me.

CHAPTER 17

Maximus blocks my kendo stick. I don't strike rapidly like last time. I wait. He blocks my next attack and swings at me. I block, grinning at my success. Maximus thrusts his shoulder into my chest, knocking me back.

We go back and forth, attacking and defending. None of us land a hit. He's focused, putting effort into his moves unlike before. This is the first time I've seen him sweat.

We stop. I breathe heavily in and out of my nose until I get my heart rate under control. I climb up the rope really fast. I jump to the next rope. It's in my hands, but slips before I can squeeze it. As I fall down, I grab the rope, stopping my fall. I climb up the rope and reach the top.

Controlling my breath during sprints, I focus on the sound of the dummies moving across the room. I avoid them. On some sprints, I barely bump into them, staying on my feet and pressing forward. At the end of the session, I stand straight up with my hands on top of my head, allowing the air to circulate fully.

As time goes on, my knowledge from the monolith comes to me more naturally. I don't have to force myself to remember it. My mind becomes a sponge, soaking up knowledge about weapons, armor, hand to hand combat, endurance, and much more. The more I learn, the better I train. This allows me to apply more of my knowledge to my training.

My sparring sessions with Maximus are longer and faster with a mix of different moves between us. I last longer, keeping my breathing under control. I land my stick on his shoulder. He swings at me. I dodge, and poke his chest with the stick.

"Time," he states.

He hands me a briefcase. Inside is a sword that glows on the edges.

"This will be your weapon for the matches," he reveals.

There's a button on the hilt. I press the button. The edges of the sword heats up.

"This is dope!" I cheer.

"It's from me. It was something I used for another purpose."

I strike the dummies in their vital parts with excellence. We spar with our swords, this time turning the battle shields on to protect our bodies.

My knowledge pays off more. I block more of his attacks as only a few hit me. My sword lands on his chest. The battle shields protect him. Landing a hit excites me too much because as I pause, he shoves me, this time dropping me to the ground.

"Don't get cocky," he says.

I jump back up and continue. I'm in a puddle of sweat when we finish. Waiting for him to compliment me, I receive nothing. I shake off the brief disappointment as my progress excites me. Forget patrons, I'm going to be unstoppable.

**

"You should see the kids, they say 'Nova is going to run them ova.' They love you," Atlas compliments.

I chuckle, covering my mouth to hide my huge smile as I blush.

"It must be lonely sharing a house with people who want to kill you. Only if you had a familiar face," he mentions.

I see what he's trying to do. He wants me to ask him to visit like it's not his idea.

"This is your 2nd hologram call. It must cost you a lot to do these," I bring up.

He stumbles over his tongue. Hopefully he realizes that money issues will make a trip impossible.

"I've been working more hours which is why I should come visit," he continues.

"Atlas I don't know," I hesitate, shying away from the hologram projection. "It's a long trip."

"I'm not a little kid. I can travel. What's-." He cuts himself off. His tone changes into an assertive one. "Why don't you want me to be there for you?"

"I don't want you to waste your time. You may come here for nothing. You shouldn't get your hopes up."

He gasps in offense.

"Have faith in yourself," he urges.

"Faith isn't something that comes easy in a place like this."

"Then let me be there for you, encouraging you all the way."

"You have dreams Atlas, but this is no fantasy."

The doorbell rings.

"I have to go."

"Nova please-."

I cut off the hologram. I can't stand talking to him anymore about the subject. Atlas at my side would be nice, but he doesn't have the stomach for this kind of violence, let alone in person, especially if I get killed. I can't even imagine how Lyssa's family felt watching her die, or how the other families felt.

I open the door, finding Elpis on the other side. Her face is pale without makeup. Her eyes are bloodshot.

"May I come in?" she pleads.

I let her in. She paces back and forth, fumbling with her hands.

"I have to tell someone, but everyone here is to themselves. After seeing you talk to Lyssa, I feel like you're the only one I can talk to."

"About what?"

"I had a dream I got on stage during the interviews and told the world what they've done to us."

"It was just a dream."

She pauses with a lost gaze.

"Elpis, it was just a dream, right?" I worry.

"I don't know," she guesses.

I worry at any moment her head will explode. For a guy like Blaze, this is enough to push the button. I place my hands on her shoulders.

"Elpis, you know that's not smart."

"What else do I have to lose?" she whimpers.

"Your head?" I remind her.

She chuckles faintly.

"If the ring doesn't kill me, I'll spend my entire life as a slave. Detonator or not, it won't matter. But if they knew the truth, even if I die, maybe things would change."

"These people aren't worth losing your life over. They'll go on with their lives, forgetting what you died for. What we do in the ring is for our survival, nothing and nobody else."

She stares out the window, leading to the balcony. My floor is several stories high.

"Elpis."

She doesn't respond, eyes lost on the balcony as if she's day dreaming. She smiles.

"I guess you're right. It was just a stupid dream, that's all," she chuckles weakly.

She plods away. The confident stride she had during the interviews is gone. I fear for her life. The suffering she's going through to consider an idea like that is unimaginable. Is this how we all feel?

I step onto the balcony and look down at the ground. I never realized how high my suite is. One fall, and splat, everything would be over. I can't believe it's so easy to end things. The opportunity creeps at every corner yet we don't do it. No, not tonight. I go back inside for bed.

**

The next morning Blaze calls us to meet him at the front lawn. A huge cloth covers a giant rectangular object, standing many feet in the air.

"Valkyries, it's my honor to reveal this year's memorial for the fallen," Blaze announces.

He takes off the cloth, revealing a giant headstone. It features the names of the dead Valkyries from round one.

There are no tears. This isn't a funeral. The memorial serves as entertainment for the audience, and a reminder to us that only one of us will avoid the wall.

"Does anyone want to say anything? Cameras are always on," Blaze snickers.

Athena steps up. It surprises me she cares enough to speak. She spits on the ground. Never mind.

"Look at these names. All of you will be on here," Athena declares. She points at Ira. "Especially you, freak!"

Ira smirks. Athena storms away.

"Man I love this show!" Blaze cheers.

Everyone leaves, but I stay. I stare at Lyssa's name. It hurts me, knowing I'm the reason she's on the wall. Yes, it's kill or be killed, but I can't help, but feel responsible for her death. I try to forget her and move on, but she plagues my mind. I march off, hoping she won't ever come back.

Training resumes. I can't land my sword on Maximus as he hits me with ease. I never struggled this much since my synch, but now I'm sloppy as training feels harder. The difficulty makes me mad. It's like I'm a rookie, stepping into the training complex for the first time. Maximus grabs my arm and tosses me to the ground.

"Pathetic! The matches are within days, and your fighting sucks!" he grills.

I pound my fists into the mat.

"I am trying!" I yell.

197

"Trying isn't enough. What's going on with you?"

"Nothing."

He looks me dead in the eyes. I look away. Lyssa comes back into my mind. No, not this again.

"It's the girl," he declares.

"What?" I stammer.

"The one whose brains you bashed in like a watermelon."

"Her name was Lyssa!" I scream.

He smirks.

"You need to forget about these people. They are not your friends," he asserts.

"Like I said it's nothing. Let's go," I snarl, grinding my teeth.

He walks away from me.

"Training's over," he says.

"I'm ready!"

"If you want my time, earn it. Come to me when you're actually ready."

He leaves me feeling stupid. I throw my blade, yelling.

***

I visit the headstone. I don't know why I feel guilty about Lyssa's death. They never show how Valkyries cope with killing. We see the celebrations and glory, but not the mourning. I read in a book by one former winner that she had heard Valkyries crying at night. A couple years back, another winner, Morta, hanged herself. She left a note, asking God for forgiveness. There's no way I'm the only one who feels dread about murdering someone. The others are just better at hiding their pain.

A drop of liquid falls from the sky, hitting my face. The sky's clear. It can't be rain. The liquid splashes over the headstone, hitting my hair. Wiping my hair, I smell the liquid. My nostrils flare at the strong acidic smell - nail polish remover.

I go to the other side of the headstone. Ira splashes bottles of the remover on the headstone.

"Hey! What are you doing?" I demand.

She takes out a lighter with an evil smile.

"Benzene and acetone, nothing when alone. But together it's doom, when they go boom," she sings laughing.

She clicks the lighter, turning on the flame. I tackle her to the ground, knocking the lighter out of her hands. We tussle, rolling on top of each other in the grass. She head-butts me. As I'm disorientated on the ground, she runs for the lighter.

I jump to my feet. We grab the lighter at the same time, tugging for it. She laughs. She bites my hand, forcing me to release the lighter. I grab her head and smash it into the headstone. She hits the ground. I chuck the lighter into the ocean.

"No!" she screams.

"It's over, you psychopath," I gasp, catching my breath.

I keep my eyes on her, anticipating the fight to continue. She's on her knees, sniffling. She breaks out into tears, crying like a helpless child.

I don't care about the headstone. With the remover in my hair, I don't want my body to be on fire. I can kill her right now. It wouldn't be the first time a Valkyrie got killed outside the ring, but I'm done fighting for now. Going back inside, I look over my shoulder just in case.

**

Tonight is the announcements of the 2nd round matches. It's based off of popularity and patrons, so off the bat I know it won't be in my favor. Blaze is on tv, giving his energetic presentation. He gives a recap, featuring training sessions and interviews. The focus shifts to my scuffle with Ira. The cameras didn't catch the beginning that reveals why we fought, but it's enough for him to talk about.

"Look at them go! I guess some people can't wait to get it on," Blaze laughs. "And now, the moment you've all been waiting for."

A holographic bracket appears next to him. I look past all the other names in search of mine. I see my name and look to the name next to it. It's Ira.

"Tune in tomorrow for these exciting battles!"

I turn off the television. How ironic?

**

I arrive to my training floor. Maximus raises his eyebrows at me.

"I'm ready," I declare.

"We'll see."

We spar with the real swords. We wield two blades, something I learned from the synch. Our swords clang. I move faster than before, hitting him without getting hit. I finish with a good session.

"Tomorrow there's no stopping. There won't be any pleads. The fight stops when one of you is dead," Maximus asserts.

**

Standing on the suite's balcony, I look to the night sky. This could be the last time I ever see the moon. What if I die tomorrow? Am I ready to meet my parents? I think about what I might say to them. I'm sorry I wasn't a better daughter. I'm sorry I'm the reason you died. I close my eyes as thunder rips through the sky. No this won't be the end of me. I'm not ready to die yet.

CHAPTER 18

It's quiet in the hover car as we ride to the arena. I expect Venus to rave like usual, but she matches the silent atmosphere radiating from Flavius, Maximus, and I.

My match is scheduled to be third, so we left early. Each round takes place one day a week. Since it's the 2nd round, it's going to be busy with 8 matches in one day. Unlike the last round, the fights won't happen at the same time. All eyes will be on one match at a time.

My heart beats fast, and goosebumps appear on my arms the closer my fight approaches. This is controlled tension. Not to the point where I can't think, but the opposite. I am focused, knowing the unease will not go away, so I try to embrace the feeling.

I think about the conversation I had with Atlas this morning. He wished me good luck, believing that I will make it to the next round. As much as I enjoyed him contacting me, it's sad he was the only one who did it. I wish I could talk to Luna. It's my biggest fear to die without telling her how I feel, and to never see her face again.

The car steers around the mountains. Another island comes into view. On this island stands an enormous coliseum. It's bigger and more magnificent than any structure I have seen in my entire life. The coliseum covers the entire island, dwarfing the surrounding islands and buildings around it.

Hotels stand on the smaller islands nearby, harboring people from all over the world who came for Last Valkyrie. Every year the show brings in thousands of people to Delos. Whether they bought tickets or came to experience the city, people flock here.

This year, Delos brought in fifty billion dollars in counting from tourism and advertisement. The entire world is watching.

We walk to the front of the coliseum where hundreds of people stand behind barricades, cheering and chanting. Cameras are flashing. I wish we go in the back, but my managers suggest the front is good for press coverage.

A robot rolls up to us, looking like SED, but with more colors. It scans our faces.

"I am happy to welcome you to Battleborn Arena," the robot enthuses.

We follow the robot. I survey the energized crowd that's filled with reporters and fans hungry for action.

"Nova!" a reporter calls out. "You're predicted to be killed inside a minute. How does it feel to be ranked so low?" she pries curiously.

My mind stumbles as I hesitate to speak, struggling for the right answer. Someone laughs. A group of young men wearing Athena shirts laugh at me.

"Hey Nova, how about you bend it ova. So ugly, you need to wear a mask like it's Octoba," one rhymes.

I step towards them, but Maximus grabs my arm.

"Forget them. Don't engage with fools and make yourself look like one."

"I'll be a fool if I don't. What about patrons?"

"There's a time and place for everything. Can't have patrons, if you get killed today. Focus on the task at hand."

"What's the matter, can't speak without daddy?" the guy snickers.

"Hey!" Venus calls out, marching up to him.

Venus punches the man, dropping him. Cameras flash at us. Venus grabs a camera from a reporter and glares into it.

"You see this man lying on the ground right here? That's going to be the fate of all of Nova's opponents!" Venus declares.

"And that's why we have her," Flavius says as we walk off.

"Thanks," I told Venus.

"Oh dear it's nothing. It's all part of the act," she laughs.

The robot leads us to my dressing room under the arena. On the table is a black one piece suit. Its design is similar to wet suits surfers wear. It's covered with pads. I feel the nylon texture as I stretch it. I tap on the pads. They're hollow, slightly hard, but not thick enough to provide much protection from a blade. The suit isn't much different than my training gear. Other than the simple pads, it offers no protection.

"This is what I'm going to fight in?" I ask in offense.

"This is what you wear when you don't have patrons who build actual armor. Remember your training, don't get hit, and you'll be fine," Maximus says.

He has a way of making things sound easier than they are.

"Dear, I'm sorry about the look," Venus apologizes. "The texture makes it hard for us to give you any kind of design for it."

"She can worry about how she looks when she survives," Maximus adds.

Venus shoots him a glare. Maximus hands me my sword from a compartment in the wall. He retrieves his sword and armor. We spar. I train to perfection, hitting his battle shields while blocking and dodging his attacks.

The television displays the countdown to the opening ceremony. It's a little bit under 30 minutes as commentators speak about the event. The tv is on mute. We train until the countdown hits 0.

"Time," Maximus says.

Maximus unmutes the screen. We turn our full attention to it. A montage plays, showing clips of Last Valkyrie's evolution throughout the century. The early years after the revolution when Last Valkyrie was a battle royal in the nuclear wasteland of New York City. In those days there were no live audiences, patrons, or interviews. People watched from home.

The years the tournament format was first introduced with one on one death matches, bringing in the first live crowds. The creation of the Siclades Islands which became the one and only home for the show, bringing in the global fame it has now.

The voiceover speaks about the glory the Valkyries risk their lives to attain, painting the show in a magnificent light. The montage ends. The live aerial feed of the arena displays. It shows the cheering thousands in attendance.

"Ladies and gentleman," the announcer speaks throughout the entire stadium. "Please stand as we honor the Corporate States of America with the Song of Juturna."

Everyone freezes at the screen, not moving. A little girl steps to the microphone in the ring as everyone stands. She looks no older than 12, wears a white dress, and has a face as soft as an angel. She opens her mouth and sings.

'The chains have been broken.'

'Bringing life to the soul.'

'With light from the sky.'

'Shining all over the world.'

'The star they worshipped.'

'Now lies in ashes.'

'With its beauty broken.'

'The false king it once was.'

'Now they see, now they hear.'

''Now they feel, now they live.'

'A lasting reign.'

'Now they fall, now we rise.'

'Now they die, now we stand.'

'A lasting peace.'

'Pain was for yesterday.'

'Joy is forever.'

The roar of the crowd shakes the roof. Venus sheds a tear. It amazes me how each year they find a different child to sing. Each time it's beautiful.

The cameras show crowds watching from all over the world. Crowds in Times Square, London, Tokyo, and other major cities. You don't have to be a diehard fan of Last Valkyrie, but when the Song of Juturna plays during the opening, you watch. It's the unsaid law of the land because nothing else embodies the CSA, and the effect it has on the world like it.

Even if you aren't American, you pay your respect. It's encoded in our brains like second nature. The first match is starting to begin. Maximus orders me to pause my training and watch.

Bellona's up. She marches to the ring to a dead crowd. She has no entrance music or theatrics. She focuses on the ring, holding only a shield.

"Bellona is an interesting Valkyrie," the commentator Fox states. "The sheer power she has makes up for her lack of personality and words. We saw that during the 1st round."

"Power worked for her before, but it ain't gonna cut it in the ring," the other commentator Brom says. "You need patrons, proper training, and great equipment, if you want to survive this. That lone wolf act can only get her so far. Today we're going to see it end."

Pyro shoots up from the top of the ramp. From the fire steps out Hybris in a fire proof suit. She takes off her suit and helmet, revealing her armor. In her hand is a long metal chain hooked to a curved blade. Dancing to the ring, she swings the blade in the air, hurling words to the crowd.

"I'm on fire tonight! I'm the baddest on this show! Nobody can touch me!" she boasts.

The crowd throws roses at Hybris. She earned a handful of patrons for her brashness, claiming the Valkyries are nothing to her. The internet lit up with fans and critics when she mocked Bellona's late mother who had committed suicide.

Her armor is bright and thick, providing protection for her body. The suit, weapon, and even the pyro is paid for by her patrons. I can only imagine how plain my entrance will be.

"Compared to what Hybris has, Bellona might as well have brought a slingshot!" Brom laughs.

Hybris shoves her blade to the camera.

"I'ma cut her up," Hybris teases.

They meet in the center of the ring, face to face before the bell. Bellona keeps her head down as Hybris dances up and down, amusing the crowd.

"Tell mommy I said hi," Hybris laughs.

They go back to their corners, and the bell rings. Hybris swings the blade. Bellona puts the shield up, taking the hit. Before Hybris can pull it back, Bellona grabs the chain and yanks it forward, propelling Hybris towards her. Hybris screams in fright. Bellona decks Hybris in the face with the shield, knocking her to the ground covered in blood. Hybris' teeth fly out. The crowd awes as Bellona mounts Hybris and bashes her face in with the shield.

"Oh god!" Fox shrieks.

"Bellona is turning Hybris' face into a mud hole!" Brom yells.

Bellona brings the shield down on Hybris' throat, slicing her head completely off. Hybris' head rolls as blood spurts out her body, painting the canvas. Bellona lifts Hybris' head in the air, roaring with her bloody shield. The crowd erupts with cheers. Fox comes up to Bellona with a microphone.

"Bellona, how-."

Bellona storms past him with her trainer. The camera rolls back to Fox.

"Well like they say, actions speak louder than words," he states.

Blaze enters the ring. He picks up Hybris' head by the hair and swings it in the air.

"Who wants her head?!" he yells.

The crowd goes ballistic as he tosses it to them. The camera shows the crowd fighting over the head. I'm in disbelief at the entire fiasco. As a kid it was a spectacle, but knowing I'll be in it soon, is unbelievable. I finally see the nature of this show for what it is. It's barbaric and so are the people cheering it on. Maximus turns off the tv.

"Come on, continue with your training," he states.

Flavius places his hands on me.

"We'll be in the crowd just like at the reception, but try not to look at us," Flavius says.

"Kill that crazy girl," Venus adds.

I smile with a nod. They head off. I continue with my drills. The robot comes in minutes later to take us out. Walking through the hall, the crowd's noise grows louder. I breathe deeply, trying to calm my nerve. It's more than the fear of death that causes anxiety. Despite my training physically and mentally, I don't come to terms with what I'm about to do. I guess none of us do.

I step through the curtains. Bright light invades my sight. The noise turns into unified booing. My eyes scan the crowd, taking in the angry faces.

'You're going to die tonight!'

'You can't fight!'

'It's going to be ova Nova!'

Maximus puts his hand on my shoulders.

"Focus," he urges.

I shift my attention to the ring. It's called The Oval due to its shape. It stands 15 feet in the air. It has no ropes or cage, only spikes at the bottom. If a Valkyrie falls out the ring, she is instantly impaled to death. This is to ensure that the fans get an exciting death no matter what. Valkyries fall to their deaths all the time.

I ignore the booing, turning them into background noise. I try to see this as one of my fights back home. A fight to the death to add to it. I think back to my school fights. Thinking back to them and seeing how light they were compared to this calms me down.

As the ring gets closer, I try to feel immersed in the environment, but I'm still worried. I'm not a warrior ready for battle. I step on a disk. It levitates, bringing me and Maximus into the ring. Blaze stands in the middle. My managers are in the front row. Flavius nods as Venus waves.

Boos turn to cheers. The spotlight shines on Ira who walks out in bright orange armor, more vibrant and fortified than mine. She holds two daggers. Makeup sparkles her face. Silver eye shadow gives light to her jade eyes. She holds up her daggers in the ring as the crowd chants her name. Her craziness has captured the fans. A microphone floats from the ceiling into Blaze's hands.

"Fighting out of the black corner, from San Francisco - Nova the Star!" he announces.

Boos fill the arena.

"And from the orange corner, from parts unknown - Ira the Maniac!"

The crowd cheers. The robot ref calls us to the center of the ring. It goes over the rules, reminding us the fight won't end until one of us is dead. We look each other dead in the eyes. My face is expressionless, staring into the devilish eyes of Ira. She grins and licks her lips.

"Your blood is going to taste good," she taunts.

"Remember your training," Maximus says.

We touch weapons and go to our corners as everyone leaves the ring. The robot asks if we're ready. We nod. My heart pounds tremendously.

"Let's go!" it yells before flying into the air.

Suddenly my nerves calm, and all the anxiety goes away. As soon as the bell rings, Ira rushes in, taking me by surprise. She strikes, one dagger after the next, relentless. I can only backup, avoiding her daggers. I lunge back, but the separation doesn't hold as she keeps charging. I almost lose my footing as I step near the edge of the ring. I catch my balance and run along the side as Ira pursues.

"What are you doing?!" Maximus yells.

"Keep rushing her, don't let up!" her trainer orders.

"Scared aren't you? You're going to die just like Lyssa!" Ira laughs.

Lunging forward, she thrusts both daggers at my chest. I block them. She corners me. Her deranged grin shows.

"You're ready to die?" she laughs.

My eyes drop to her feet, remembering what I learned from the monolith. She jumps towards me, leaving her entire body defenseless.

Stepping to the side, I grab her hand and knock her other dagger in the air with my sword. Controlling her wrist, I swing her towards me. She gasps. I drive my sword through her face. It rips through the back of her head.

The crowd goes silent with a gasp. Ira twitches as her blood drenches my blade. She's either still alive, or it's her motor functions working one last time. I pull my sword from her head. She drops to the ground with a hole ripped through her face, leaving it disfigured.

"Not before you," I utter.

A piece of her brain hangs on my sword. I shake it off. It splashes in her blood. The bell rings. My team enters into the ring as I stand there amazed. The robot comes over and scans Ira's corpse, confirming what we all know. Her trainer shakes his head with disappointment.

"Ladies and gentleman, your winner, Nova!" Blaze announces.

There is a mix of cheers and boos. As the robot raises my hand, I can't help but smile. I'm still alive. Maximus gives me a simple nod as Flavius claps. Venus hugs me, squeezing the breath out of me.

"Oh dear you did wonderful!" she praises.

Brom comes up to me with his microphone.

"Nova, you have been criticized for how timid and reluctant you were in your first fight. Do you feel like all of that has changed now?" he asks.

"Uhhhh," I stutter in confusion. I can't think of anything to say. It's all going by so fast. I was fighting for my life a minute ago. Now in a blink of an eye, I have an interview. My brain goes limp. "I...."

Maximus grabs my arm.

"What are you doing?" I ask as we leave the ring.

"Saving your image."

Venus appears on the tron, giving an interview in the ring.

"It's exactly what I told you. Nova was going to put that crazy girl in the ground!" Venus boasts.

The crowd laughs. Questions fill my head as we are all back in the dressing room.

"Why did you stop me?" I ask Maximus.

"You stumbled over your words. You can't afford to look like a fool."

I sigh. No matter what I do, it never impresses him.

"We're her managers. We decide how she appears to everyone, not you," Venus tells.

"My job is to keep her alive. She was going to fold and lose whatever support she just gained, again," Maximus retorts.

"You made her look like she can't speak for herself!"

"Maybe you should have done a better job at that then."

Venus gasps in offense. She opens her mouth, and judging by her expression, she's going to let Maximus have it. Flavius steps in.

"Maximus I appreciate what you did. It's your job to make sure Nova performs to the best of her ability in the ring,"

Flavius says. Venus' mouth drops, looking to Flavius for an explanation. "But please understand that this is a team effort. Nova has a say in what she does as much as we do. We need to work together for her survival."

Maximus' face doesn't move at all as he and Flavius stare at each other with unmoving eyes.

"Know what you want to say next time," Maximus asserts to me.

"You're not going to congratulate me on winning?" I ask.

"I'll congratulate you when you win the entire show."

He walks off. My self-confidence shrinks. It's as if I didn't even win out there. I feel small. Venus puts her hand on me.

"It's okay dear. You have nothing to be ashamed of. You did great today. You'll run them all over."

It's not a lot, but Venus' effort to cheer me up is uplifting. The relief of surviving is short lived as it won't be long before I have to fight again.

I thought some weight would be removed after winning, but the pressure only increases. No doubt Atlas watched. What about Luna? How do they feel about seeing me kill someone? I know everyone back home is cheering. At least I'm still alive, and that beats being dead.

CHAPTER 19

The Valkyries gather at the training complex on the top floor. We were instructed to meet here with our ring weapons. Reporters from major news outlets are here as well. Training hasn't started yet, and they're already flashing cameras at us. We were told today's training is going to be different. Instead of individual sessions with our trainers, today we are going to be trained by a former Valkyrie. It's a surprise.

Whoever she is, she's bringing in so much attention with the media outlets, and attention means patrons. Normally when we train, we are filmed by the cameras we cannot see, to prevent distractions. With all the cameras in front of us, today's training will be about putting on a show. A perfect opportunity, one the Valkyries have in mind.

The doors swing open. Gasps come out as we chatter with each other in surprise at who it is. Carrying a metal staff, Astra comes in. She's dressed in fully plated armor that covers her entire body.

It's thick and bulky, more fortified than anything a Valkyrie has ever worn in training and combat. The armor weighs her down as she trudges, but she walks steadily in it.

"Hello Valkyries. I want to congratulate you on making it to the 3rd round. It's my honor to train you and teach you the skills I used to help me win the show," Astra says.

The flashing lights pick up, now irritating our eyes as we cover our faces. Astra notices our discomfort. She gives a nod to her bodyguard.

"Soter, please," Astra says.

Soter goes up to the reporters.

"Would you all mind turning off the flashes? It's hurting their eyes."

The flashes stop. The armor around her neck forms into a helmet, covering her head and face.

"Now then we can begin. Whoever wants to step up first may do so. We'll go one at a time from there."

Silence sweeps the air as nobody moves. Our faces show a mix of hesitation and contemplation. I don't know if it's her armor causing the second guessing. With all the attention and cameras, millions are watching this training, and nobody wants to make a fool out of themselves.

Sitting back is as harmful to a Valkyrie's reputation as poor performance. This is a mistake I can't make. I step up. Athena does so as well. On instinct I step right in front of her, blocking her from Astra's view, asserting my position to everyone.

"Nova," Astra acknowledges.

I draw my sword. Our weapons clash. I take the offensive as she defends mostly. Despite my speed outpacing her, Astra blocks well. It seems like a stalemate will ensue until I push Astra's staff away and strike her chest. Her armor absorbs the hit as my blade bounces off. Astra keeps fighting without any sign of damage.

Speeding up my attacks, I hit her all over her body. My attacks do nothing. We keep fighting. Astra rams her staff into my chest, knocking the air out of my body. I fly hard into the ground. Astra helps me up.

"No legal armor in the ring can take all those hits. Your armor is against the rules," I complain.

"That's true," Astra says.

"Then why have us train against it, if we won't encounter it in the ring?"

"To put you in a scenario in which your attacks are useless, forcing you to find other ways. If you can succeed against this, you'll be better off in the ring." Her helmet rescinds. She smiles at me. "You did very good Nova. I enjoyed that."

I limp away, regaining the air that was knocked out. Athena glares at me. Paying no attention to her, I focus back up front.

"Next person," Astra says.

One by one they step up, put up a fight, and Astra knocks them down. None of our attacks do any good. Even her helmet absorbs hits, taking Bellona's shield like it's nothing. Astra remains unbeaten.

"You all should be very proud of yourselves," Astra compliments.

Our panting stops as she speaks. Everyone forgets their fatigue and stands straight up to face her. The respect and admiration we have for her radiates throughout the room. For me, I don't admire Astra for her accolades and status. Winning Last Valkyrie doesn't command respect from me, but it's what she went through that does. She is a survivor of this mayhem, representing what it truly means to be strong. Only the Valkyries can understand what that feels like yet only one of us will know.

"All of you possess the qualities to be the Last Valkyrie. Whatever happens, may glory find you in this life or the next."

"Hey Astra, how about a picture with the Valkyries?" a reporter calls out.

"Of course!" Astra enthuses.

Her armor opens up. She steps out, wearing a smaller battle suit. It's a black skintight one piece, covered with chrome plates. It's the armor she fought in last season, still with the marks from the fights. She joins us in the middle. We clutch our weapons for the pose.

"Alright, say Last Valkyrie!" Blaze says.

We repeat the phrase with smiles. The cameras flash. Anguish, fear, and dread lurk behind our fake smiles. The world needs to believe we enjoy this.

I feel only Astra is genuine. Even with the sweat on her face and her hair tied, she blossoms with a natural beauty that's unmatchable.

We go our separate ways as Astra talks to the reporters. Some Valkyries are called for interviews. Their personalities and abilities keep them in a good light. No reporter approaches me. No matter how great I perform physically, my image is tainted by the Lyssa fight. Any mishap is blown out of proportion, and any success is minimalize. This doesn't upset me, only motivates me more. After getting changed, I head outside where Astra and Soter are.

"Today was great wasn't it my lady?" Soter asks.

"Indeed it was. They showed skill and determination. And what did I tell you about that 'my lady' stuff when nobody is around."

"Of course, Astra," Soter chuckles.

How does she do it? How is she compassionate after all she went through? It can't be a front for the cameras. This is who she is. The mystery to the cause of her character boggles me.

"Astra!" I call out.

"Hi Nova. Good job today again. What can I do for you?"

"I have a question."

"My lady, we have a charity event," Soter mentions.

"It's fine, we have time, Soter." She turns to me. "If you have any more questions on fighting, I won't be able to explain it all."

"It's not about the show. It's something more personal."

Her smile slowly fades away.

"Soter, I'll meet you inside," she speaks.

Soter leaves.

"Why did you-."

"Remain a Belenus?" she answers. "Why would any of us continue to give our lives to them after we win?" She turns her gaze to the ocean as if to relive the memories. "We come from nothing. We have nothing, but the desire for more than what life gave us. After all the pain and suffering you go through to stay alive, you wonder if there's something greater for you."

The ocean rushes up against the rocks.

"In the end when the confetti falls and millions love you, what can you go back to? Nobody you know treats you the same. Friends and family don't want you, they want the Last Valkyrie. All we ever want in life is more, and even that's not enough," she confesses.

***

I'm at my door when I hear footsteps approaching fast. Athena marches towards me.

"You think you're cool for what you did earlier?"

I hesitate to speak, trying to figure out what she means. It hits me.

"You're still tripping about me cutting in front of you? What difference does it make? We all went. Get over it," I groan.

I open my door when she yanks my arm towards her. I pull my arm back and clench my fists. The urge to use her face as a battery ram against the door is strong, but unless she attacks me, it's pointless to fight. We glare at each other.

"Don't ever make me look stupid again, or you won't have to wait for the fights to taste your own blood."

She stomps away. It's so easy to take her out from behind, but with the cameras everywhere, everyone will call me a coward. I hope she gets killed. What a devil.

My phone buzzes with a notification. My run in with Athena is making rounds on the internet.

'@hardhat104 - lmfao Athena really punked Nova. Idek how Nova is still alive.'

'@neverbeenshot - My grandfather can last longer in bed than Nova will next round.'

Not all comments are bad. I have some supporters and fans, but the hate gets more attention, so they talk about it more. You can't satisfy everyone. What was I supposed to do, punch Athena and fight her in the hall? Bettors and patrons don't like it when fights happen outside the ring. It messes up their numbers. I had to think smart for once.

I need a drink now. I hit the button and wait for my server. At any minute she will come through the wall. I wait, but she doesn't come. That's odd. She's usually fast. I hit it again, but nothing happens. Before I can press again, the wall opens up. She trudges out. Her eyes are red and strained with bags underneath.

"Can you make me a Martian Martini?" I ask politely.

She nods and plods to the kitchen. With sloppiness, she spills much of the juices on the counter when making the drink. She constantly drops the vegetables. Her strained eyes, messy hair, and lethargic movements all make sense.

She's drained, over worked from whatever they make them do when they're not serving us. I'm forcing her back into more unnecessary work.

I feel bad. Who am I to be ordering her around like she's beneath me? I'm no better than her. Fate puts us on different sides of the coin, but we're both slaves.

She comes over with my martini on the plate. She fumbles the plate, dropping the glass on the ground. Eyes widening, she trembles at the mess and broken glass. A fearful look pours over her like she's expecting me to punish her. Is that what happens to them? Do they get beat for making mistakes?

"It's fine. It's just a drink. I wasn't thirsty anyways," I say with a smile to reassure her.

She sweeps the mess.

"No, leave it. I'll get it."

It must be years since she had something to drink. I pour her a glass of orange juice. She backs up.

"Oh right, the mask," I say.

I loosen the mask. It's a simple hook and loop strap. It comes off. Syringes with yellow liquid covers the inside of the mask. No need for a lock when the serum make the servers too docile to take it off.

"Here," I offer, handing her the juice.

Her mouth drops and she panics, panting loudly. This is the most animated she has been.

"Corvin! Verona! Where are you?!" she screams. "They're coming!"

She clutches my shoulder.

"Please I have to find them!" she cries. "I have to-."

I put the mask back on her face and seal it. She shuts up and calms down instantly. The submissive look appears once again in her eyes as she awaits my order. I wish she could be a person again.

"It's okay. You can leave now," I whimper.

She walks back where she came from with her head down. My suite taints my appetite for a drink. I need to get out. I'm heading to Delos.

The show's hover car takes me to Delos. This is one of the so-called 'benefits' of being a Valkyrie. We get to call our own automated hover cars to take us wherever we want on the islands. They only go to the islands, so visiting home is out of the question unless permitted to do so. There's no point in them keeping us close. They can hear everything with the bombs in our heads.

The bar I'm going to is very high on the recommendations. With a hoody on my head, I move by pedestrians, making my way into a bar. Hopefully nobody will recognize me.

"A Martian Martini please," I tell the bartender.

He comes back with my drink. I swipe my credit card, not giving him the chance to get a good look at it. He observes me.

"You look familiar, have I seen you somewhere?" he asks.

"I don't think so."

I drink as he remains in my peripheral view looking. He shrugs.

"Athena!" he blurts out.

"No," I sigh.

"It's Athena!"

"I said-."

He points at the door where people gather taking pictures. In the middle of the crowd is Athena.

'You're bad!'

'We love you Athena!'

She acknowledges their compliments with nonchalant waves, not too invested in them as she continues walking.

"Hey Athena, it's all on the house!" the bartender calls out.

"Thank you," she says heading to the bathroom.

This is unbelievable. I want peace, and Athena has the same idea. First my drink gets ruined at my suite and now here. Her presence spoils my desire for a drink, serving as a reminder how much my life sucks. I want to lash out. I need someone to blame for my foul mood.

Her. This is Athena's fault. Who does she think she is? I scorn at her as she walks into the bathroom. I bet she thinks she's better than all the other Valkyries. I'll show her. I slam my drink down and march to the bathroom.

She washes her face, looking down as I stand behind her. She sees me in the mirror. She pauses, briefly surprised and then scorns at me.

"What do you want?!" she grunts.

"Your blood all over my hands!" I snarl.

"What did you say to me?" She shoves me. "Who do you think you're talking to?!"

"I don't care how many little fans and patrons you got. You ain't nothing! Your act is just to hide how pathetic and insecure you are. If you got a problem with me, we can solve it now."

Dropping her purse, she ties her hair.

"Too bad there aren't any cameras to catch me killing you. I'll just drag your corpse out and take pictures with it! More patrons for taking out the weakest!" she declares.

Screw the consequences. I'm infuriated. I just want her dead. We step towards each other. The door swings open, breaking our attention. A group storms in. A tall woman with a scar running across her face leads the group. She's blind in one eye.

Athena drops her hands, gasping at the group. She's shocked to see them as if she recognizes them.

"Pixis, you're-."

"Alive?" the tall woman responds. She points to me. "Get her out of here."

Two of the individuals rush over and grab me. They escort me out the bathroom. They go back inside, shutting the door. A dose of clarity hits me as my anger fades. With a clear mind, I feel foolish I engaged in a conflict, thankful I got out of it. Unfortunately for Athena, I can't say the same. Whatever beef they have with her, is not my problem.

I head for the door, but halt at the tv. Round 2 highlights play as people in the bar cheer. If Athena dies tonight, they won't even know because they're too busy watching tv. This is how they view us. They're oblivious to our pain and suffering. We are nothing more than entertainment to them.

Astra was right. They don't love us. They love their dopamine. We're too good for these people. I barge right back inside the bathroom. The assailants hold Athena by the arms as Pixis faces her. My entry catches their attention.

"Girl didn't get the memo," Pixis says. She nods to one of her associates. "Take care of her."

The man lurks towards me with a knife. My eyes focus on his blade, calculating his move. He goes for my chest. I step out the way and snap his arm. Grabbing his head, I smash it against the mirror and drive it into the sink. A piece of the sink breaks off. He is motionless in a puddle of water and blood.

With the distraction, Athena slips her hand free and elbows a goon in the jaw. As he staggers back, I tackle him through the bathroom stall. The back of his head smacks against the toilet seat. He twitches as blood pours out the gash on the back of his head.

A woman rushes at me with a knife. I catch her hand. Pushing back and forth with the knife, our heads are close to each other. I head-butt her. Her grip loosens. I push the knife into her throat. She gags as I drive the blade up her throat. Her blood spurts onto my face. I push her corpse down. Athena dodges Pixis' knife strikes.

"Pixis, please stop," Athena begs. "I never meant to-."

Pixis keeps striking at Athena. Athena ducks and uppercuts her. The knife drops. Athena grabs it and stabs Pixis in the side of the neck. Pixis drops to her knees, holding the knife in her neck.

"Pixis, I'm sorry. It was my fault-."

Pixis takes out a gun, stopping Athena in her tracks. I kick Pixis in the face. She hits the floor. The knife goes deeper into her neck. Her blood pours out on the floor. A gloomy look casts over Athena's face as she stares at Pixis' corpse. She sniffles, holding back her tears.

"We have to go," I say.

She doesn't move, staying in her trance. I have to leave now before someone walks in. I don't fear the authorities. They won't do anything. It was in self-defense, and nobody messes with Valkyries. Still, the media frenzy this will cause will be a big distraction for me, if I'm caught. I leave the bar. Athena follows right behind.

"Hey!" she calls out. "Thanks."

We go our separate ways, without looking back.

CHAPTER 20

Normally I would have my server make me some coffee, but I'm done using her. I make my own coffee. It feels good and taste better, knowing it came from my hands. I drop my coffee, startled at Maximus on the couch. He's stretched out on the couch as if it's his house.

"How did you get in here?" I stammer.

"You forgot to lock your door. You alright?"

I think back to the brawl last night. The images of the blood and brains are still fresh.

"What are you doing here?" I grunt.

"We're going to train."

"Train? That's hours from now."

"Call it a special event."

He hits the server button. My server comes out with her obedient eyes.

"I would like a cup of coffee. Moon brewed please," Maximus says so politely.

"No you don't. You don't order her to do anything." I turn to her, softening my tone. "It's fine."

She skedaddles off.

"We really have to do this now?" I groan.

"Do you have somewhere else to be?"

I grab my shoes.

"I guess not," I sigh.

Outside, Maximus walks in the opposite direction of the training complex.

"The complex is that way," I say with irritation.

"I know."

I roll my eyes at the sky. I wonder if disobeying my trainer will get my head blown off. Fans would love to see that. I follow him to wherever he's leading me to. We get to the shore of the island where there's a boat. I think he's going to give me swimming lessons.

"Help me push this into the water," Maximus says.

We push the boat far enough in the water for it to float then we jump in.

"You know how to row a boat?" he asks.

I nod as we paddle. At first we paddle without direction. The mansion leaves my sight as we steer in a new direction. No sign of life is near. Dozens of islets surround us. We maneuver around them. I have no idea where we're going, but whenever he makes a command, I follow. At times it seems like the boat is too long to make the sharp turn, and we'll flip overboard, but we turn perfectly.

"You seem to know your way with a boat," Maximus marvels.

"I had some experience."

Sometimes dad took the family fishing. Whenever we went, we never used an automated boat. He always wanted us to do things the old fashion way when it came to nature. While everyone else dropped an electric tube in the water to kill nearby fishes, he made us use a fishing rod. 'Technology can't save you all the time. You have to use what God gave you,' he said.'

As we paddle, the scenery changes. Stone igloos on an island come into view. People dressed in tan robes drift around on the island. Some kind of retreat, a getaway for the people of Delos I suppose. We get to the shore. Slight soreness hits my arms from rowing, causing me to roll my shoulders. We grab a crate from the boat. The crate is wide, but not that heavy. I carry it with one hand without too much effort.

The inhabitants' faces come into full sight. They're people of different ages, all with dark circles under their eyes. It's as if despite their different ethnicities, they ended up sharing the same sullen look. Many are skinny with little meat on their bones. A man grills a dead bat at a nearby hut. This isn't a getaway. They're too poor and malnourished to be from Delos. They live here.

"The map of the islands doesn't show people living here," I say.

"That's because these people are unknown to the world. The natives of the Siclades Islands," Maximus reveals.

"The ones in Delos came here first?" I say, now unsure.

"Tell that to their ancestors who were taken from their homes and forced to build the islands only to be left behind. Not the fairy tale they teach in schools, is it?"

This is far from the common notion that companies funded new cities in uninhabited parts of the world. People volunteered to build the cities in search of a new beginning. The immigrants came together and created the Siclades Islands. There was no forced labor. The story paints a beautiful picture where everyone prospered back then on the islands. It's all a lie. What they taught us in school, what society believes, none of it is true. The others scorn at us.

"Why are they mugging us?" I ask.

"We wear the clothes of their oppressors."

"My family were miners. I didn't oppress anyone."

"Nova, to them anyone more fortunate than them is an oppressor, and that's everyone."

It's mostly adults who glare at us. Some kids play outside, embracing the fun. Their spirit is too youthful to let the misery overwhelm them. Kids play soccer with a rusted robot's head. The head rolls to my feet. The kids wave at me. I kick it back to them, sure that it's what they want. They kick it back. Giggling with excitement, they await my next move. Deciding to play in their game, I kick the robot. We go back and forth, kicking the robot. One kid runs towards me with the robot, trying to get it around me.

Stepping up to defend his advance, I laugh. This game excites me. Nothing else matters right now, not the training or the fights. For the first time in a while I'm happy. I steal the robot from the kid with my foot, ending the game. He reaches into his pocket. He opens his palm, revealing a necklace made out of bamboo and stone.

"Thank you," I say, taking the necklace.

We approach a man who grills a squirrel and a bat. Maximus and the man acknowledges each other with nods.

"Show us the way," Maximus states.

The man takes the smoke pipe out his mouth and spits. The pipe is made out of bamboo. He puts herbs in his pipe and continues smoking.

"What do you have to offer?" the man snarls with no interest.

Maximus grabs salmon from the crate and drops it on the table. The man's dead and beat eyes light up with a joy that's foreign to him. He prances up and down. Calming down, he wipes the smile off.

"It's going to get cloudy soon. May start raining. You should head out before it does," the man answers.

"Excellent," Maximus says.

The sky is blue. The sun shines bright with no clouds in sight. If Maximus paid the man fish to predict the weather, then Maximus just wasted some good salmon. We walk through the village, going into the woods. We walk on a thin dirt trail. It's the only visible path. The more we travel, the less the path is visible. Trees surround us as the dirt trail is no longer visible.

I think we're lost, but Maximus leads the way as if he has a map inside his mind. We go in between trees, uphill, then downhill. After walking through the forest for some time, the trees stop appearing. We enter the flat lands. Mountains surround us. We're in the open now.

"Tell me, do you still blame the Hyperions for your father's death?" Maximus asks.

"I own some of the blame," I sigh with my head down.

"Reach into the crate."

I'm surprised to find my sword along with bulky armor and metal arm gauntlets. Maximus puts on the exact same armor then grabs a thin simple sword. This has to be a joke, there is no way we can spar out here.

"We don't have any battle shields," I say.

"That's why we have the armor."

"Did you forget? We can't train without the shields."

"How is this any different than in the ring? We may not be fighting to the death, but we can still train like it."

I hesitate to move towards my gear.

"You want to get rid of fear, get out of your comfort zone," he asserts.

I grab my gear.

"I'm not afraid," I declare.

Wearing armor and wielding swords, we circle each other.

"You must learn to focus your anger on your opponent without losing control," he states.

We begin sparring. Our swords clash against each other. His torso is open for a hit. I take it, but he blocks with the gauntlet. We jump back, leaving numerous feet between us.

"Don't blame the Hyperions or yourself for your father's death," Maximus announces.

I charge at him, he blocks my strike again and looks me dead in the eyes.

"Blame your father."

I halt. In my freeze, Maximus snatches my sword out of my hand and tosses it. I let loose, swinging at him. There is no technique. I just want to punch a hole in his face, but he dodges easily.

"You can be angry all you want. Your father was still a fool," Maximus scorns.

My sword is close. I part from Maximus and pick up my sword. I strike, but he blocks.

"My dad was doing the right thing!" I scream.

"The right thing?!" he yells in offense.

He knocks my sword in the air and kicks me in the chest, sending me to the ground. I block his sword with my gauntlets.

"The right thing in this world is like searching for snow in the desert!" he declares, striking at me.

He backs up, allowing me to get up. He stands between me and my sword.

"Morals don't matter to the enemy. Only victory," he proclaims.

I charge at him. He swings, but I duck underneath, sliding towards my sword. As I pick it up, he rushes towards me. I trip him to the ground. I jump to my feet and point my sword at his chest.

"I won," I declare.

He smirks like he knows an inside joke I'm not getting.

"The only thing you won is another lesson on humility."

I realize, I'm standing over his legs. His legs clamp on my ankle, taking me down. I fall into a puddle of water. We get a camp fire started from tree bark. I dry and warm myself. I'm still shaking from the cold water although my clothes are becoming less wet. Maximus stares at the fire calmly.

"You have more potential than your parents could ever have," Maximus says.

"You didn't know my parents."

"I know the anger you feel, blaming yourself for their deaths. The loss of your love ones hurts you so much, you wish you never knew them, so you wouldn't have to suffer," he laments.

Something catches his attention as he points past me.

"Your next lesson will be catching that pig," he says.

"Pig?" I question as I look. "What pig?"

When I turn back around, the kendo stick smacks me on the side of the head, knocking me off my feet. Colliding with the ground, I black out.

CHAPTER 21

I open my eyes to a gray sky. My head hurts as I groan. Rubbing on it, I feel specks of blood. How long was I out? The sky was blue, and now it looks like it's about to rain. Oh my god! The man Maximus gave the fish to was right.

Wait, where's Maximus? I jump to my feet. My head swivels around, looking for him. I only see the forest. The crates are gone. All I have is my armor and sword. He could be going to the bathroom in the woods.

"Maximus!" I scream.

I wait, but there's no answer. I call out a few more times. Nothing again. There's no way he left me out here. Why did he pull that cheap shot? If it was to test my reflexes, why would he dip out?

Maybe it was an accident. Perhaps he hit me too hard and thought I was dead. But why leave? If anything, he would have kicked me until I woke up and then training would have continued.

There's only one explanation I can think of, it's the obvious. Maximus, wanting to get rid of me, left me here to die. He was always cynical of me since the beginning. This morning he was displeased with how I had let Athena run up on me. 'She made you look like a fool in front of everyone,' he said.

But if he wanted to get rid of me, why didn't he just finish the job? A simple cut with his sword, and nobody would have suspected he killed me. Unless he wanted me to suffer first. He knows I'm unfamiliar with this place. With the gray sky, there's no sun for me to follow. I can't believe it, that maniac planned this from the start.

Many questions run in my mind, but I put them aside to find a way out of here. With no sun, I'm lost. This can't be happening. Do Blaze and the people behind the scene care I am lost? No doubt they're listening through the tracker inside me. This must be entertaining for them. I'm in the middle of nowhere, so there are no cameras for the audience to see through. Help's not coming, I have to save myself.

Think Nova, which way did you come? All the directions are the same, leading to the forest. Looking everywhere, I hope a path will look familiar. I look for a hint that one path is better than the others. Maybe one that looks less creepy, has better looking trees, or just gives me a gut feeling that it's the best option. Nothing comes. Growing tired of looking around, I set my eyes on the mountains. If I can get there, I will see the entire island and know where to go. I pick up my sword. Screw it. I walk into the forest towards the mountains.

I don't let my mind wander. With no Maximus as a guide, I look everywhere to check my surroundings. There weren't any animals on our way up here, but that doesn't lower my guard. The chances of me running into an animal are low though. If it happens, I have my sword.

When the Siclades Islands were created, engineers drained parts of the ocean to elevate the underwater islands. Companies wanted the islands to look as natural as possible, so they brought over hundreds of land animals. Unfortunately, many died because they weren't compatible with their new environment. Besides the birds who migrate here naturally, it's rare to see a land animal outside the zoo unless it's imported food. Every now and then, there are sightings of possums, raccoons, or elks in Delos, but I can't bet on it out here.

Leaves crunch under my feet as birds chirp. Many times there are too many trees and bushes blocking my path, forcing me to change directions. Being in a tight space limits my ability to react quickly if anything happens. The more space I have, the more I can see what's coming. Going towards the mountains, I aim for the paths that grant me the most space.

I wonder if there are any cameras filming. I doubt they're out this far in the middle of nowhere. If they are, the fans wouldn't care about me. If anything this would be entertaining. My haters would be jumping out of their seats, waiting to see if I die of starvation or thirst first. That reminds me.

My stomach growls, giving me discomfort. Man, anything would be good at this moment. With no animals around, I have to rely on the plants. I can't eat any berries, not knowing if they are poisonous or not. Food is going to be out of the question for a while. With my canister gone, the only thing I can do is wait for rain and catch drops in my mouth.

I travel for a little bit over an hour, assuming the afternoon is here. My feet are slow as I'm sluggish, feeling tired. The hunger in my stomach turns into pain. Each step causes pain in my gut. I forget my hunger, coming across a bush full of berries. They look like the kind of berries you put in a blender. My mouth waters at the idea of eating them. I can feel their sweet juices drenching my dry tongue. No! I can't lose my life over hunger. Looking away from the berries, I keep moving.

If this carries on any longer, I won't make it to the mountains. I halt, hearing a sound. Paying more attention to it, it becomes clear. The sound of a water stream hits my ears. Not just water, but a rapid flow of it. I rush towards the sound. The sound grows louder as I run. I come across a river flowing downstream.

Dropping my sword, I dive my head into the water. The water hits my face, cleaning it. Water pours into my mouth. When my mouth gets full, I swing my head backwards, allowing me to gulp. I repeat this motion, taking big gulps. My belly gets full, taking away my hunger.

The bushes move, causing me to stop. I reach for my sword when a deer comes out. I can't believe it. The deer walks up to the water and drinks, ignoring me. It must be one of the few animals that didn't die off here.

This is my chance. I lurk towards the deer with my sword. It doesn't notice me approaching. Its attention is stuck on the water, drinking peacefully. I raise my sword, ready to attack when a small deer comes out of the bushes. It drinks next to its mother. Hesitating, I stare at them. A part of me wants to kill them really bad, but I let it die as I lower my sword and turn around. The wilderness doesn't care about ethics, but it's hard for me to forget them even out here. That's why I'm a fool.

Looking at the river, something clicks inside my head. It's all going downstream. It eventually leads to the ocean, and the ocean means the hut village. I have no idea how long the river stretches, but this idea outweighs the mountain one. Okay, Nova you got this. I walk, following the river downhill.

More hours go by as I follow the river with no sign of it ending. At times I drink water to replenish my body and stabilize my hunger. I can only drink so much before getting full and having to go to the bathroom.

Will I ever get out of here? Maybe this is the end. I've been out here for hours with no sign of civilization. The more ground I cover, feeling I'm getting close, the more the forest seems to extend, trapping me here. Only my feet keep me moving. At this point, I don't think about going home. The action of moving consumes my spirit like an automated machine. No thoughts, just the focus on a simple action and doing it forever.

It rains heavily, but it doesn't bother me. Continuing, my mind scans the environment. The scenery looks familiar. I recognize certain trees and paths. Seeing these paths, more things become familiar. This was where Maximus took that long pause, staring into the sky as if he was considering where to go next. I follow this path, beginning to remember all of it. My footsteps pick up as I gain confidence. Jogging with newfound energy, I move without hesitation. Everything is coming back. I feel myself getting closer then I see the hut villages.

"Yes!" I cheer.

I drop to my knees in the middle of the village with joy. The inhabitants go on about their business, ignoring me. The rain and heavy clouds are gone, bringing the pink sunset. My relief ends, seeing our boat is gone. Of course Maximus took it. I can swim, but in my state, I will drown from fatigue. I go back into the village, looking for help.

"Hi, I need some help," I say to a man.

He scorns at me and continues walking. I approach a woman carrying a basket full of plants, but she hurries off. With each person I come across, they frown at me, turning their backs like I have the plague.

"Hey you!" a voice calls out.

It's the man Maximus gave the fish to. He waves at me to come over.

"Your friend left you," he snickers.

"Do you have a boat? I need to get off this island."

"A boat huh?" He rubs his raggedy beard. "That depends."

"On what?" I irk, growing irritated.

"If you have something to offer in return."

"I don't have any animals for you to eat. I'm sorry."

"Pity. You corp-hounds want it all, but will give nothing," he snorts. He shoos me away. "Come back when you have something to offer corp-hound."

A corp-hound is what the misfortunate call the wealthy. It's derogatory, but I feel honored to be called it for the first time in my life. I slam my gauntlets on the table.

"Take them in exchange. You can kill some animals with it."

He squints at the gauntlets, inspecting them which is pointless because he's no expert. As far as he's concerned, they're sharp enough to cut flesh, and that's all that matters.

"Sold," he announces, taking the gauntlets.

He hands me a key.

"I have a boat around the corner," he says.

"Perfect, thank you."

My fingers are within inches of the key when he pulls it back.

"What are you doing? A deal's a deal," I stammer.

"I said you can have the boat. I never said you can have the key to unlock it from its cage. That is another trade."

"What?!" But I don't have anything else," I whimper.

This lying dirty man has my blood boiling so bad, I should knock him out and take the keys. Even if I had my debit card on me, it would do him no good. The moment he steps in Delos, they will call the cops on him. He strokes his beard once more. His eyes light up at my sword.

"Your sword for my key."

"I can't," I gasp, clutching it.

"Then I guess you can't get off this island."

"Please, I gave you the gauntlets. Just let me have the key. I have to get back," I plead.

"Should have thought about that before you came here, corp-hound."

I yank on my hair, trying to control my anger. I'm not giving up my sword. I don't have any patrons. If I lose this, there's no telling if I'll get a new one. I'll be stuck with a training sword against superior weapons. That's assuming for some crazy reason Maximus will still be in my corner. I need my sword, and I need that boat. This old geezer leaves me no choice. I take my sword out its metal sheath and point it at the man's throat. His face turns pale as he freezes.

"You listen here you backwoods low life old man," I snarl, staring down his soul. "You will give me that key and the boat, or the kids will be playing soccer with your head after I cut it off!"

His eyes flare with fear.

"You wouldn't hurt an innocent old man would you?" he quivers.

"I've killed many people. You'll scream the loudest as I bathe in your blood!" I declare.

Shaking, he hands over his key, almost dropping it. I snatch it and my gauntlets. The boat is in a shed nearby. The wood is chipped, and the paddles are broken. It's smaller than the last boat, but I have to use all my strength to push it into the water.

"You corp-hounds are all the same!" the man barks.

"I don't own anything," I retort.

"Doesn't matter. You sleep and eat in their cities, you are one of them! Get out of here!"

I keep pushing. The boat trudges as I push it out. The inhabitants are looking at me, mumbling insults. They keep their distance from me. They're probably too scared to do something even with their numbers. I'm glad they're frozen with fear. Their numbers against my exhaustion - I don't know if I can take them all.

Pushing the boat out, I see the little boy from earlier. His joyful eyes from before are gone as he looks at me with sorrow like I crushed his dreams.

"I'm sorry," I grieve.

I hand him the gauntlets. When I get near the water, the inhabitants form a large group behind me. I'm ready to reach for my sword. They stop at a distance, watching me get into the water. There's no time for rest until I'm far away from the island.

I paddle away. My fatigue and the broken paddles make maneuvering the boat harder than before. The huts are out of sight, so I take a break, resting back. The pain those people go through has to be brutal. To live out here in despair, right next to the most advanced cities in the history of the world is a tragedy. Their view of the world is one of misery. Their experience with me will only taint that picture even more. Maybe we're all bad, and I'm just as terrible as my captors.

I arrive to the mansion, leaving the boat at the shore. I go around towards the back to avoid anybody. On the way to my suite, I encounter nobody. I pause at my door, hearing classical music from the inside. I open the door slowly.

Maximus drinks in the kitchen. Taking out my sword without making a noise, I tiptoe behind him. His back faces me as he drinks. Killing him is a matter of life and death. He'll do me more harm than good if he stays alive. I know how to fight on my own. He's useless to me now.

"You're really going to strike me down with a gift I gave you," Maximus says.

I freeze in shock. He turns around, sipping his tea with calmness.

"The maid knows how to make some good tea," he compliments.

"You monster! You left me out there to die!"

"Hardly. From the looks of it, you're still alive."

"You don't know what I had to do to survive, who I had to-." My voice faints, thinking back to the poor man I threatened. I take a deep breath. "Why?"

"Why not?" he gloats. "Go ahead. Strike me down. I left you in the woods. I'm in your house, drinking your tea. I bet that makes you angry, doesn't it? Take your revenge."

I step towards him, ready to strike.

"Come on Nova! You pathetic excuse for a Valkyrie! I bet your parents were just as weak as you. That's why they're dead!"

My anger hits a boiling point, but suddenly settles. I don't move. This is too easy, I realize. I'm not that stupid.

"I'm not playing your game. You're going to tell me why," I assert.

He raises his eyebrows. For the first time, he's surprised. He pours the liquid down the sink. It's only water.

"Turn off music," he calls out.

Silence fills the room.

"I wanted to test you today," he reveals.

"We always train."

"Not physically, but mentally. After seeing what Athena did to you, I didn't want you to get too distracted like you did with Lyssa. I needed you to focus."

"So you threw me into the wild to strengthen my mind?"

He nods.

"Seeing the anger in your eyes, I know it worked." He sticks his arms out. "Are you going to kill me?"

"I really want to!" I declare.

As much as I want to kill him and hate what he did, I think back to what I gained from it all. The insults and the training, all of it made me stronger. He's tough, but he's my trainer. I still need him. I lower my sword.

"You know where the door is," I grunt.

"Training at the same time," he says.

I smile. That's the Maximus I know. The aching in my stomach comes back. I run into the kitchen and eat almost everything in sight: meat, cheese, breads, and fruits until my belly is full. I take a shower. The steamy water soothes my battered body. I'm ready for bed when the doorbell rings.

"We already said training would be-."

I halt, seeing Octavian at the door. His height towers over me.

"Octavian," I stammer.

"Did I catch you at a bad time?" he asks.

I realize I'm still in my towel.

"No, it's fine," I stumble, still trying to collect my thoughts.

Where am I at?

"I just want to say thank you," he says.

"For what?"

"Oh come on Nova. Your gift was amazing, but you don't have to be too humble about it. It came in the mail today with a letter from you."

He takes out a tiny chest that rests in his palm. He opens it. A little glass ballerina sticks out. It moves in circles as a chime plays from it. He smiles at the display.

"Exactly how my mother liked them. She never was a fan of the holograms. You really did your homework," he praises.

"I like to read bios," I lie.

My heart beat picks up. I pray he won't ask any more questions about it. I don't know anything about music boxes. He gulps.

"I didn't come here just to thank you. There's a show at the opera house tonight in downtown Delos."

245

"You're asking me out on a date?" I gasp.

He blushes, trying hard not to smile even more.

"I know I'm supposed to make a big announcement, but forget the rules tonight," he laughs.

I laugh as well, but it's fake.

"Let me think about it?" I guess.

"Oh. Okay, just let me know," he utters as his forehead scrunches up.

He walks away with his pondering look. What did you do, you idiot? It's a date. Every Valkyrie wants a date with the Chosen One, and you just turned him down. What are you thinking? He's at the end of the hall when I jump out.

"Wait, Octavian!" I shout.

"Yeah?"

"I would love to join you," I chirp with a huge smile.

He grins.

"Awesome. My car will come by at 7pm. You're going to love the show, Nova."

When I get back inside, I slide down the door. I breathe heavily. Who in the world gave him the music box? Lord knows it wasn't me. Minerva? I'll ask her later. For now, I have bigger things ahead.

"Oh my god, I have a date with Octavian Hyperion," I blurt.

It troubles me even more that I don't know if it's a good or bad thing.

CHAPTER 22

"You have a date with Octavian?! Look at you!" Venus cheers.

"With it being unexpected and at night, all the eyes will be on you. It's a great opportunity for you to connect with Octavian and the world," Flavius informs.

"Thank you," I say at their holograms.

I look at the ground.

"When you pull this off, you'll have all the patrons. I'm talking about the top swords and armor. You'll be unstoppable Nova!" Venus sings.

"We have to get a dress ready quick and come by," Flavius mentions. "Are you alright Nova?"

"It's just a lot to think about," I say with a fake smile.

"Well get ready because the fun has begun!" Venus enthuses.

The hologram ends, leaving me alone with my pestering thoughts. The reality of tonight settles in. All I can think about is him. Not Octavian, but the one he resembles so much – Augustus. I'm going on a date with the son of the devil.

My managers come over. They take me through the same process they did the night of the interviews. This time, they don't go overboard with the makeup. They give me enough to sparkle. My dress is purple with stars.

"Excellent isn't it?" Venus asks.

"Of course," I sigh.

"Nova, is something wrong?" Flavius wonders. "Ever since you told us about the date, you seem bothered.

There's no point in lying anymore.

"I can't do this," I gulp.

"I know this is a big opportunity. Octavian has the looks to make a married woman forget her vows, but you can't let your nerves get the best of you girl," Venus gushes.

"It's not him. It's his dad,"

"Augustus?" Flavius stumbles.

"My dad fought for him in the Siege of Hyperion Industries."

"Nova, it was an act of bravery," Venus praises. "I'm sure-."

"It was murder!" I yell. My voice instantly lowers. "I was there. Augustus didn't give us the backup we needed, and people died because of it."

A sullen mood sweeps the room.

"Nova, I had no idea about it. I'm sorry," Venus consoles.

"I can't face him. Every time I see Octavian, I see Augustus, and it reminds me of my dad. I don't know if I'll breakdown, or go off on Octavian," I whimper.

Flavius places his hands on my shoulders.

"Nova, listen to me very carefully," he says seriously. "You may cry out there tonight. You might even make a fool out of yourself, but you must never go off on Octavian, or blame his family especially in front of the cameras."

"But there's only one rule on this show."

"There's an unspoken rule also. You never go against the Chosen One."

My managers glance at each other nervously.

"Every so often there's a Valkyrie who does," Venus says timidly. "They want to stand out, cause drama for ratings, or in rare cases, they can't take it anymore. They don't get their head blown off. Instead they have an armor malfunction, or their weapon goes missing before the fight."

"I can't go on the date," I groan.

"Yes you can. Put on the best character you have and give them a show. It's just for tonight," Flavius insists.

My eyes stay on the ground as I don't move. I can't do this. Anything, but a date with Octavian.

"Then cancel the date. Nobody knows it's going to happen, so there's no trouble," Flavius offers.

That'll work. I won't be losing anything. I'm already at the bottom of the barrel. It beats embarrassing myself even more.

"So sad. This could have propelled you so far in the rankings," Venus sighs.

She's right. This is a once in a lifetime opportunity. I won't get another chance like this. I look up, standing straight.

"I'm going. I need the patrons, so I'll give them a date to remember," I declare.

"That's my girl!" Venus praises.

As soon as they leave, I run to the bathroom and throw up. All that food I stuffed in my mouth comes out. I taste the cheese I had. Staying in the bathroom for a little bit longer, I throw up more. Tonight won't be easy. It'll be like fighting in the ring.

CHAPTER 23

Octavian waits for me outside the mansion. He has a black luxury hover car. It's wide and has features unlike the plain cars the show uses. This car, like Astra's, signifies wealth and power.

"You look beautiful," he compliments.

"Thank you."

I don't overly show gratitude, not wanting to give off the impression I need his compliments. I'm still humble enough to smile and appreciate the gestures. He opens the door for me. He waits for me to get inside first. The car takes off. Sitting across from each other, I try not to keep eye contact for too long. I don't want to stare, but it's hard to look at anything else when it's just the two of us. He's bolder than me, keeping his eyes on me. Not in a weird way, but one with interest.

"Didn't anyone tell you it's rude to stare?" I joke.

"I should take a picture and hang it up," he quips.

I chuckle. This isn't acting. He really makes me laugh. This is a good way to forget I don't like him.

"Do you have a collection of music boxes?" I ask.

"I lost them over the years. Do you have anything your parents gave you that you really loved?"

"I had a necklace from my dad," I mumble.

"What happened to it?"

"It was stolen from me about a month ago." I catch his frown. "It's no big deal. That's what happens when you ride the bus in downtown SF."

The cameras could be on us at any moment. I can't afford to have one slip up, one awkward moment that will make me look stupid. I need to keep the energy alive.

"You're a fan of the opera?" I assume, turning to him completely.

"My mom use to take us to see it a lot. That's why I love it so much!" he exults. "Where did your parents use to take you?"

"The beach, fishing, the forest. They wanted us to explore. It was simple, but special," I say.

"It's the thought that counts." With a sigh, he looks out the window. "Sometimes I wish I experienced more of the simple life."

We arrive to the opera house. A long line stretches out to the sidewalk.

"We're going to be waiting forever," I note.

He chuckles.

"Nova, when you're with me, you'll never have to wait." He steps out first and takes my hand. "Shall we?"

We walk past the line. I take note of the many people in line. They wear tuxedos and ball dresses. This isn't like the interviews where people dressed in flamboyance for the cameras. Their clothes tonight are professional with a simple yet sophisticated style.

I catch glances with the people in the line. At first they look offended that they're being cut, but their expressions quickly change to acceptance when they recognize us. We approach the host. His face lights up with delight upon seeing us.

"Mr. Hyperion, how do you do?" he asks cheerfully.

"Great tonight. I take it you have a seat ready for my friend Nova and I?"

"Of course sir!"

A waiter comes out.

"Show Mr. Hyperion and Nova to their seats please."

As we walk past seats, people stand to greet Octavian. We can't walk for more than a few seconds without being stopped by someone who wants to shake his hand.

'How's the family Octavian?'

'Give the big man my wishes on his new release.'

'I hope your father likes the gift I sent.'

'Our stock prices are going up since you guys acquired us. Thank you!'

Person after person, Octavian shakes their hands. He greets them with a few lines to make them laugh before going onto the next person. I can't tell if he's being genuine or just a charlatan for the masses, but he comes off smoothly. The way everyone gravitates to him, he has the style of what the old civilizations called a politician.

"You have a lot of friends," I awe.

"My father does. They're all his friends, so that makes them mine," he explains with humility.

We make it to our seats, high on a balcony with a few other people. A middle aged older man leans over towards Octavian.

"Octavian, how's everything going with you son?" the man asks.

"Leon all is well," Octavian greets with a handshake.

Unlike the quick handshakes he gave the others, Octavian and this man embrace each other with a firm one. Octavian doesn't wear the quick smile that turns off as soon as he's done greeting someone. This smile is truly authentic.

"How's business going?" Leon wonders.

"Same as usual, booming with our new releases."

Both men look out towards the stage as they speak.

"I'm talking about the military business. The longer Josev Yanga isn't found, the more money we have to spend sending troops to the colonies," Leon grunts.

"As long as all the other execs have the same resolve as my father, we have nothing to worry about," Octavian boasts.

"This isn't about resolve. Sending armies and equipment across the Solar System is a lot of work. It's not a good look to our customers. They come to the colonies for a new life. That's not how they feel when they see soldiers marching in front of their homes. Something needs to be done about Hades Hammer."

Octavian's smile leaves as he clenches his teeth.

"My father knows what he is doing." Octavian smiles at me. "Go ahead, drink."

I take a sip in order to not seem awkward while keeping my ear to the conversation.

"Some of us aren't as confidence as your portrayal," Leon continues. "The occupation has been going on for too long. Perhaps if your father sought out a diplo-."

"This will go how he wants it to go," Octavian asserts, raising his voice. He lowers his voice with a more friendly tone. "Let's not waste this precious time for business in front of my friend."

Leon acknowledges me for the first time.

"I'm sorry for not seeing you. Please accept my apologies," he comforts, reaching out his hand.

"It's fine. You're all just passionate that's all."

"I like that," he admires. "You look familiar. Have I seen you before?"

Before I can answer, he speaks again.

"You're Nova, the Valkyrie. Pleasure to meet you."

The conductor appears on stage.

"Ladies and gentlemen, before we start, I would like to welcome our honorary guests tonight. Octavian Hyperion, and from Last Valkyrie, Nova!" he announces.

The spotlight shines on us. The entire theatre claps. Not wanting to overdo it or do too little, I follow Octavian's simple wave to the crowd. With the usual broadcast of opera houses, the viewers of the show, and Octavian's presence, so many eyes are on me tonight. I just want to play it safe and make it through the night. That will be enough for some patrons.

"We give our blessings to you and your family. The success of the Conclave benefits everyone," the conductor praises.

Taking my hand, Octavian stands. I bow with him. These aren't diehard fans of the show like the common people who worship the Valkyries. They aren't even fans of Octavian as the Chosen One, but they acknowledge him as a Hyperion. To them, he is power, something they want or despise. For the moment, I share this power with him.

"Before we start the show, I want to follow up on a special request we received earlier," the conductor speaks. "The theme for tonight's performances is the Conclave. In celebrating it, we will honor the people who served. People like Nova's father."

"What?" I gasp.

"Everyone please rise."

I slowly get to my feet in disbelief.

"What's going on?" I ask.

"It's my gift," Octavian rejoices.

The orchestra plays Juturna's Song. A huge portrait rises from the stage. My heart drops at the figure on the portrait.

"Dad," I weep.

The portrait is the length between the stage and the ceiling. In the painting, my dad wears his uniform, shining in the gold background.

The applauses are endless, not slowing down. As they grow louder, I can't hear my increased breathing. My eyes water, not from tears of joy, but of anger. These people celebrate my dad like he was a hero when he was betrayed and murdered. He died for their society, the same society that looked at him as scum. Tonight they celebrate him, only to forget him tomorrow. They are liars. Elite monsters who only care about feeding their egos. I want to slaughter everyone in the theatre and cool off in their blood. I can't take this anymore.

Holding back tears, I storm out. Marching down the street, I ignore cars and stoplights. I stop at an overpass where a pond is underneath me. It's quiet unlike the busy streets nearby. I'm alone with the calm water. The peaceful scenery gives me tranquility. My frown reflects at me in the water. Two doves float by, lifting my mood a little bit. Footsteps approach.

"Nova, are you alright?" Octavian wonders.

"I'm fantastic," I choke, wiping my tears. "It was just unexpected."

I keep my gaze at the pond, hiding my face from him and any cameras that might be around.

"You did like it did you?" he asks.

Oh please why does he have to ask that? Can't he just be satisfied with my lie, so I can pretend everything is great?

"Your father was a hero."

"Stop talking about my dad!" I yell. He steps back, startled. Remembering who I'm talking to, I change my tone. "Please don't talk about him."

"I don't understand. Everyone loves him. You should be proud."

"Proud?" I snort. "Proud he's being used as a token for your big parade to make you feel better. None of these people love him. Not you and especially not your dad."

He tilts his head.

"What does he have to do with anything?" he stumbles.

I glare at him. His ignorance infuriates me, and I can't pretend any longer.

"They didn't give their lives to protect Hyperion Industries during the siege. It's all a lie."

"That's not true," he mutters.

"I was there. Your dad refused to send reinforcements!" I yell.

"He wouldn't. He's a good man," Octavian defends.

"Then why did my dad die? Why didn't the company help our families? Tell me!"

"I don't know," he whimpers.

The insecurity strongly shows in his voice as he cowers back.

"You don't even believe your own lies. You're just like him. An egotistic lying elitist who deserves to burn with the rest of your family!"

He's speechless, opening his mouth in hurt. Screw his feelings, he deserves worse. I storm past him. Rage consumes me, putting me in a trance void of logic. I don't care about the show. With so much anger, I am insane. I stomp in the street, ignoring the red light. Cars honk at me.

"Go drive off a cliff!" I scream.

My heart pounds. My head is on fire as my ears ring. A big jumbo tron on a building catches my attention. On the tron is a replay of my meltdown. My voice sounds off for blocks through the speakers as pedestrians watch. I didn't realize how furious I was. I look like a complete fool on the screen.

This brings me back to reality as I begin to cool off. I get my breathing under control as my anger disappears, giving me a clear head. I become more aware of my actions. What did I do? Losing patrons is the least of my concerns. I put my whole life in jeopardy. Thinking back to what my managers told me, there's no telling how the show will deal with me. I'm screwed.

I call my hover car with my phone. My awareness turns into embarrassment. I can't believe I said all those things. My anger made me bold, but now that it's gone, little Nova is back. I wish I played it safe and never spoke. I should have told Octavian everything was great. When I get back to the mansion, I come across Elpis in the hallway.

"What did you do?" she murmurs.

Ignoring her, I continue towards my suite, but she follows me. Girl, just take the message and leave me alone.

"They're not going to let you survive the 3rd round now. Why would you throw it all away?" she pries.

She puts her hand on my shoulder. I punch her, sending her back a few steps. Holding her mouth, she's astonished.

"Worry about yourself!" I growl.

Without looking back, I go to my suite. I have nothing to explain. I'm the one in pain. Storming into my suite, I drop down on the floor and cry. Nobody can save me. I want my parents. I want someone to hug me and tell me it's going to be alright even though it won't. They're going to fry me.

CHAPTER 24

I am slow to answer my hologram the next morning. The emotionless face of Irma appears.

"A hover car will pick you up to take you to XVN headquarters," she says.

"What's going-."

Her projection cuts off. Great. The hover car waits for me outside. I look out the window towards the water as last night replays in my mind. I wish I never went on the date in the first place. If only I had bit my tongue a little longer. I should have swallowed my pride, smiled, and went back with Octavian to enjoy the opera. The fans could have loved me. Now I await a fate that won't be in my favor.

I wonder about my punishment. Will they sabotage me in the ring? A bullet between the eyes sounds plausible, allowing them to pull the 'she disappeared' story. Torture is up their alley, with Irma as the punisher, and Blaze enthralled by it all. I dread the anticipation as my stomach sinks and my palms sweat. Why did I have to be so stupid?

When I wake up from my nap, I see an XVN sign outside the window. I head to the skyscraper in front of me. The people in suits bring back memories to the Siege. I approach the front desk.

"Hi," I speak hesitantly. "I'm-."

"I know exactly who you are!" the lady cheers. "Just take the elevator to the top floor, and Mr. Neroburn will be with you."

Her delighted response startles me. It's not sarcasm or fake, but genuine admiration. It must be good customer service.

The elevator ride feels forever. Looking out the window, the city drops as I elevate. The city recedes under my new height. The entire city radiates a tiny presence, being dwarfed by the magnificent size of the skyscraper. The door opens, bringing sight to the large room. At the other end sits Blaze at a desk. Irma stands next to him. A large window showing the blue sky is behind them.

"Welcome! Come on in Nova," he greets, getting up from his chair.

The walk is endless. With each step, it feels like the desk grows further from me, turning this into a painful trek. Dizziness falls over me as I feel the room tilting. I turn my eyes to the displays on the walls in an attempt to stabilize my vertigo.

One display is a rock from Mars with a boot imprint on it. I walk by a stuffed tiger. Taking up a large portion of the room in the corner is the head of the Statue of Liberty. Among the different kinds of antiques, the one that sticks out the most is the sculpture of David. I scope it out. Cracks cover its torso, the nose is chipped, and the balls are gone. So this is how they'll punish me – literally on top of the world. How theatric?

"How do you like this place?" Blaze chuckles.

"Just get it over with. Do what you have to do to me," I sigh.

"Do you think you're here for punishment? Nova, I'm appalled you would think I'd do such a thing," Blaze awes sarcastically. "You my friend have been the talk of the town."

Holographic projections shoot up from his desk. A news clip plays from the holograms.

"Nova, once a joke of Last Valkyrie, is now an overnight sensation, taking the world by storm with her recent outburst," the news reporter tells.

The video of my rant has over fifty million views already. My name is featured in many headlines in the news. They love me on social media.

'Oh my god, Nova snapped. She's dope!'

'Nova, like she ain't messing around anymore. That's what I'm talking about.'

'That's how you do it girl, you show them wassup. Yass queen!'

I'm ranked as number one out of all the Valkyries, leaving me stunned at my new status.

"Maybe you might win after all. Congratulations," Blaze cheers. "You're bringing in ratings, so you can still play."

He reveals the detonator in his hand. My heart jumps, thinking back to that unlucky girl who got her head blown off.

"Oh calm down. This is for something else!" he laughs. "As long as you keep your mouth shut, you'll be fine. Unless you want a front row seat with mommy and daddy."

I charge at him. Irma jumps in and kicks me in the jaw, sending me to the ground.

"Wow! Make sure to cover that up, we don't need you looking beat in front of the cameras!" Blaze enthuses.

Staggering to my feet, I spit out blood. My jaw rings with pain as my head is hazy.

"You're a monster. It must be so easy and fun for you to watch us kill each other!" I scorn.

His smile goes away. A look of dismay appears.

"But I shouldn't expect anything more from an emotionless psychopath like you."

Blaze gets up from his seat slowly, staring at me with a haunted look.

"You think I want to force you to fight that I like this? In the beginning, they ran pilots and accepted volunteers. But when the Valkyries saw the deaths, many got scared and quit. The matches had to be fought to the death in order to compete with the other shows, but with no cast, there was no other choice."

"So all this is for ratings and money?" I scorn.

"Wake up. When has it been about anything different?"

News clips appear on his desk, showing bombings on Mars, riots, and long unemployment lines.

"The world has always been on fire, and we control that fire with the products we sell. We give people an escape from reality, and the world goes on," he asserts.

"Tell that to the Valkyries."

"It's a sacrifice. The gladiators of ancient Rome never got to enjoy their society."

As I trudge away, his laughs plague my ears. I rinse the blood out my mouth at a water fountain. Someone tugs my shirt.

"Excuse me, Ms. Nova," a tiny voice murmurs.

It's a little girl, no older than five, staring at me with innocent eyes.

"Can I get a picture with you please?" she asks.

Behind her is a lady smiling. Biting my tongue, I nod.

"Of course!" I welcome.

The lady snaps a picture with me and her daughter.

"Can I be like you when I grow up?" she asks.

I look into her eyes, seeing a world of innocence. What fantasies did her mother give her to make her dare to ask such a stupid question? I bet she tells her daughter to believe in her dreams, that the world is a loving place, and anything is possible. Judging by the wide grin on the mother, she's just as stupid as her daughter. Their ignorance is disgusting; it's a disgrace that they believe the lies. I hide my resentment with a smile.

"You can be anything you want to be," I charm.

CHAPTER 25

The next few days are surreal. In less than 24 hours, my managers book me for so many photo shoots, interviews, and appearances. I even have my own commercial, featuring yogurt. It's been years since I ate yogurt. I forgot the taste.

News stations do segments on me, talking about my life before Shed Court, and when my dad was alive. Despite all the attention, I put the focus back on the people of Shed Court, to shine light on their struggles. An entire episode of the Felix Neptune show features me.

"I have to ask now, do you find Octavian attractive. Don't worry, we won't tell?" Felix snickers.

The audience giggles as Octavian's picture shows on the tron.

"I'd say he's a low 8, but that's only because I still plan on marrying him after this."

The room bursts into laughs, and I join in. What happened to the angry Nova? The one who raged against Octavian and his entire family. She's still here, but her time in the lights is gone. I could only play the mad woman for so long before it got stale and bored the fans. I had to change my persona up, using humor to entertain.

It's not just the fans treating me different, but even the Valkyries. I can tell by the subtle looks on their faces. Passing them by in the mansion or at the training complex, some wave at me, while others quickly smile. Not all admire what I did as they give me glares.

They don't hate or disagree with what I did. They feel the same way. They don't like all the spotlight on me, shutting out their chances for more patrons. This new attention comes with a price. Wherever I'm at, I keep my head on a swivel, watching just in case a jealous Valkyrie wants to take me out.

"You better watch out for them Valkyries. Don't want to end up like Niobe," Venus says.

Niobe was a Valkyrie, who during the interviews, in an attempt to get the spotlight, made out with the Chosen One. Her plan worked, everyone loved her, but only too much. The other Valkyries did not like the idea of being showed up. Later that night, the Valkyries stomped her to death in her room. She was kicked in the face over 100 times and was still kicked after she died. They found her teeth lodged in her stomach.

My managers take me to a shop in Delos where a patron has paid for me to get new armor. We walk through the laboratory, seeing the different kinds of armor.

"These are all prototypes, so we'll do the design later," Flavius says.

They all look the same to me, plated armor on top of skintight wear, fortified with materials that make them strong and durable. All are massive upgrades from the basic one I fought in. My old one offered me as much protection as a t-shirt. That was what I got for not having any patrons.

One suit can emit a poisonous gas. It also releases an anti-toxin back into my body, leaving me immune to the poison. My problem is the anti-toxin is 95% effective against the poison. The 5% scares me. Another one sends out an electric pulse. It's great, but I have to get close enough to my opponent for it to work. The numerous suits are all excellent, but the drawbacks are too big for me to afford in the ring. One catches my attention.

"How about this one?" I ask.

"This one absorbs melee attacks and stabs to a certain degree," the tailor explains. "It sends out a concussion wave in proportion to the hits it takes. So if it's a small hit, it'll send out a smaller wave after a certain amount of small hits. If it's a big hit, it'll immediately send out a bigger wave."

"What's the catch?"

"It's more flexible, enabling more speed, but it's not as durable as the other ones."

Speed versus durability. Durability is a huge priority, but I don't want it to slow me down. Besides it can only take so many hits. No armor is indestructible, so I don't want to fight with the feeling I am.

"I'll take it."

Venus claps. As long as it gives me protection beyond the basic ones, it'll do.

"You're going to love the design Nova!" she cheers.

***

My training quarters is filled with new equipment. I have training robots and access to virtual reality that simulates the fights. New weapons are on the racks. One is just a hilt. I press the button, igniting an electric whip.

"This is awesome!" I exclaim.

Maximus and I set up to spar.

"Do you even know how to use that thing?" he asks.

"How hard can it be?"

I ignite the whip and swing at him. He blocks it with his sword. I swing again, this time wrapping the whip around his sword. He pulls his sword back, pulling me off my feet. I land on the ground.

The next round I grab the gauntlets on the rack. They shoot out concussion blasts. I fire at Maximus. He runs to the side, dodging them. The gap between us shrinks. I hold onto the handles, charging up the gauntlets. Bigger blasts emit out, barely missing him. They propel me to the ground. The impact with the floor knocks the air out of me.

I hold a simple looking shield in the next round. I hit the button on the inside, and a streak of fire comes out. Maximus dodges the flames, jumping out the way and blocking. I grow angry as he dodges. The force of the flames is too strong for me to handle, throwing me off balance. The flames spin out of control, going in all directions.

"No!" I gasp.

I throw the shield down, stopping the flames from coming out. Maximus shoulder bumps me, dropping me to the ground. The room's on fire. Exhaust shoots out the walls, putting the fires out. Nothing is damaged as all the equipment and weapons remain the same. Maximus helps me up. I jump to my feet in frustration. He chuckles.

"What's so funny?"

"The weapons don't make the warrior. You can have all of these toys, but they don't mean anything," he says.

"Patrons are a bad thing now? You've been on me about them this whole time."

"Yes, but if you don't know how to use these weapons, they become burdens rather than gifts."

This is something to think about as I leave.

**

"So we have a shoot with Temporal Magazine. Raven Gammon wants to do an interview. Oh I got you booked to make a guest appearance on Die by Day," Venus tells me with excitement.

I sigh. More appearances, more love, and more patrons. All of it feels heavy on me now.

"Nova, what's wrong now?" Flavius asks.

"I appreciate all that you are doing along with the support, but it's starting to become too much."

"You don't like this?" Venus gasps.

"No, I love it. I'm getting better armor now, and I'm thankful for it. But all these interviews, shows, and equipment can take away from what's really important. I just don't want to overdo it, that's all."

Venus' eyes lower like a sad puppy.

"But we have so many things scheduled," Venus whimpers.

"Then we'll go for her. We can speak for her. It'll show that Nova is very dedicated to training. The fans will love that," Flavius adds.

"I suppose that'll work," Venus sighs.

"Thank you for understanding," I say.

With the extra time, I can train more. I head to training.

"How many weapons will it be today?" Maximus asks.

I take my sword out from the casing.

"Just one," I declare.

We spar. There are no mistakes this time. I handle my sword perfectly, going through the routine with excellence. Training's over. Despite how good I am, Maximus laughs.

"What's so funny this time?" I question defensively.

"Out of all the things that boggled my mind on this show, I still don't understand how you got a date with Octavian."

"Excuse me? You don't think I was worthy?"

"From the rankings, there was no reason for him to pick you especially out of nowhere. How did you do it?"

I think back to that music box, still wondering who gave it to him.

"I don't know," I falter.

"Maybe it was Minerva, or a guardian angel."

I contact Minerva through the hologram about the gift, but she knows nothing about it. Who and why? Why did someone help me all of a sudden when I was at the bottom of the barrel? Then it crosses my mind. Of course. I should have known. I know who.

I knock on a suite's door. Sweat glistens my hands as I wait for it to be answered. I hope I'm not wrong. Athena opens the door. She mugs me.

"What do you want?" she questions.

"It was you. You gave Octavian that music box in my name."

She says nothing, keeping her uninterested gaze on me.

"I'm only here to say thank you."

"Save it Nova!" Athena snaps. "I didn't do it because I like you. I owed you that's why."

"For what happened in the club," I answer.

She goes to close the door, but I put my hand on it.

"I just want to know one thing. Who were they? Why did they attack you?"

She balls her fists, not hiding her frustration on her face. This is my cue to leave, but I don't. She's either going to tell or strike me. It's not because I care so much about her life, but what happened impacted me. It thrusted me to a new level. I at least need to know why.

"Let's just say where I use to work at things went sideways, and we had to escape. They were my friends, but when it came down to it, I left them to save myself," she explains.

Her gaze turns sullen as she stares at the ground. I think back to the Siege. Athena snaps out of her daze, giving me a scorn.

"I'll consider that story as my last gift to you. Next time we're this close, one of us is dying," she declares.

She slams the door right in my face. Tonight, Blaze announces the matches for the 3rd round. I see my bracket. Next to my name is Elpis. I throw my glass of water at the floor.

"Oh come on!" I groan.

I wish my opponent is someone who makes me mad, or doesn't speak to me. It would be easier to kill them then. Lyssa was in the moment, and Ira was a maniac, but Elpis, there's nothing to hate about her. I actually feel sorry for the punch. I don't know if I can kill her.

CHAPTER 26

In the locker room, I gaze at my reflection, wearing the shining black and blue armor. It's thick, fortified with strong fibers, and flexible enough to allow me to move freely. I feel weightless in it. Stars paint the back of the armor. This is Venus' design. She went for a space look, symbolizing a supernova. I was reborn, brought back from death and ridicule she told me. I have to give it to her, she knows how to make me look stunning.

"Your opponent gives you no reason for you to hate her. That might make it hard to kill her, but I have a reason," Maximus says. He gets in the side of my face "She's in your way of victory. She means to kill you. She doesn't want you to see your friends and family again. Do you want her to kill you?"

"No," I utter.

"What did you say?"

With a glare, I swing my head to him.

"No!" I scream.

"Good because the battle doesn't care about feelings, only who's left standing," he declares.

He's right. It's time to stop caring about these people. The world doesn't care about our circumstances, so why should I? It's either me or them.

As I march to the ring, the audience cheers. They say my name, throw flowers at me, and some even declare they love me. The love is great, but I treat the cheers like boos, with no attention as I set my focus on the ring.

When everyone clears the ring, Elpis and I meet face to face with focus. The show dubbed this fight The Golden Girl vs the Rising Star. It's all for show. In the end it doesn't matter what they call us. Only one name matters – winner.

"I didn't mean to punch you, but I do mean to do this," I declare.

"May the best Valkyrie win," Elpis says.

My sword touches her bladed disks.

"Let's go!" the robot yells.

At the sound of the bell, I charge. She throws one of her disks at me. I deflect it. Our swords collide.

"Behind you!" Maximus yells.

I can hear her other disk moving in fast from behind. I jump out the way. She catches her disk. She aims for my throat, one disk after the other.

I dodge the blades, backing up. Rushing in, I take the offensive. The speed of my attacks forces her to go on defense. She blocks, crossing the disks to make a shield. Sparks come out as our blades grind against each other.

I thrust my shoulder into her chest. She stumbles. I aim for her chest. She blocks with one disk, bringing the other one into my gut. Her blade cuts against my armor, but doesn't penetrate it. She presses to no avail. My armor shoots out a concussion wave, sending her back. The crowd awes in surprise at the work of my armor.

She looks at me from head to toe, trying to make sense of what happened. Closing her eyes, she takes a deep breath. She throws both of her blades sideways. They fly pass me. I rush in.

She stands still, anticipating as the hum of her blades get close. Sweat covers her face as I get closer. The blades are right behind me.

"Drop! Drop!" Maximus screams.

I drop to the ground. The disks fly by me, going towards Elpis. She gasps as her disks come back to her, severing her head. Her blood splashes in the air as the crowd goes silent. Her head drops to the floor with her surprised expression.

The crowd roars. Standing over Elpis' body, I feel no remorse. She is dead, and I don't care.

"Your winner, Nova!" Blaze yells.

Fox approaches me.

"Nova, congratulations on your win. You won in an amazing fashion with agility, cunning, strength, and speed. How do you think you were able to do it?"

"I just have a good trainer who shows me a lot of different tactics for the fights," I answer.

"Our minds are still on what happened with you and Octavian a couple nights ago. Can you tell us more about the history between your family and his?"

The crowd quiets as I think. Now that the fight is over, I can afford to let loose and have fun.

"I'll make sure Octavian is a good boy and behaves after I win this show. Right now I'm set on my next opponent," I gloat.

The crowd erupts with cheers, chanting my name so loud, it shakes the arena. Maximus nods at me. Back in the locker room,

I place ice on my stomach. Elpis' disks left a big bruise. My stomach cramps.

"They said this armor was supposed to protect me," I complain.

"It did more than just protect you, it saved your life. Had you been wearing your old one, Elpis would be playing jump rope with your intestines," Maximus says.

I gaze into the mirror, seeing the fire in my eyes. I'm poised and ready for the battles ahead.

CHAPTER 27

The nightmares stop. No Lyssa, no dead Valkyries, nothing. I sleep peacefully like a baby at night. The only interruption comes one night when I hear a loud knock. It comes from the balcony window. I don't believe it. Octavian is here with a hover car floating behind him. I storm over.

"What are you doing here?" I gasp.

He lowers his head, gulping.

"I have to talk to you," he mumbles.

If this is for the cameras, I won't give him the satisfaction of having the audience see his act. It's best to let him in where the cameras won't film. I step aside, letting him in.

"You have nothing to say to me," I scoff.

"I'm not here to give you words, but a gift."

He reaches into his pocket.

"If this is your way of apologizing, you can take it and shove-."

I am cut off as he tosses a necklace to me. I catch it. It's my necklace. I'm speechless. Dumbfounded with many thoughts racing in my mind, I trip over my words.

"How did you-?"

"When you told me your necklace was stolen about a month ago in downtown SF, I had my father's people look into it. There are cameras everywhere. After so many traces, leading from one thing to another, the thief was found."

"What happened to them?"

"Let's just say they were taken care of along with their family," he declares.

I don't even want to imagine how the crook met their fate. It's worse that their family got involved, but I don't have the opportunity to shed tears for them. Different emotions overwhelm me: joy, relief, and even sorrow. I shut my eyes, preventing tears from falling out. I can't let him see me cry. I want to thank him, but not after all I said and felt about him. It'll make me look foolish, if I go back.

"This means a lot," I snivel.

I stop myself short of saying thank you, but he knows how I feel as he smiles. The windows bust open, sending glass everywhere. Individuals dressed in black tactical gear and helmets jump in.

"One of yours?" I ask.

"No," Octavian gasps.

They fill the room, marching to us. Octavian punches one, but the others shock him with cattle prongs. He hits the ground, knocked out. I punch one. The others throw me to the ground. One puts their knee on my back, pinning me.

"Help!" I scream.

A sharp pin hits my neck.

"We got it," one says.

A tiny metal ball hits the floor covered in blood.

"They won't be finding her now."

Voltages surge through my body. I shake into darkness.

CHAPTER 28

I hear meat being brutalized, beaten to a pulp like someone's hitting a punching bag. A mix of whimpers and grunts surround me. Slowly blinking, glimpses of light peek into my eyes. My first reaction is to get up, but the ropes keep me bound to the chair. My hands are tied behind my back. I open my eyes completely.

I'm in an abandoned warehouse. I try to pick up sounds from the outside, but I hear nothing. The beating continues. Tied to a chair, Octavian soaks in his own blood as a man pulverizes him. Bruises cover Octavian's face. His eyes are swollen. The blood from his mouth pours all over his shirt. The man's associate stands in the corner, enthralled by the beating. I get a good look at the two. Dirty white shirts and ripped pants. They both have rough hands and rugged faces.

Not the kind that are left to roam the streets of Delos. They look like they've been through a lot of mess. The one doing the beating has a scar on his cheek. The other one has a tattoo of a skull on his neck.

"We can do this all day pretty boy," Scar grunts.

"Leave him alone," I mumble.

My jaw muscles are stiff from the cattle prong, rendering my speech useless. Scar keeps beating Octavian. His fists smash into Octavian's nose. Blood gushes out. Moving my mouth around, I start to gain more control of my muscles.

"Leave him alone!" I yell.

The pair laughs.

"Glad you could join us." Scar yanks Octavian's hair. "If you don't want your boyfriend to get his face smashed in any more, you better make him talk."

"You won't get away with this. They'll find us," I threaten.

Scar smirks, unmoved by the threat.

"I don't think so. You remember that pain you felt in your neck. We removed the tracker," Scar declares.

"What?" I gasp.

I'm actually disappointed that a bomb is no longer in my head. The mayhem on the show is mercy compared to being killed by these goons.

"I told you already. I don't have higher access to Hyperion Industries," Octavian groans in pain.

"Then give us his money! I want it all!" Scar barks.

Scar beats Octavian to a pulp. When the pounding ends, Octavian leans over, wheezing as his blood creates a puddle.

How these people got a hold of us in the first place I don't know. The tracker should've alerted the show I was in trouble. Now, they have no idea where we're at.

I remember I still have the bracelet that boy gave me. I wear it to bed each night. With its sharp edges, there's a chance it can cut through the rope. I move my hands against the rope, making sure not to go too fast to draw attention, and not too slow to be of no use.

"We'll do this the old fashion way. Call your old man," Scar orders, taking out a phone.

"He doesn't give out his personal cell phone. There are so many people I have to go through just to speak to him," Octavian wheezes.

"Aren't you the perfect family," Scar taunts.

Scar grabs a blowtorch from a bench.

"You better start talking, or it's going to get real hot in here on some Salem hype!" Scar barks.

"They were hanged," Octavian mutters.

"What?"

"Women were hanged at Salem, not burned, idiot," Octavian scorns.

"Rich boy got some brains on him," Scar chuckles to Skull.

They laugh. Octavian spits blood in Scar's face. Slapping the blood off, Scar grows enraged. I worry for Octavian's life, causing me to fasten my speed on the rope. The rope loosens as I keep rubbing my hands. That's good, keep going.

"You know what? You have tough skin. I wonder if she's as tough as you," Scar says, turning to me with a wicked smile.

"No leave her alone!" Octavian yells.

I gasp as I rub faster, not caring about the subtleness of my plan. Octavian struggles against his restraints, trying to get out.

"I'm going to kill you!" Octavian screams.

Fire comes out inches near my face as Scar toys with the blowtorch. I can feel the heat as I turn my face away. My hands are almost free.

"It's time for a makeover," Scar chuckles.

"No, please! I don't have anything," Octavian begs.

My hands slip free. I smack the blowtorch back at Scar. The flame burns his face. He howls, falling to the ground. Skull reaches into his pants. I grab the blowtorch. As Skull aims his gun, I press the handle, igniting a huge ball of fire. The fire torches Skull completely. He's on fire, screaming and running through the warehouse. He drops as the fire blackens his corpse.

Scar charges at me. I press the handle, but the fire doesn't come out. It's empty. He tackles me to the ground. He chokes the air out of me.

"I got you!" he howls.

The side of his face is burnt. His skin peels, revealing his blistered flesh. I jam my thumb into his wounds. He screams, letting go of my neck. Getting to my knees, I pick up the torch. I smack him with the torch, breaking his jaw. Toppling him, I pound his face in with the torch. With each hit of the metal, his face caves in.

I picture he's Blaze. It feel so good beating a man to death without consequences, to finally let out all my anger. Nothing resembling Scar remains. His face is disfigured. A chunk of his tongue lays on the ground that he bit off during the beating. Blood soaks the torch. Octavian's groans snap me out of my trance.

"Let me out please," he whimpers.

It's easy for me to beat him to death with the torch and blame it on the goons. I think about all the misery his family caused, not just for me, but for so many others. I clutch the torch harder. He deserves to get beat. The torch drops from my hands. I untie Octavian. Enough with the killing today.

"Nova this is my fault."

"Save it. We need help."

"They took my phone from me."

Scar's phone is broken. Skull is charcoal. There's no point in checking. We go outside. Abandon refineries surround us. The skyscrapers of Delos are far off in the distance.

"Where are we?"

"Southside Delos. Far from home," Octavian says.

We go into an area filled with apartment complexes. They are old and rundown. As we walk through the street, a large group forms in front of us, blocking our path forward. They wear the same red jackets and white face paint.

"I got this, just stay behind me," Octavian gulps.

He takes the lead, meeting the leader in the middle.

"Look what we got here! Some outsiders!" the leader announces. "Blood Boys own this place, so if you want to go through here, you're going to have to pay a traveling tax."

"We don't have anything, we're just trying to get by," Octavian says.

The gang laughs. Scrutinizing Octavian, the leader stops laughing.

"I've seen you before," the leader asserts, glancing at the two of us. "Oh my god, you're Octavian Hyperion and Nova from Last Valkyrie! We got ourselves some celebrities!"

They cheer, slapping hands. Good now they're going to let us go.

"On a second thought, you two are going to have an extended stay here," the leader declares.

"I told you," Octavian begins. "We don't-."

"Shut up!" the leader barks.

The leader punches Octavian in the mouth. The gang laughs. Taking out a gun, the leader aims it at us. Octavian takes a deep breath.

"Listen here boy, I want everything you got!"

Octavian gazes at the leader with calmness, undisturbed by the gun. Growing mad, the leader takes the safety off.

"Are you deaf? Let's see if you can hear yourself screaming," the leader taunts.

With lightning speed, Octavian swats the gun out of the leader's hand. Grabbing hold of the man's arm, Octavian snaps it. The leader screams as the gang awes in surprise and backs up. Octavian elbows the man's nose, flattening it. Blood floods out.

Octavian chops the leader's throat, crushing his windpipe. The leader drops to his knees, wheezing. Octavian knees him in the face. As the leader lays unconscious on the ground, Octavian pummels him with punches.

The gang does nothing, frozen in fear. The leader's breathing stops. Octavian stands up, blood dripping from his hands.

"Anyone else?" Octavian asks.

The gang runs off. I hesitate to speak, stepping back as Octavian stares at the corpse. This man in front of me is a stranger. He's not the charismatic Octavian the world knows. He killed on instinct like someone flipped a switch. He turns to me, breathing heavily from the whooping. His eyes are low as if he's

284

possessed. I'm afraid. He closes his eyes. When he opens them, his breathing is back to normal as he's calm. He takes a phone from the leader's pocket.

"I'm going to call for help. We should find a place to stay first," he says.

The trance is over, and Octavian is his normal self. There's a lone apartment in the corner, more devastated than the others. The windows are broken, and the door's missing.

We tiptoe inside, checking our surroundings. It's void of any furniture or sign of life. Holes are in the walls and floor. The wooden floor creaks with our steps. A foul stench hits my nose smelling like waste.

"I don't think anyone lives here," Octavian assumes.

He gets on the phone and goes to another room. After a few minutes, he comes back.

"The network's police were looking for us. They're on their way."

For Octavian this is a blessing, but for me, it's nothing to get too excited for. I'm saved from this prison only to go back to another. Octavian looks in a broken mirror nearby.

"Wow they really messed me up," he enthuses.

He laughs at his reflection as if it's the funniest thing he has ever seen. I doubt he ever got punched before.

"Is this funny to you?" I ask.

"It's been a day!" he laughs.

"Oh I bet getting tortured and almost killed is so thrilling for you," I snort.

"Nova, would you relax? We escaped death, and now we get to go home."

As soon as he says that, he realizes his mistake.

"I'm sorry, that's not what-."

"Home?" I question. "You call that island a home? That may be your playground, but that's our prison!"

"I'm sorry," he apologizes.

He reaches out, but I swat his hand away.

"No! You don't know how it feels. You've been privileged your entire life. You seek adventure to give you some kind of street cred, but you'll never know how it feels to be us."

"Why because I was born with a silver spoon in my mouth?" he asks defensively.

"Being born rich isn't your crime. Your indulgence in our misery is. You sit from the comfort of a chair and watch us kill each other. This is all a game to you, but for us, it's life or death. What do you know about pain?"

"I had my fair share of it," he mutters.

I laugh.

"The only pain you go through is deciding which Valkyrie you want to marry. I couldn't even see my mom before she died because your people locked me up!"

He frowns, lowering his gaze. I march up to him, getting in his face.

"You smile for the cameras, saying you love this show. What kind of man gets off watching women kill each other? You're just like Blaze. At least he doesn't pretend to be a decent person. You don't even know who you are, but I'll tell you. You're a cold heartless monster!"

He looks up at me, revealing the strain on his battered eyes. He takes off the ring on his hand.

"This was a gift from my bride," he says, smiling dimly for a brief moment. "All I wanted was my own life. But my father wanted me to be the Chosen One in order to better public perception of our family. When I wouldn't, he had her thrown on the show. I watched an axe split her head open."

He pulls out several more similar rings.

"For seven years, I watched someone I love get thrown on the show to die. My father said it was a punishment for my disloyalty. He promised the only person I would fall for would be a Valkyrie. So tell me Nova, what would you have done for the ones you love?" he weeps.

I step back as my scowl leaves, and my anger fades. I wish I could take back all the things I said and thought about him. It twists my stomach, knowing how much I hate him.

He doesn't earn my sympathy easily as I still blame him, but it's hard for me to stay angry. A gust of wind blows the leaves outside. Numerous XVN police cars descend down. The cops come in by the dozens.

"Octavian and Nova. Stand still," one says.

As they scan us, one has their hand hovering over their gun.

"It's them," one announces.

He moves his hand away from his gun. As we walk towards the door, a cop gets in front of me.

"Ms. Nova, stand still please."

He takes out a medical gun and puts it to the back of my neck. I feel a pin in my neck again. The tablet in his hand beeps as a red dot appears.

"It's live."

They escort us to different cars. I want to say something to Octavian, at least apologize, but it's too late. We are too far from each other now. They lead me to a white hover car without their logos. Maximus surprises me, waiting inside.

"Why are you here?" I stammer.

"You're my Valkyrie. When they showed the footage of your kidnapping on the balcony, I wasn't going to sleep until you were found," he says. "But there's something else, and I wanted you to hear it from me first. XVN found the conspirators. It's Hades Hammer."

"They're in Delos?" I gasp.

"No. The show claims they found a holdout in the huts I took you to."

This isn't good for the people on that island. Any connection to Hades Hammer calls for a full armed presence. An occupation is bound to happen there.

"They're going to tear that island apart looking for them," I gulp.

"No, Nova, they won't have to," Maximus cautions. "They're going to bomb it to dust."

CHAPTER 29

I clutch my seat, preventing myself from falling down in absolute terror from what I heard.

"They want to make it explosive for the cameras," Maximus says.

"But there are innocent people down there."

"The world doesn't see innocent when it comes to Hades Hammer."

"Hades Hammer? The people who kidnaped me were in tactical gear. They had a device that took out my detonator. The show struggled to find us, but found the culprits and a cell just like that? This seems all too convenient for ratings, don't you think?"

He looks up as he rubs his chin, contemplating the possibility.

"Please tell me you don't believe this," I beg.

"It makes no difference. What's done is done," he declares.

I get up to argue when a loud roar rips through the air. Above us, dozens of hover crafts soar, armed with rockets.

"No!" I scream.

I grab the steering wheel. It's locked.

"We have to do something," I plead.

"It's in autopilot! Sit down before you get us killed!"

I ignore him, hitting all the buttons. There's no logic in my brain, just the need to do something. The thought of those people being burned alive fills my head. The old man, the little boy who gave me the bracelet, all those people are going to die. It's not fair.

"We have to do something!" I yell.

I feel a strike at the back of my neck. I release the steering wheel. I wobble with dizziness and collapse on the floor.

**

I wake up on a surface smoother than the hover car's floor. I get up from the couch. Wooden walls surround me. A breeze of air gushes in, bringing my attention to the doorway it comes through. Maximus stands in the doorway, looking outside.

Staggering to my feet, I look around. The plain cabin lacks any décor as it just has a bed. I falter towards him, still regaining my balance. Out the door, a dark cloud of smoke fills the air.

"They've torched the entire island. Turned it all to dust," Maximus gasps.

This is the first time I've seen him breathless in utter shock.

"We should have went there," I say.

"It doesn't matter anymore."

I slam my fist into the wall.

"It always matters! I could have saved some people!" I bark.

"And then you'd be dead like the rest of them! You'd be doing your opponents a favor!" he shouts in my face.

"Isn't that what you want? You left me in the woods and gave me no slack. What difference does it make to you if I live or die? Do you get money if I win? Is that what this is about? Don't worry, you'll be back next year, berating another Valkyrie, so why do you care?"

He backs up and relaxes. I wait for a response, but he stares at me with a calm gaze. My anger subsides, turning into confusion at the sudden pause.

"If I win, I get the same thing they promised you - freedom," he says.

Sighing, he walks to the wall where a picture of a woman and a child is at. He gazes at it.

"I wasn't always doing this. I had a family, but they were taken from me, so I sought vengeance. After I got my revenge on my enemies, I didn't stop. I slaughtered their families, friends, even their children," he grieves. Cutting himself off, he takes a deep breath, hesitant to speak. "I didn't recognize who I was, and prison was the only place for me. That was when XVN came to me with an opportunity."

He tells me the truth. All the trainers are prisoners serving hard time with life or death row. Serial killers, terrorists, traffickers; the worst of the worst. If their Valkyrie wins, they go free with ten million dollars, no strings attached, no bombs, nothing. If they lose, the trainers go back to prison, waiting for the next year's Valkyries. Many trainers don't return because they get killed by angry prisoners who didn't get the opportunity.

"You were going to give up on me and go back to prison?" I ask.

"I've done this for over 20 years. What's one more year," he reveals.

CHAPTER 30

Tonight is the Felix Neptune show, featuring the last four Valkyries: Me, Hera, Bellona, and Athena. Waiting behind the curtain with the others, I stand tall and poised. I've been on this stage several times, each time my confidence grows. I have this in the bag.

The curtains open, bringing forth the clapping crowd. Felix hugs us. The show starts off with the usual pleasantries to warm everyone up. Felix compliments us on our looks and performances, and throws out a few jokes about dead Valkyries to get the audience to laugh. He begins with individual questions. He talks about Bellona's way of finishing opponents quickly.

"What are your secrets?" Felix asks.

"Milk," Bellona answers with no emotion.

"That must've been a strong cow," Felix jokes.

The crowd laughs. He asks Hera about losing her hand in the ring and having it replaced with a robotic one.

"Now I can be an official citizen of Delos. I hope they let me in the country clubs," Hera teases.

For Athena, he asks her about the night at the bar.

"You were spotted at Club Blood Moon. That same night multiple bodies were found in the bathroom. All of the victims lived in the Bronx. Is this a coincidence?"

Athena raises her eyes to the ceiling, exaggerating her thinking. This gains chuckles from the audience and Felix.

"Um," Athena says innocently. "They must've been some fans of mine and wanted to reenact the show."

After the audience settles down, Felix turns to me.

"Nova, I want to talk about what's on everyone's mind. The kidnapping."

My chest tightens. I wish he started with a joke, but the kidnapping was aired. Everyone wants to know.

"What can I say? I've been getting use to death lately," I suggest.

The audience chuckles.

"But this wasn't some match. We're talking about Hades Hammer. How does it feel to have almost been killed by those savages?"

"Savages?" I question, wiping my smile off my face. "You call the people on those islands savages?"

"Before a couple days ago, the world didn't even know there were people living so far out there. We don't know what kind of people they were. They could have been hiding nukes, for all we know," Felix explains.

His tone is no longer a joking one. The light hearted energy in the room is gone.

"Why does everyone believe whatever story they're told by XVN?" I ask.

"What do you mean?"

The Valkyries' faces turn pale. They turn their disturbed gazes to me as if to warn me. Hesitant to speak, I turn to my managers behind the curtains. They shake their heads in panic.

"Who knows? Maybe they had nukes and were a lot dangerous than we thought? Why call them savages? I say they're monsters," I assert.

Felix nods as people clap.

"It's amazing you survived. I take it the third date with Octavian is cancelled now?"

I force myself to laugh even though it's fake, but it's authentic enough to fool everyone.

"I want to play a game," Felix announces. "It's called who looks like a terrorist." Pictures appear on the screen behind us, showing the people from the villages. "We were able to get these photos taken from XVN fighter planes before the bombings. So let's play shall we?"

The audience claps and cheers. I tremble at the screen. The pictures show the hut people before the bombings. They were hanging clothes, playing soccer, gathering plants, and going about their normal lives with no idea of the atrocity looming over them.

The audience plays the game, picking which one looks like a terrorist as Felix eggs them on. The next minutes are painful to endure. Watching this, sickens me to the point I feel like I will throw up. None of the Valkyries laugh. The boy who gave me the necklace appears, playing soccer.

"He looks like a little terrorist junior in the making!" Felix taunts to the crowd's delight.

"Enough!" I yell, standing up. The crowd falls silent, looking at me in astonishment. "You laugh at the murder of children yet you call them savages. Why? Because they look different than you, come from a different culture, so it's easy to believe they're terrorists? We call them terrorists, and they call us oppressors. The only savages are the people in this city!"

Mouths are hanging in shock. They never heard this before. It shatters their false world. Cybernetics are in the seats. With all their implants they might as well be robots. No emotion, just shells pretending to be people. I storm off stage, ignoring my managers.

Mascara runs down my cheek because of my tears. The person in the mirror is unrecognizable. What have I become? I play by their rules, smile for the cameras, make everyone laugh, and still they treat me like an object. How can they be shocked at what I said?

They expect us to smile after all the abuse we go through publicly and behind closed doors. I punch the mirror, shattering it. Blood drips down from the cut in my palm. Bellona stands behind me.

"What?" I growl.

"It was a good speech," she says.

My eyes stay on the shattered mirror as she leaves.

Rain splashes the window as I look out from the hover car. My managers are quiet, facing away from me. I don't have to see their faces to know their disappointment.

"This won't be like the date with Octavian. It's one thing to go after the Hyperions, but you berated the entire show. That's going to make Blaze angry," Flavius cautions.

"I don't care about patrons anymore. What difference does it make now that I have my weapon and armor?" I groan.

"What you did was close to breaking the golden rule. Blaze won't forget."

"I'm ready for whatever they have for me."

We arrive to my mansion.

"I hope so," Flavius sighs.

I get to my suite. Blaze appears on the television screen with a special announcement.

"I know the 4th round starts next week, but I decided to do something different. With how fire Nova was tonight, it's best to give the people what they want now. Nova will fight tomorrow at 9am. Her opponent is Bellona," Blaze announces. He grins, waving at the screen. "Sleep tight everyone, you don't want to miss it."

My fight is in less than 12 hours from now. This is payback for what I did. Fighting a dominating Valkyrie like Bellona on a short hand notice, without training is Blaze's idea. Flavius was right, but this is no punishment for me. Fighting Bellona is a challenge I welcome.

CHAPTER 31

In the dressing room, I am fully dressed in my armor, wearing a new helmet with a visor. The helmet is a gift from one of my patrons.

"She's all strength. No technique or defense. Use her power against her," Maximus asserts.

Bellona comes out to a mix of cheers and boos. Ignoring them, she stares at the ring. She doesn't play the crowd game or seek patrons. All she does is destroy her opponents. Some like her simple style, others don't.

It appears that Bellona was given a gift as well. Instead of her shield, she wields a long mace with spikes. It's her morning star. I anticipated a fight between my sword and her powerful shield, a true battle of attacks. With her morning star, this will be a war.

"Look directly at her when she gets in," Maximus tells me.

Our eyes are set dead on each other. Our noses are only inches apart.

"Your story ends today," Bellona states.

She shoves her mace against my sword, pushing it back.

"She's limited," Maximus says, leaving the ring.

I nod, bouncing up and down, ignoring the crowd chanting my name.

"Let's go!" the robot yells.

Yelling, we charge at each other. Our weapons collide, sending a thunderous boom throughout the arena. A shock surges through my hands from the collision as I grip harder. We stand our ground.

She swings wildly, trying to take my head off. I back up, dodging the mace. The air gushes in my face from her haymakers. She screams ferociously with each swing. She steps on my foot, stopping my retreat.

I head-butt her, smashing my helmet into her skull. She stands still, only more enraged. I gasp, in disbelief at her durability. She slams her mace into my chest. My armor sends out a giant concussion wave, launching us back in the air.

Hitting the ground, my chest stings with soreness. My air isn't fully back in my lungs as I hobble to a knee. Bellona charges at me. There isn't enough time to get to both feet as she swings at me.

I duck and strike her leg. My blade slides off her armor, without doing any damage. Her mace slams against my helmet, sending me flying across the ring. Using the momentum, I roll to my feet. My head raves in pain as my helmet is cracked. It's useless now. I toss my helmet off.

As our weapons clash, my headache grows. She pushes me backwards, forcing me to give up more ground. She's overpowering me.

I hit the button on my sword. It heats up and glows. The more Bellona slams her mace against my sword, the more her mace deteriorates from the heat. Bellona is too distracted to see her mace weakening as it presses against my sword. She swings at me again. I put my sword up. Her mace breaks on impact. She gasps and swings at me. I sever her hand. Her blood pours out her stump as she howls.

She head-butts me in the face. I feel my nose break. Bellona runs to the other side of the ring, holding her bloody stump.

"Oh no!" she cries.

It's hard to breathe out my nose as I wheeze. Blood floods out my nose into my mouth, tasting like iron. My headache increases as I see two of her. I shake my head, letting me see just one Bellona who stands there like a wounded animal.

I creep towards her. Desperation shows on her face. She knows she's helpless, but I won't rush in and make a mistake this close to victory.

A shield drops down from the ceiling and falls at Bellona's feet. They must really want her to win, or me to lose. The crowd boos.

"You can't do that!" Maximus barks.

Bellona places her shield on her stump. A streak of fire shoots out of her shield at me. I jump back, putting my sword up. Deflecting the fire, I charge at Bellona. The fire runs out. She runs away from me.

As I chase her around the ring, she wheezes. I slice her across the back. My blade slides off again, but dents her armor. I keep slicing all across her armor. Each strike sends her forward, slowing her down. Her armor wears out as it cracks, revealing her bruised back.

I raise my sword over my head and bring it down on her back. Her armor breaks. My sword slices her skin. She hits the ground and raises her shield faintly. I kick the shield away. The audience stands on their feet, chanting my name. Bellona spits on the ground.

"Do it!" she snarls with anticipation.

I bring my sword down on her head, splitting it down the middle. The two pieces of her head slide from each other, spilling her brains out on the mat.

The crowd erupts in cheers. I hobble as standing up exhausts me. Lights flash, irritating my eyes. The strain to my eyes is unlike any pain before. Barely able to see, I rapidly blink my watery eyes. Blood pours down my head. Maximus touches my shoulder, holding me up.

"I got you," he says.

Fox runs up, shoving his mic in my face.

"Nova, that was amazing. How do-."

"Give her a break! She just went through a war!" Maximus snaps.

"Thank you," I stutter.

"Rrrrrrrr uuuuuuuuu," Maximus says.

"What?"

All the sounds are muffled to my ears as I can't hear what he's saying. The only thing I hear is the ringing in my ears.

Stumbling, I reach out to him. It feels heavy just to move a muscle. The weight of this force sends me down. Crashing to the floor, I splash in the pool of blood. Finally some rest.

CHAPTER 32

I'm underwater. Murmurs surround me. Blinking, my vision becomes clear. I see people in white lab coats. A wall of glass separates us as I float in water. The need for sleep reigns over me, forcing me to close my eyes. I want to sleep forever

I wake up again with the sun light shining in my face. My head rests on a soft pillow. I'm in a hospital bed. I groan from morning tiredness, yet my body feels fine. I don't feel the pain or headache. My breathing is normal. I touch my nose. They've fixed it.

"How do you feel?" Maximus asks in the corner.

"Better than I was in the ring. What happened?"

"You had a concussion, fractured skull, and internal bleeding in the brain. You were in a coma for three days."

"Only three days?" I gasp.

My quick recovery boosts my confidence, making me feel a little bit invincible.

"One of your patrons gave you a healing tank to speed up the process. If you didn't wake up, it would have been considered a forfeit, and-."

He doesn't continue. The hesitation tells me a forfeit results in death. Athena and Hera are fighting live on tv. Both are bloodied and battered without weapons. Hera grips Athena by the throat with her metal hand, dangling her in the air. Just as Athena's about to pass out, she thrusts her thumbs into Hera's eyes. The force pushes Hera out of the ring. She falls with Athena.

I jump off the bed, eyes glued to the action. Falling, Athena grabs onto the edge of the ring. Only holding on with her hand, she dangles in the air as Hera holds onto her feet. Athena tries to crawl back into the ring, but Hera weighs her down. Athena grabs her double blade nearby. The camera zooms in on Hera's frightened face.

"No, I don't want to die! It's not my fault!" Hera pleads.

"Shut up!" Athena barks.

Without hesitation, Athena slices Hera's arm off, sending her falling to the floor screaming. Hera's screams end when the spikes impale her. The crowd screams Athena's name as she raises her arms, embracing her victory.

Watching Hera's death is gut wrenching. Athena could have gone for her head, but instead she chose to make it painful. She is sending a message not to the world, but to me. She wants me to see what she's capable of as a warning for what is to come. Blaze and Irma comes in.

"Maximus, Nova," Blaze greets.

"What was that out there?! Outside interference is against the rules!" Maximus yells.

Blaze bows his head.

"I want to apologize. That was wrong of me. I was upset about the night show and wanted Nova to pay," Blaze gulps.

He hands me a gold pen.

"Please accept this gift as my apology. America was bought with this pen in the Great Purchase. I used it to sign checks, but it's yours now."

Not grabbing the pen, I scowl at him. After everything he's done, he can take his apology and shove it. I want to stab him with the pen so bad. Maximus nods at me. He knows how I feel. I smile at Blaze.

"Of course," I welcome.

I take the pen. Blaze is unpredictable. Making him angrier would be harmful to my survival. The sullen look on his face lights up with a grin.

"That was good for the cameras!" he cheers.

He skips off. He laughs so loud, I hear him in the hallways.

"I want to kill him," I scorn.

"Forget him. You have one true enemy – Athena."

CHAPTER 33

Tonight is our last appearance on the Felix Neptune Show before our fight.

"Do not go off script this time," Venus grunts.

My managers spent hours covering up for me, doing interviews and press releases to apologize for my previous behavior. Flavius was kind, claiming the stresses of being a Valkyrie had gotten to me, and I managed to cope with them.

Venus played the child angle, saying a kid from the villages had looked like a kid from Shed Court. It had been in the heat of the moment she claimed. Everyone ate it up, sympathizing with me.

I don't understand why my image matters this late in the show, but my managers say it always matters. With the final match, everyone is on edge, and I don't want to give anyone a reason to hate me. Considering the tricks in my fight with Bellona, it's best not to throw any additional roadblocks in my way.

"Go out there like you own the crowd," Flavius says.

The door opens. I walk from one side of the stage as Athena comes out the other. We both wear red tunics, draped in gold togas. The set up for the stage was changed, dropping the big curtain entrance. Meeting each other in the middle, Blaze stands between us. We stare at each other for the face off.

"Okay that's good," Blaze says.

Athena and I shake hands and go to our seats where we shake Felix's hand. This night doesn't have the optimism of the first interviews, or the joking manner of last time. There are no hugs or couches.

Our dresses were swapped for tunics, and the entrances were changed to give a more serious aura. The audience shares this energy. There are no cheers, only clapping. People of Delos aren't the only ones in the crowd. There are people from all over the world.

My managers didn't spend time on makeup or getting my hair done. Wearing my afro, my look shows I mean business. Athena wears her hair in a bun. Her face is bare of makeup as well.

"Welcome ladies and gentleman, we have one of the best fights in Last Valkyrie history!" Felix announces. "So who has the first question?"

The questions are mostly about the fight and our preparation such as training, patrons, and dieting. I reveal that the island changed my eating habits. Eating meats and vegetables gave me abs. Despite the delicious sweets and fatty foods the mansion has to offer, I avoid them for clean nutrition.

Over indulgence in certain foods harms performance in the ring. I contribute part of my success to drinking water and avoiding wine with the exception of the first interviews. I don't tell them about the monolith, giving all the praise to my trainer and managers.

The questions shift to our personal lives, coming from people who work for podcasts and gossip magazines, the ones who feed off of celebrities' lives.

"I've been in contact with some friends and family," Athena says.

They ask for more details, but she doesn't give any. They ask me. Atlas comes to mind.

"Some friends," I reply.

We answer more questions. We keep laughter to a minimum even when Felix says a joke which is less frequent than previous times. There is no glamor to this. The straight forward questions allow us to be ourselves rather than play a character.

"I have a question for Nova," a man calls out.

They bring the mic to him. He isn't dressed up like everyone else, or even wearing a buttoned shirt. He has a wild beard and bags under his eyes like he hasn't slept in weeks. He probably spent all his money just to get here, dying to meet me.

"Why did you do that to my sister?" he asks.

"Who's your sister?" I respond, leaning over.

He stares at me with unflinching eyes.

"Bellona," he utters.

The audience gasps as I look over to my managers who are shocked. This kind of question requires a script to stick to in order to answer. Without one, I'm stuck, afraid of saying the wrong thing. He awaits my answer. I breathe deeply, focusing on him, seeing him as a man who lost a loved one.

"It wasn't personal," I say sincerely.

"Say that to her son who now has no parents because of you!" he rages. "This entire show is a joke! People give their lives for what? She had a life and decided to give it all away for this?!"

Security rushes to him. He knocks their hands away.

"You need to calm down!" a guard orders.

The man snatches a gun and aims it at me. The crowd screams, dropping to the floor for cover.

"You monster!" he cries.

Bullets fire, tearing his body up. The guards shoot him even as he's on the ground.

"Secure!" they yell.

My eyes remain frozen at the horrific scene as I don't move. They put handcuffs on his corpse. My managers run over to me.

"Nova, are you alright?" Flavius gasps.

I say nothing, seeing the bullet holes in the man's body. His corpse locks me in a daze.

"Nova," Venus says.

His dead eyes look at me with the same emotionless look he had before. I feel he is still alive, cursing me for ruining his life. I turned some kid into an orphan. This is my fault. Venus touches my cheek.

"It's not your fault dear, you hear me? Everyone has a family, remember that," she comforts.

She hugs me, burying my face into her chest. I want to cry, but I fear what that will do to my image. I hate myself even more for not having the guts to be myself even in a time like this. I still care about the superficial.

"Now the kid won't have an uncle either," Blaze snickers to Irma.

The guards clear the auditorium to clean up. As we wait backstage, Blaze and Felix talk.

"Continue the show? Blaze someone just died," Felix argues.

"Which makes it even better to continue. Think about all the viewers who will be tuning in tonight now!"

"Somethings are worth more than ratings."

Blaze smirks.

"You know, your contract is up for renewal. It's going to be very hard to continue your son's treatment without a job," Blaze taunts.

"You wouldn't," Felix quivers.

"You've been doing this for what, 20 years now? It's about time we have some new blood don't you think? I guess Flynn will just have to rely on some vitamins to keep him healthy."

"Blaze, I'm begging you don't."

Blaze's grin stretches.

"You have nothing to fear as long as you get up there and put on a show for the world."

"Of course," Felix gulps.

"Good boy," Blaze cheers, patting Felix on the cheek.

The show continues. My managers remind me to stick to the script like usual. We come out on stage with a live audience as if nothing ever happened, but it's so hard to pretend. The man's dead body is still fresh in my mind, but I have to smile for the cameras.

"Ladies and gentleman," Felix hesitates. "We have crew members at Bellona's house where her son Anton is at. We'll be on the air with him."

A little boy appears on the giant screen. He has fat cheeks and puppy eyes. The room awes at the boy, but it's not from the live crowd. The audience is dead silent, sharing distraught from the shooting. The reactions are added sound effects from the stage. They're meant to trick the world in believing we stand behind Blaze's sick antics.

"Hey Anton, how's it going?" Felix asks with extreme passion, the kind an adult has when speaking to a child.

"Good," Anton murmurs.

"Do you know who I am?"

"You're that man who talks a lot on tv."

The sound effects laugh.

"That's right," Felix chuckles, sounding so fake. He pauses, closing his eyes briefly. "I have some bad news to tell you. It's about your uncle," Felix hesitates. A camera lights up with the word Osric. "Osric has passed away."

Anton doesn't react as if he has no concept of death.

"Did you kill him?" Anton asks.

"No, of course-."

"I'm talking to her," Anton says. The projection on the screen points to me. "You killed my mom. Did you kill my uncle too?"

Everyone looks at me for answers. I trip over my tongue, faltering to speak. Not even my managers give me any signals on what to say. This is all for shock value. What am I supposed to say? I enjoyed killing his mom, and she died like a screaming coward? Blaze would love that. I look directly at him on the screen. This is no time for nonsense even for a child.

"Anton I know what it's like to lose your mom and feel like you're alone in the world. But you must be strong. Take your pain and make it mean something because the world doesn't care about our suffering. Can you do that?" I ask.

"I think so," he guesses.

"Good because-."

"And we're out of time folks!" Felix announces. "Anton we wish you and your family blessings to come. Take care!"

The fake claps pour out as Anton's feed ends. Nobody has the stomach to ask or answer any more questions after the distasteful act. For the remainder of the show, Felix entertains us with skits from crew members. The stage pumps out more fake noises to hide over the fact that nobody's laughing.

As this continues, members of the audience leave. Before it's over, there's nobody in the attendance, yet the fake reactions still come. The one thing me and Athena have in common is our silence, reflecting our hate for the antics.

**

I get home and dial Atlas through the hologram. Since he has to use a holo booth, and our phones can't make calls to people outside the show, I have to wait for him to be notified and then go to a booth to pick up. I know right? Our phones can't contact other people, but the holograms can.

I guess they know a lot of people can't afford holograms, so it limits our range of contact, while making it seem like we have freedom. Normally Atlas calls, making it easy for me to pick up since the hologram is in my room.

I need to hear his voice. I wait for over ten minutes. With each ring, I doubt he'll answer. I go to cut it off when his image digitizes in front of me.

"Nova is everything alright?"

"I can't do this without you Atlas. I need you here."

He blinks rapidly.

"What about getting hopes up?" he stammers.

"I don't care about what I said before. I was being stupid. No matter what happens tomorrow, I need someone in my corner." I look down, hesitating to speak the next words. "Someone I care about."

"Is this what you really want?

"I can have my managers book you a trip."

"I'll be there," he promises.

I have to hold back my tears. After all the pain I caused for our families, friends, and especially him, he still cares about me. Atlas is the kind of guy who can go through so much pain and suffering, and still have compassion for others. He will never leave your side no matter what.

"Thank you Atlas," I weep.

"No, thank you Nova."

Lying in bed, I gaze at the stars through the glass ceiling. This could be my last night alive, the last time I ever feel a pillow behind my head. Athena will be a tough opponent. From the footage, she has speed, strength, and technique. She's resilient and relentless.

No matter how much they threw at her, she came back. An all in one package, making her the toughest Valkyrie, not just out of my opponents, but out of the entire season. Could this be the end for me? Every match could've been my last.

Things are unpredictable, and anything can happen. It's a miracle I made it this far. There is no way I would have imagined this back when I was locked in that white room. A shooting star flies by. It reminds me of the ones Atlas and I would see at night when we were kids. Maybe I can watch more shooting stars with him.

The idea brings joy to me, and also lights a fire to my heart. This can't be my last night. I have too many people to live for: Atlas, Luna, Ms. Blackford, and all of those people at Shed Court. Tomorrow will not be my end, it'll be my reckoning.

CHAPTER 34

Last Valkyrie chants blow up the stadium, shaking the locker room's ceiling. It's a ritual for the crowd to chant before the finals, but it's never this loud. The unexpected first round, my rants, the kidnapping, and the shooting give fans mania like no other season.

The final ceremony features a performance from world renowned singer Vanya Locke. It comes to an end, thus making my entrance near.

"No matter what happens out there, I'm going to miss you dear," Venus weeps.

Her tears touch my neck as we hug.

"We did everything in our power to help you. We couldn't help you in the ring, but I hope we made a difference," Flavius says.

"You did," I reassure, giving him a hug.

"We'll see you after the bell," Flavius assures.

I always wonder where they came from, and how they ended up on the show. Sometimes I questioned their morals for being on the show as they know the evil behind the scenes.

Despite my assumptions, everything they do is for my benefit. Even Venus' obnoxious comments, and Flavius' monotone at times, it's all for me. This is enough for me to consider them as friends.

"I want to thank you. For taking me this far. No matter what happens, I'll always be thankful for what you've done for me," Maximus reveals.

His words stun me.

"Maximus, this was all you. If it wasn't for you, I wouldn't be here," I confess, wanting him to know the importance of his actions.

He smiles with surprise as if it brings him great joy to know he's important to me. Putting his hand to his mouth, he belches as his eyes water. He takes a deep breath, holding back the tears.

"It has been an honor to be by your side, watching you come this far. Your parents would have been very proud of you," he gushes.

I hug him very hard and long. Burying my face into his chest, I hear his heart beat. I let a few tears out. I feel he's doing the same. A security guard comes in.

"Ms. Nova, you have a visitor."

"Atlas! I'm so-."

I stop speaking, seeing the one who comes in. The tremendous surprise it causes me, makes my stomach drop. At the door with a face bare of makeup, showing how beautiful she is without it, stands Luna.

Silence surrounds us. My gaze is on her as she hesitates to move forward. She takes one step. We run to each other. Embracing with a hug, we hold each other tightly. I bawl, not caring how loud it is. I let it all out as she does the same. It feels like ages since I have seen her beautiful face.

"Luna," I stammer, trying to get more words out.

"Nova, I don't want to hear it. I will never forgive you for what you've done, but you are my sister, and I will never stop loving you," she whimpers.

"I'm sorry."

"I don't want your apology, I want your promise. You promise you'll come back to me. Promise it."

"I will," I snivel, nodding my head.

She stops at the door.

"I'll see you on the other side," she weeps with a smile.

"Always."

I wipe my tears. Shadow fighting with my sword, I focus on the fight ahead. Love, family, and friends aren't occupying my mind anymore. All I think about is killing Athena and becoming the Last Valkyrie.

CHAPTER 35

Before stepping on the disk, I look to the crowd. Luna is near the front row. She looks with anxiety and caution. Coming from Shed Court, this kind of atmosphere is alien to her. I nod at her. Octavian sits in the VIP section in the front with his family and friends. Augustus isn't here.

Athena goes to an elderly man in the front row. She kisses him on the cheek and bows. They close their eyes as the man says something. As we stand in our corners, Blaze arrives in the middle.

Standing next to him, short with a face full of plastic surgery is Hermes Fortuna. She owns Omni Media which is the parent company for many media companies around the world including XVN. Funny, Athena and I could have been fighting over one of her children. She has a scowl on her face. I know it angers her that her family didn't win the lottery to be the Chosen One of this season.

It's been 5 years since their family was picked. They could assert executive power and become the only Chosen One, but fans would grow bored which is the reason their shareholders don't allow it. Looking back, I'm actually glad they didn't get picked. Her entire family, male and female, either has cybernetics, plastic surgery, or some drug addiction.

"Ladies and gentlemen it is now time for the final hour to commence!" Blaze announces to the cheers of the crowd. "In the gold corner, she started slow, but has taken the world by storm. She's controversial, always has a trick up her sleeve, will make you bow to her as she kills you. From San Francisco, Nova the Star!"

The crowd roars as I raise my sword.

"Fighting in the red corner, she's small, but her fire isn't. What she lacks in size, she has in her sword. She has the rage of a bear, the power of an ape, and the heart of a lion. If you're not amazed, that means you're already dead. From the Bronx, Athena the Tasmanian Devil!"

Her name is met with roars, rivaling the magnitude of mine. The stadium stands united in their love for the two of us, trading chants of our names.

Meeting in the middle, our eyes stick on each other with an intense focus. The narrative the show pushed leading up to the fight was that we hated each other since Astra had visited. Athena was one of the top Valkyries and hates me for taking her spot. They wanted us to feed into this story by dissing each other. We didn't bite, not caring about the drama. Only victory matters now. Hermes stands between us.

"I want to congratulate you two on making it to the final round," she says. "One of you will become the Last Valkyrie, so give these fans and the world a match they deserve. Touch weapons, and may glory find you in this life or the next."

Our blades touch.

"You got this Nova," Maximus declares, slapping me on the back.

Looking dead ahead, my nerves calm. The sound of the crowd becomes background noise. All the hype around this match doesn't matter. It's time to go to war.

"Let's go!" the robot yells.

We circle the ring, sizing each other up. I lunge forward, striking with speed and intensity. Her defense is fast. She goes on the offensive, striking at me. Her blades keep coming as I defend against both of them in a rapid fashion.

I stagger back in retreat as the onslaught continues. Each time she strikes, her arm over extends, giving me the chance to yank it. I hold back the urge as it would leave me vulnerable for her other blade.

Planting my feet, I keep my defense. We pull our swords back, setting up for a heavy blow. Our blades collide, creating a loud clang. Vibrations run through my bones. We press against each other with our swords. Neither of us move.

She spins, striking at my feet. I jump in the air. As I come down, she trips me with her foot. Catching my fall with my hand, I roll, barely missing her blade. As she pulls her sword back, I see an opening. Jumping to both feet, I slice her face.

She screams in agony. The crowd gasps in shock. I go for her throat, but she jumps in between my shoulders with a head-butt. I stumble off balance. She thrusts her sword into my gut. My suit releases the concussion wave, blasting Athena back.

The impact of her sword feels like a bowling ball to my stomach as I stagger in pain. The pain, so excruciating, brings me to a knee. I clutch my stomach. My hands feel wet. There's blood all over them. Oh my god, I've been cut. The wound is a few inches deep, not pouring out a lot of blood, but the longer this fight continues, the more this will be a problem.

We hobble to our feet. The crowd gasps in surprise at the wound I left on Athena's face. She has a deep scar running from her eyebrow to her chin. Dark red blood gushes out her eye, drenching half of her face.

There is no sign of pain on her face, only anger as she scowls at me with an animalistic rage. Huffing and puffing, she charges, letting out a battle cry. She unloads a brigade of strikes, faster than before. They're too fast and strong for me to block, so I jump out the way.

She doesn't let up. Her rage numbs her to the pain. Each time I dodge, my gut irks with pain. Athena's strikes are fast, but also off target now. The blood and vision loss mess up her balance.

I don't have to dodge so quickly anymore. I take leaps to get out of the way. Not choosing to strike back, I wait for my opportunity patiently.

Only I see the battle changing as Athena swings. She spins. I jump back, allowing her to complete her spin. When she does, I bring my sword down on the middle of the hilt, severing her double blade into two. She freezes in disbelief. I stick my sword in her throat. She immediately clutches my sword as blood drenches her hands. Athena collapses as I take my sword out.

I smile at Maximus. I've survived this nightmare. Waiting to hear cheers of my victory, I hear nothing. Maximus doesn't rush over to me in celebration. He stands still, looking dumbfounded.

I stop in my steps, trying to figure out why nobody's reacting to my win. The sound of gagging hits my ears. I turn around. Coughing up blood, Athena is on her knees with a pale face. Shaking, she motions me to come back and fight. I lift my sword and march towards her.

I go for a swing at her neck, but stop at a sudden force in my gut. This time, the pain is deeper in my flesh. I look down where Athena's sword has impaled me. Blood pours out. Shaking, Athena presses her sword further into my belly. I scream, feeling like my guts will pour out if she drives her sword deeper. Her blood loss hinders her strength.

I slice Athena's neck. My blade stops in the middle of her throat. The wound in my gut weakens my ability to cut her head clean off. I step back, leaving my sword in her throat as her blade is in my gut. Adrenaline wears off as the pain surges. I yell. We both collapse in the pool of our blood.

The audience stands, silent in anticipation of what's next. It feels like fighting against gravity just to stagger to my feet with the pain. I hobble over to Athena who gets to her knees, keeping my distance just in case. Athena reaches out faintly towards the old man with her blood soaked hand.

"I'm sorry," she mopes.

He breaks out in tears. Athena looks up at me.

"If the world was a better place, we may have been friends," she wheezes with a smile.

I grab her sword and take a deep breath.

"I would have loved to," I say.

I slice her throat, from side to side, opening up a deep gash that sprays her blood all over my face. Her body remains still on the ground as her eyes stare out, soaking in blood. This is no trick. She's not playing possum. I am the Last Valkyrie.

CHAPTER 36

The confetti hasn't fallen yet as the crowd remains silent. With the sword still in my flesh, and the blood increasing, nobody knows if I will survive, not even me. A medical robot enters into the ring.

"Hold still please," it says.

A beam of heat shoots out of its eyes at the sword. My insides heat up as the metal melts, leaving only the shard in my gut. The robot clamps its hands on the shard and yanks it out as I shriek. I clutch the hole in my stomach as more blood spills out. I sweat profusely, feeling disorientated. Add me to the list of Valkyries who died after winning.

"Don't worry, I'm here," Maximus comforts. He helps me up. "This is going to hurt."

My heart races. The robot seals my wound with its heat ray. I let out a cry as my guts feel like they're on fire. The wound is sealed, but I'm still in pain. A needle emits from the robot's chest. I shoot back. The last thing I'm going to take is a needle from this show.

"It will lessen the pain," Maximus offers.

I step forward as the robot injects me. In a few seconds, the pain decreases as my movements become more stable. Blaze joins us in the ring.

"Ladies and gentleman, your winner and the 75th Last Valkyrie, Nova the Star!" Blaze announces.

The crowd breaks into cheers. The confetti falls, and the fireworks shoot out. My managers hug me.

"Girl you were awesome out there! You had me scared! I thought I was going to pass out for a minute!" Venus cheers.

"Thank you for everything," I praise.

"We should be thanking you," Flavius admits.

"Maximus we did it," I say, hugging him.

"No, you did it," he resounds.

A tear falls from his eye.

"Are you crying?" I stammer.

"I have allergies."

I chuckle, nodding just to give him the satisfaction. The ring lowers to the ground. People fill the ring. Reporters and suits all congratulate me, taking pictures. It's more of a blitz than a celebration. Everyone wants to get their fifteen seconds of fame with the Last Valkyrie. Even now, they're already treating me different.

'Can I get an autograph?'

'My daughter is having a birthday party, and she's a big fan. Can you swing by?'

'We're having a fundraiser, your appearance will bring in so many donors.'

'You're going to need an agent. I have managed the biggest stars in Hollywood.'

They don't ask how I'm feeling, or if I'm still in pain. Everyone wants to see what they can get out of me. This doesn't surprise me. Astra was right. Guards rush people out the ring. I'm surprised they didn't do that earlier especially after Osric. Luna tries to get in, but a guard blocks her.

"Let me in, she's my sister!"

"Luna!"

Seeing I recognize her, the security guard steps out the way. We hug.

"I told you I was coming back," I say.

"I know."

Guards clear the ring completely, leaving only the ones who are meant to be in. Fox comes to me for an interview.

"Nova, I know you're in pain with a lot of things running through your mind, so I don't want to storm you with so many questions. Congratulations on your victory."

"Thank you sir."

"Is there anything you would like to say?"

He hands me the mic. What can I say? For the first time, I don't have to play an angle to win fans over. I think back to the beginning, remembering the ones who didn't even make it out the trials. The world doesn't remember them. They are labeled as missing.

For the fallen Valkyries, it makes no difference how fans will remember them. Their families won't ever see them again, and the worst part about it all, they'll believe the Valkyries had a choice.

"Honestly, Fox, the only thing on my mind right now is the other Valkyries who didn't survive. Their lives should not be forgotten in my celebration. That is why as part of the reward money, I will be giving a million dollars each to the families of all the Valkyries this season," I reveal.

The crowd gasps as everyone looks at me in disbelief. Fox's eyelids go up.

"The remainder of the money will go to Shed Court. It won't bring back the fallen, but it's the least I can do."

"That is so kind of you. You are a class act. Ladies and gentleman, Nova!" Fox praises.

The crowd cheers. This will bring a profound fame and status to me, but I don't care about the love from the world. This isn't for them. Octavian's seat is empty. I can't find him in the crowd.

"Where is Octavian?" I ask Maximus.

"He left when you were declared the winner. Said he had something to take care of, but will see you before the coronation."

My heart sinks, thinking about the coronation where I will be married off to Octavian. Surviving this show is a consolation prize because the chains will never be broken. My life is entering in a new chapter of oppression.

CHAPTER 37

With the detonator out of my head, a sense of freedom, although temporary, dawns on me. I don't have to worry about my head exploding. This makes me wonder how the show makes sure no winner tells. I may never know, but in no way will I find out. There are enough things to stress about. My new life with Octavian looms as the wedding is in a few days. I have to make the best of my last days as Nova before I become Nova Hyperion.

Venus and Flavius are off, coordinating the wedding with the show. The cameras for the show have stopped playing since my victory. They'll be on again for the wedding. I don't trust the show. There could be hidden cameras anywhere, so I stay alert.

I roam the entire mansion for the first time. It feels different, hearing no footsteps, or cries of other Valkyries late at night. I come across the living room wall where I entered from the night of the 1st round.

It feels like ages ago when I was locked in that room and bashed Lyssa's brains in. A lot has changed. Wandering past the suites, I think back to my conversations with Valkyries. Zuri who gave me her condolences for my 'baby'. She told me she had lost a child too. Bellona crushed her skull in the third round. So this is what victory feels like, to be at the top, alone with nobody to share the joy with.

The television plays a tribute to all the dead Valkyries, featuring a special on their lives and where they came from. I watch them all, but pay closer attention to the ones I fought. Lyssa lost her parents in an airport bombing done by Hades Hammer. Ira was in the religious cult Oracle of Fire where she suffered abuse at the knowledge of her own parents. She was the sole survivor of a fire at a resort that killed the entire congregation. Elpis was a former addict to e-dope. Bellona's father was killed by police in the farmer protests in Ohio. Athena worked at a hospital that was burned down by rioters during the Bronx Riots. Fifty people died at the hospital. These were my enemies, but with their stories, for the first time, I see them as people.

I dial Atlas through the hologram. They gave me my phone back, but I like seeing Atlas in life size.

"How did you get Luna to come down here?" I ask.

"I didn't. She always wanted to see you. We watched your fights together. She just never knew how to face you," Atlas reveals.

"Thank you." I blush, but it breaks my heart, remembering my lie. "There's something I need to tell you. The baby-."

"I know."

"How?" I gasp.

"My mom was pregnant with my brothers. I know when someone has a child inside them."

"But you believed me when we spoke that night after the interviews."

He shrugs.

"I just wanted to keep up the story just in case somebody was listening."

I clutch my chest. After all he did for me, sticking by my side, no words can show how much I am thankful for him. I wipe my tears.

"You can thank me by not forgetting us little people at Shed Court and visit often," he teases.

"Of course. I'll find time after the coronation," I chuckle.

"Wedding. You don't have to hide what it is from me. Live your life Nova."

I can tell he has come to terms with my new life. I haven't felt myself since I was kidnapped, but Atlas' support means the world to me. It's the one thing that assures me not everything has changed. It gives me some peace. I just have to see one last person.

**

Luna opens the door to her hotel room. She immediately steps aside to let me in. Her packed bags are on the floor.

"You're leaving already?" I ask with astonishment.

"I came here to see you. Now that you've won, it's time for me to go back home."

She stuffs her clothes in the bags, ignoring me.

"Luna, it may not seem a lot, but I still need you here for the wedding."

Throwing her clothes down, she mugs me.

"If you wanted your family to be with you, you should have thought about that before you left," she snarls.

"Luna that's not fair."

"And what you did to us was?"

I'm speechless. She has a right to be angry. She shakes her head.

"You never loved our family like I did," she utters.

"What?"

"You were always too busy for us. When mom needed help, you were nowhere to be found. I had to step up!"

"I had a job. I was busy providing for our family," I retort.

"Here's a newsflash for you Nova. Work is no excuse to neglect your family. We all have responsibilities."

"Like you? You're a teenage girl who skips class and does drugs. Don't talk to me about responsibility."

As soon as the last words leave my mouth, Luna frowns, and I instantly regret saying them.

"So that's what you think about me?" she whimpers with a weak chuckle.

"Luna I'm-."

"Forget waiting, I'm out."

She picks up her bags and heads to the door. No not like this. Our relationship can't end like this, her hating me because of a lie. I beat her to the door, placing my hand on it to block her exit.

"Are you going to stop me now?" she growls.

I hug her and whisper in her ear.

"Come with me, and I'll tell you why I really left."

She looks at me confused.

"Just tell me," she says.

I shake my head and silently say no. She drops her bags.

"Okay," she states.

We take the hover car to the mountains where Maximus and I trained. I take her far away from the car.

"Nova, what's going on?" she groans.

"You'll know soon."

I make note of the path we take as we go deep into the forest. This time I remember. The hover car is out of sight. I stop. She folds her arms, patience running thin.

"Are you going to tell me now?" she demands.

I take a deep breath and proceed to tell her everything.

CHAPTER 38

Staring at the ground in a daze, Luna's speechless. She claps her hands around her mouth, shaking.

"It's been one big lie," she murmurs.

She drops to her knees. Planting her face in the dirt, she sobs an ocean of tears, rocking her body. She jumps up, throwing her arms around me.

"I didn't know!" she cries.

"Don't blame yourself. It's not your fault," I assure.

"We have to tell," she whimpers.

I jolt back with my mouth hanging.

"No!" I gasp. "If the show finds out-."

"They won't! The detonator is out. They can't harm you," she argues, wiping her tears.

"Luna, listen to me." I clutch her shoulders. "They are very powerful. Telling people will draw a lot of attention, and they'll know it was me."

"Then what do you suggest we do?" she snaps with assertiveness. Her tears fade. "We can't just do nothing!"

"I just wanted you to know I didn't have a choice. I couldn't live my life with you blaming me."

"You have a choice now. You can save-."

"The world? What do you hope to happen from this?" I question.

"I don't know. But it has to be good," she falters.

"If we let the truth out, they'll think we're crazy, or worse, they'll go crazy themselves. It won't make a difference. The ones on top will always win."

She shrieks at the sky.

"The ones on top killed our parents and enslaved you!" she argues. "Not everyone experienced what you went through and lived through it. Are you really going to marry a Hyperion after all they've done to us?"

"I have no choice."

"That's not true Nova!" she screams.

"You haven't seen what I've seen. The bodies, the screams. The pain I had to go through," I mutter. I run my hands through my hair, thinking back to the many deaths. All those bloodied corpses at the trials flood my mind. "I don't want anyone I care about to go through that."

"But more people will. They'll be taken from the street and forced to go through that terror. You may not know them, but they will suffer, and you chose not to do anything about it."

Her bravery comes from her ignorance. It's something I wish I had. They took so much from me. I can't afford to lose the one thing I can't live without.

"I'm sorry," I say, tears flooding my eyes.

"So am I. I'm going to tell Shed Court and then the world."

"No."

I reach my hand out, but she slaps it away.

"Do not argue with me. You will take me to the airport, or I will find my own way off this island, and I'm not too familiar with this place. Some people still care," she declares.

She marches off in the opposite direction from the hover car.

"Luna stop being childish and get back here!" I demand.

She ignores me, heading further into the forest.

"You don't know what's out there!"

The trees begin to block my complete view of her as I can only see her red shirt.

"Okay Luna, I'll take you!"

She stops and turns to me.

"If that's what you want!" I whimper.

She heads back towards me. Her arrogance overpowers me as I'm helpless to stop her. Whenever my sister sets her mind on something, there's no turning her back. This is the only way I can get her home safely for now.

The ride to the airport feels longer than it actually is. A dreadful silence fills the entire ride. There is still no point in talking. This hover car belongs to the show, so I can't be too safe and believe they're not listening somehow. We arrive to the airport.

"Where do you get your strength from?" I ask.

"From you."

I keep my eyes on her as she sulks away, watching her until she becomes lost in the crowd.

CHAPTER 39

Two hours pass, and I'm still staring at my wall. Empty wine bottles litter the floor. My desire for love caused all of this. I should have been satisfied with Luna visiting me, us having a broken, but alive relationship. None of it matters now. I fear the show will find out I told. My bigger fear is what people will do when the truth comes out. I hope nobody dies because of my mistake. Now I see why Valkyries never tell and how the show keeps it that way – fear. It's not the fear of our heads exploding, but the fear of the world finding out the truth for its own sake. What I might have unleashed is worse than any harm done to me. The doorbell rings. Octavian is on the other side.

"It's bad luck to see the bride before the wedding," I say.

"At this point, any luck is good. I should have been there to congratulate you. After all we've been through, I didn't know how to do it. My absence wasn't a good look for us."

"Us? There is no us. Just what we show for the cameras," I chuckle, shaking my head.

Dropping to my couch, I stare at the wall again. He approaches, but I pay him no attention. He gets on a knee.

"Are you proposing? Kind of too late for that at this stage don't you think?" I laugh.

"Nova please be serious," he groans.

I shrug.

"Today is the last day of my normal life. I'd like to enjoy my last moments of whatever freedom this is with some bliss."

333

He punches the couch. The plush absorbs the hit which makes him look silly. Planting his face in his palms, he sighs.

"God I should have done more as the Chosen One. There's no way people are going to believe we're happily married."

I shoot up from the couch.

"Are you still going with that act?" I cringe. "The show's over."

"It's never over. It's more than just ratings. It's about power and control for our families," he cautions.

The worry on his face breaks with chuckles. He plops down on the couch and picks up a half empty wine bottle. Taking heavy gulps of the wine, he finishes in a few seconds. He gazes at the ceiling.

"Society hates big business, but depends on our creations. Last Valkyrie was created to shift the attention. Putting a global sensation in our family like you makes people forget they hate us in the first place. That's how we keep them from rising up."

"But you don't do that. It's just your family and the others," I say.

"I wish that was true."

He plods to the door with his head down. Sitting alone, I grab another bottle and drink my problems away.

CHAPTER 40

I call Luna throughout the entire day. She doesn't pick up, I try Atlas and some others, but no one answers. This bothers me. As much as I try to focus on the wedding, all I can think about is Shed Court. There's nothing out of the ordinary in the news, indicating Luna told. Did she tell them? Are they ignoring my calls out of disbelief or anger? If they're angry, I understand.

After the wedding, I will visit them. I tell my managers and Maximus I'm going to Shed Court quickly before the reception. They have a cover story for my absence. I have to get to Shed Court. I hope Luna calmed down and didn't say a word. I concentrate on the wedding. It's no good to dread every minute of today.

Beautiful. That's the image staring back at me in the mirror. The white wedding dress illuminates me. My straight hair runs down my back. Unlike the extravagant look I had at the interviews, this is a simple, but lovely look for the occasion. Maximus wears a blue tunic with a bow. This is the closest he'll ever get to wear a tuxedo. His beard is combed and groomed, giving him an appealing look. He grins at me.

"What? Never seen me in a dress?" I ask.

He hands me a scroll. It has Omni Media's symbol on it in red.

"Dear Maximus," I read. My eyes scan past the parts congratulating him on my victory. "As part of the agreement, you have been granted a full pardon and ten million dollars in a new bank account."

I stop reading, seeing enough.

"You're a free man," I praise.

"All because of you."

I give him a hug. The pardon is no surprise, but seeing it be official makes me happy.

"Now, let's get to this wedding," he says.

CHAPTER 41

The hover car takes me down in front of the Church of Chronos in downtown Delos. Its gothic architecture looks magnificent. There's a crowd lined up outside the church. They hit me with cheers as I step out. Their affection resembles that in the arena, but with a more sophisticated nature.

'We love you Nova!'

'That dress is gorgeous!'

'Mrs. Hyperion!'

I wave and smile at them. Behind my fake smile is anguish. I stopped blaming the people for their ignorance, but I don't share their love for this affair. They are children at the circus. They come for the animals without knowing the abuse. Cameras are visible everywhere. Putting on a show for the world will forever be my life.

Holding up my skirt, I trudge up the long stairs leading to the church. The high heels make me hesitant to walk normal, in fear I might trip and fall. When I get to the top, the two heavy metal doors open with a bang. A gust of air blows into the church. Everyone is on their feet, facing me.

The violin plays, covering Juterna's song. I start my trek down the aisle. Flower girls and ring bearers follow behind me. They are children of the Hyperion family. I keep my eyes forward, ignoring the many faces, none of whom I recognize. I feel their eyes on me, giving me the urge to face them, but this would show how nervous I am.

I want to get to the end of the aisle so quickly, but I have to walk slowly to look confident. It's not lady-like to panic. We're told to look happy and smile during a wedding. Not too slow to look timid, and not too fast to look brash, my steps have to have the right pacing. I stop in between two pillars in the middle of the aisle. Augustus Hyperion steps up and takes my arm.

"Ms. Nova," he greets.

"Mr. Hyperion," I acknowledge.

My smile stretches. The fact he's the one to walk me down sickens me. I bet he knows that. Our smiles hide our disdain for each other. He's a good pretender, but I can see through that smile.

I always thought it would be my dad to walk me down the aisle. When he died, I imagined it to be Mr. Archer. I never imagined it would be the devil himself.

We enter into the altar section. The seats are filled with people who are more connected with the show such as Blaze and Irma. Even a wedding can't get Irma to loosen up as she has her usual serious look. Members of the Conclave are in attendance. I wave at my managers and Maximus. Astra and past winners are in the audience. Waving at the other Valkyries, I feel like I know them. They are strangers, but feel like sisters to me, having shared the same horrific experiences.

Augustus lets my hand go at the altar where Priest Romana stands in his white garb. He's been ministering the church for over 30 years, having performed all the Valkyries' weddings since. His age shows through his many wrinkles and bags under his eyes. The priest is not a big fan of cybernetics, believing God made humanity in his image, and you can assure God isn't a robot.

Octavian stands next to me, dressed in his red military uniform from when he served in his father's space force. Stars and medals decorate his uniform. Standing behind him is his best man, his best friend Caesar. Priest Romana takes the altar as everyone sits. There's a large overhead screen behind the priest, broadcasting the wedding as the camera is currently on Octavian and I.

"Ladies and gentleman welcome. We come together to celebrate a union between not just two people, but two worlds," Priest Romana speaks. "The sanctity of our society rests upon being united. The bond between these two symbolizes that.

"We have Nova. A woman who has risen from the ashes both figuratively and literally. Octavian, who strives to uphold his heritage. As much as they seem different, they are alike. They exemplify greatness, and what we all can aspire to be."

It's painful to hold my smile throughout his monologue as he glorifies us. This feels more like a coronation than a wedding now. He praises my victories and Octavian's military triumphs. Augustus sighs when the priest calls Octavian a war hero. War hero is an overstatement for a guy who did drone strikes from a cozy office in Miami.

A cell phone rings, cutting the priest off. Venus silences her phone, and the priest continues.

"We thank our Lord-," the priest begins.

Venus' phone rings again. She looks at it.

"Oh my god?!" she shrieks.

Her mouth hangs as she trembles.

"Nova, I'm sorry," she shudders.

"What is it?"

More phones ring. Checking their phones, people gasp. All eyes are on me.

"What's going on?" I ask Octavian.

He says nothing, scanning the area dumbfounded. The broadcast on the screen instantly switches over to a news report. Seeing what's on the screen, I drop the bible. Putting my hands on my mouth, I freeze.

"No," I whimper.

Homes are in ruins with nothing remaining as dark clouds fill the air. The headline reads, *Shed Court Obliterated After Unknown Explosion. Death Toll nears 100,000.*

"It's still unknown what caused this explosion as terrorism hasn't been ruled out. Again this is the home of Last Valkyrie winner Nova," the news reporter tells. "Due to the extreme death toll and size, companies in Neo Silicon Valley are offering their assistance. We'll have more information later."

I fall to my knees weightless, bawling out a sea of tears. Luna, Atlas, Ms. Blackford, Phoebe, her child, and all those people, gone like that. Hands touch my shoulder.

"I have you," Octavian whispers, helping me up.

My vision grows blurry from the endless tears.

"Give me your phone! I have to call them! They have to be alive!" I cry.

"Nova please," he falters.

I slap him across the face.

"You're useless!" I scream.

Maximus grabs me.

"Calm down," he urges.

I throw my arms around him, planting my face in his chest.

"Why?" I whimper.

"I don't know. I'm sorry," he consoles.

Blaze comes over. The cheesy smile is gone as he frowns. I go over to him. In my state of mind, I accept any condolences, even his.

"Nova," he chokes. Leaning over to my ear, he whispers so only I can hear him. "I told you there would be consequences for opening your big mouth."

I'm motionless with a gasp. He grins at me.

"We see everything on this island you idiot. But don't worry, we'll keep you in check. I bet you wish you had your sword right now, don't you?" he taunts in a whisper.

Running my hands through my hair, I feel the pen he gave me. It's to hold my hair in place. It's sharp and pointy. I clutch it. For over a month, I dealt with his stupid grin, enduring his torment. I lived with him inside my mind, torturing me. He was proud when he blew that girl's head off. Thinking back to his laughs enrages me.

I snatch the pen out my hair. My trained reflexes are too quick for him to see me aiming for his jugular. I stab him, wiping his grin off. His eyes expand as he coughs up blood. I look him in his trembling eyes, digging the pen deeper.

"The pen's mightier!" I snarl.

He hits the ground. I jump on him and stab him repeatedly, yelling. He cries as I stab all over his chest. His blood gushes on my face. The room falls silent, too surprised to stop me.

"No!" Irma screams.

She runs at me. I square up, anticipating a fight, but she goes to Blaze who's a corpse in a puddle of his own blood. The room fixates on me in shock. A guard from Omni Media jumps out with his gun drawn on me.

"Drop the weapon now!"

Octavian steps in front of me, holding his arms out.

"Wait! Don't shoot! She doesn't know what she's doing. It's a fit of rage!" Octavian yells.

"Sir if you do not step away from the criminal, we will have to shoot you too!"

A bullet goes off. The guard's head explodes. Holding a gun with smoke coming out of it, is Augustus.

"Nobody threatens my son," he declares.

All the guards draw their guns on Augustus. Hyperion Industries' guards draw their weapons. Octavian and I stand in the crossfire. Hermes Fortuna steps between both sides with her hands out.

"Stop this! Augustus tell your people to lower their weapons!" she screams.

"You first," Augustus snaps back.

"Your daughter-in-law killed my employee. We just want her."

"She's not a Hyperion yet."

"What?" I gasp.

"You can have her, but first lower your weapons," Augustus declares.

Hermes nods at her guards, and they lower their guns. Augustus and his do the same.

"Octavian, step out the way," Augustus orders.

"Dad, no. They'll torture her!"

"She committed a crime. Now don't embarrass the family even further. We'll get you a new wife."

Tears fill Octavian's eyes.

"I'm sorry Nova," he whimpers then hugs me tightly, not letting go. "If you want her, you'll have to kill me!"

"Octavian!" Augustus shouts startled.

Octavian looks me in the eyes.

"You're nothing like them," he admits.

I give him a kiss. It doesn't even take him by surprise as he closes his eyes. I open mine. Omni Media's guards approach us.

"Neither are you," I utter.

I drive my foot into Octavian's balls. As he bends over, I shove him into the guard. I grab the guard's gun and aim it at the back of Octavian's head as he staggers to his feet. All guns point at me, Hyperion and Omni Media's.

"Nova what are you doing?" Octavian wheezes, holding his crotch.

"Staying alive!" I shriek, clenching my teeth.

Augustus and I glare at each other. He takes a deep breath and lowers his gun.

"Okay Ms. Nova, what do you want?" Augustus ask.

"The truth to come out," I demand.

"Cut the cameras!" a voice calls out.

"If these lights go out, so does his!" I declare.

Dead silence. Octavian gulps with sweat.

"Dad," Octavian whimpers.

"Do it!" the voice orders.

I slightly tap the trigger. Another inch further, Octavian's brains will be splattered on the floor.

"No! You will not send my son to his death!" Augustus barks desperately.

An older man with salt white hair stands from his seat. It's Plutus Moneta, the patriarch of the Moneta family who the voice belongs to.

"Augustus think about what is at stake here," Plutus urges with his southern raspy voice.

"Don't throw it all away," Juno Moneta, the wife, adds.

"My son's life is at stake. And I will not watch him die. Nobody touches the cameras. Nova will speak!"

All the guards lower their guns.

"The floor is yours, Nova," Augustus snarls.

"For years you believed the Valkyries were willing participants in these games. You've been lied to. We were taken from our homes and forced to fight. If we didn't, the bomb they put in our heads would go off."

Gasps fill the church down the aisle, none of which come from the section I'm in. It's news to everyone, but where I'm at, they already know the truth.

344

"This includes the Valkyries you see before you here. All of them remain silent out of fear, or the need to preserve the status their silence grants them. Your entertainment and society have come at the expense of our freedom."

"Enough!" Plutus Moneta shouts.

"This is Hyperion and Fortuna's fault. Kill them all!" Juno orders.

Moneta's guards fire their guns. The priest is the first to get hit as bullets eat his torso up, sending him crashing into a statue. A bullet strikes Caesar in the chest. As he crashes to the ground, he snaps his neck on the altar.

"Caesar!" Octavian yells.

I jump over the altar as bullets fire in all directions. Gunfire, screams, and the sound of wood breaking fill the atmosphere. Sniffling, Irma turns her attention to me. She wipes her tears with her bloody hand, scowling at me.

"You! You caused this!" she screams.

She runs at me. A bullet hits her in the chest. The bullets spare no one, hitting running bystanders. A few Valkyries get shot. People trample on each other. My managers and Maximus are gone. The Hyperions are nowhere to be found as their guards exchange fire with Moneta and Fortuna's troops. It's a three-way shootout.

A door is a few feet from me. I run to it, covering my head. Barging through it, I stumble into the alley. Screams and bullets continue. Both ways out the alley look the same. Hesitant, I look back and forth, deciding which way to go.

"Freeze!" a voice yells.

I stare down the barrel of a gun.

"I got you," the Omni Media guard asserts.

"I surrender. Just don't shoot," I beg.

He smirks and takes off the safety.

"You think I'm accepting your surrender. Killing you will be like killing Josef Yanga. I'll be a national hero," he laughs.

Out of nowhere, jumps Maximus, swatting the gun away. The guard swings. Maximus snaps his arm and smashes his head into the wall. Discombobulated, the guard drops to his knees. Maximus snaps his neck. He hands me his tunic and car remote.

"I have a crimson Jupiter 11 in the parking lot. The code is 10797."

"I'm sorry for all of-."

"None of that matters. Now go!" he orders.

Taking off my heels, I run out with the tunic covering me. People scramble and scream in the parking lot. It's pure pandemonium. Moving fast, I search for the car. I constantly press the remote. It's hard to find a luxury car when every car in the parking lot costs an arm and a leg.

A car honks. The blinking lights come from a Jupiter 11. As I jump in, a flower girl approaches the window. She doesn't speak, only staring at me with curiosity. The world stops as I freeze. My heart pounds more than ever. Please just walk away. My fate lies in her hands. I think about what I might do if she screams that I'm over here. Can I harm a child? She opens her mouth. I clench my fists.

"Thank you," she says.

She hands me a flower and runs away. The panic shields me from attention. Setting the autopilot for San Francisco, I'm not out the woods yet. A camera can still pick me up, so I lay low in the car as it gets in the air. Hover planes drop down from the sky, carrying different symbols on them; they're reinforcements for the families. With the car in the air, I leave Delos, never looking back.

CHAPTER 42

Ashes fall from the sky like snowfall. My steps through the ruins leave footprints. Blocked by smoke, the sun is a red dim light in the sky, casting a gloomy darkness. I falter over the wreckage of metal, with no clear pathway. Scanning through the debris for any sign of life, I find nothing. The twins' melted bikes are among the wreckage. Attached to the handle is an arm. Groans come nearby. Phoebe's trapped under a rock. I race over to her.

"Phoebe!" I yell.

Soot covers her face. She raises her shaking hand.

"Nova, she was asleep when it happened," Phoebe gasps.

"I'm going to get you out of here!"

"I'm going to see her soon," she chokes with a smile.

Her eyes stares at me without blinking.

"Phoebe."

There's no answer. I shut her eyes. The door to the underground pit turns. Pieces of metal are on top of the door, preventing it from opening. I throw the pieces off and open the door. The dim light of the sun shines into the pit, revealing Luna's dirty face.

"I should have listened to you," she weeps. "The missiles came out of nowhere. Is everyone alright?"

It's better for me to let her see. I help her out. When she hits the surface, she puts her hands over her mouth at the destruction.

"Oh my god, this is my fault," she cries.

"The blame is mine."

We hug. A hand sticks out of the well. I pull it up, bringing out Atlas.

"Dad! Castor! Pollux!" he yells.

"There's something you need to know," I mumble.

"Where are they?"

Taking a deep breath, I hesitate. I shake my head with tears. He grabs my shoulders.

"Tell me!"

"I'm sorry."

His mouth drops as he trembles.

"It was too late," I whimper.

He runs through the wreckage, calling for them. I want to tell him it's no use. He's a lost child in the store, crying for his parent who will never come back. He comes across the arm of his brother.

"Oh god," he gasps.

He puts his hands on his head and drops to his knees, screaming. His cries echo. His face fills with snot and tears as he whimpers.

"They were just kids," he cries.

He hugs my legs, squeezing them to death.

"Look!" Luna exclaims.

A drone floats in the sky. An ad projects from it, showing my face next to the words 'WANTED.'

"I have to get out of here."

"I'm coming with you," Luna asserts.

"It's not safe. You're only sixteen."

"I'm not a child anymore! Look around you, there is nothing left for any of us. You can't protect me anymore."

Atlas staggers to his feet, wiping the snot from his nose. He stands up straight, sticking out his chest as he clenches his fists. His eyes are puffing and red.

"We're all going," he declares.

They look at me with poise. The sister and best friend I know are falling from me. They aren't the innocent kids I grew up with anymore. It terrifies me, knowing what I'm bringing them into, but I'm done second guessing myself. I need them by my side. It's the three of us against the world.

"Okay," I answer.

Stepping into the hover car, I look back at the remnants of my home one last time, dreading the unknown path awaiting us.

Nova Will Be Back......

EPILOGUE

The crowd cheers as Felix is on stage.

"The late Blaze Neroburn's former assistant Irma is still in her coma. We wish her a speedy recovery," Felix announces. The audience claps. "It's been wild these last few weeks hasn't it?" he enthuses, shifting his tone. "With all that has been going on with Last Valkyrie, it's only fitting to bring a former Valkyrie on the show. The winner of the 45th season of Last Valkyrie, Oria Moon."

Oria Moon waltz on stage, waving at the cheering crowd.

"It feels good to be back in Delos after all these years!" Oria cheers.

"Well the last time you were here, you killed a referee, so I don't know if the people of Delos are happy to see you."

"What can I say? It was on accident. I was just happy to have won."

"Tell that to all those refs that got replaced with a robot because of your accident."

The crowd laughs.

"In all seriousness, with all the rumors and scandals going on, and people refusing to speak, I must ask. Were women forced to be on the show?" Felix questions.

"No not at all."

"So there wasn't any kidnappings, torture, and detonators inside their heads?

"Of course not. Nova is angry at the Hyperions for what happened to her family. She went on the show to seek revenge."

"It's been 18 years since your victory. A lot can change in that time. How do you know what goes on behind the scenes today?"

"The only thing that changed is-."

"How's this for a headline!" a man screams, running on stage.

He shoots Oria in the head. Felix jumps behind the table. The man shoots in the air.

"Kill them all!" he yells as the audience screams and runs away.

Security guards lay waste to the man, filling him with bullets. Felix slowly gets up in dismay at the carnage.

"Clear," a guard says.

"How many times are you going to let someone bring a gun in?!" Felix barks.

Huffing and puffing, Felix glares into the camera.

"You want to kill each other when you disagree rather than sitting down to talk? Go ahead!" Felix snarls. "Our society was founded on suffering. We've been fighting each other since the beginning of time. It doesn't matter what side you're on, or what you believe – conspiracies, what they tell you, or both. We're screwed no matter what because humanity can't stand itself. We get what we deserve, so have a goodnight!"

Acknowledgments

From the bottom of my heart I want to thank you the reader for taking the time to pick up this book and making it this far. If you would kindly do so, please leave a review on the Amazon page as reviews good or bad go a long way.

-Will SciFi

2021

www.willscifi.com

www.facebook.com/willscifiauthor

willscifiauthor@gmail.com

https://www.amazon.com/Will-SciFi/e/B08CCHDM2L%3Fref=dbs_a_mng_rwt_scns_share

https://www.goodreads.com/book/show/59088357-nova-s-blade

Nova's Blade Book 2

If you want to get updates on book 2 of the Nova's Blade series including an email when it's out, click on the link down below to sign up today!

https://willscifi.com/novas-blade-book-2-sign-up/

About The Author

Will Scifi is a pen name for an author from and based in California. He loves writing mainly science fiction that touches on themes surrounding modern day culture and society. Outside of writing, he loves going to the gym, theater, watching tv, reading comics and books, and playing video games. He thanks all of his fans for their support and highly encourages anyone who has read his work to always leave a review. Reviews go a long way in helping the author!

Manufactured by Amazon.ca
Bolton, ON